THE TRIUMPHANT
LIFE

A STORY OF LOVE AND COURAGE

THE TRIUMPHANT
LIFE

A STORY OF LOVE AND COURAGE

~ A NOVEL ~

JIN-CHEN CAMILLA WANG

Library of Congress Control Number:		2015905306
ISBN:	Hardcover	978-1-5035-6041-3
	Softcover	978-1-5035-6042-0
	eBook	978-1-5035-6043-7

Cover illustration and design by James J Wang
Cornell Beebe Lake photo on back cover: Photo by Sonja Skelly, provided by Cornell Plantations

Print information available on the last page.

Rev. date: 01/22/2016

To order additional copies of this book, contact:
Xlibris
1-888-795-4274
www.Xlibris.com
Orders@Xlibris.com
704793

To my parents
For their wisdom, vision, and inspiration
May they nod an approval from God's Kingdom

To my late husband Darrel G. Dearth
For his unwavering love I did not deserve
To him I owe eternal gratitude

CONTENTS

PART FOUR

Tragedy in the Gorge

PART FIVE

First Taste of Love

PART SIX
New Life as Husband and Wife

PART SEVEN
Last Reunion

PART EIGHT
Disasters Struck

PART NINE
Healing and Triumph

Acknowledgments

I am grateful to my co-editors Leven Chen, Christine Wang, and Tiffany Wang for their insights and suggestions. I am indebted to Grace Hicks for her invaluable input. I thank my dear friend Anita Weinstein, MD for reading my manuscript and offering me encouragement throughout the process.

My love and gratitude to my sisters, Chia-Ling Liu and Grace Hicks; my brother, Shenandoah Wang; and my sons, David Wang and James Wang; for their unfailing love and care, especially during my own dark days.

PART ONE

Out of the Lion's Mouth

I

Six-year-old Lily dashed into the servants' quarter of the stately mansion. "Mama! Communists came to my school today," she panted, out of breath. "They made teacher Mr. Lee kneel and they beat him. Blood was on his face . . ." A violent pang seized her mother. In an instant, the myriad of bombarding thoughts that had been swirling in MayAnn's mind finally came into sharp focus. She knew what she would do.

The year was 1949. China was fighting a civil war. The news had been littered with reports that the then governing Kuomintang Party of the Republic of China was rapidly losing ground to the opposing Communist Party of China, and MayAnn had been increasingly anxious about the prospect of communists arriving to her hometown XiangShan in the province of Zhejiang. That fear soon became a reality. The idyllic seaside town was to face its inescapable fate.

On July 7, 1949, a hodgepodge company of an army in communist uniform marched in and overtook the defenseless town. Suddenly, the quiet and peaceful surroundings were filled with noises and soldiers. Children ran out excitedly to watch the spectacle but were quickly hushed by their parents.

A group of one hundred and thirty soldiers came to MayAnn's carved redwood front gate. The leader of the communist group addressed MayAnn with strained politeness.

"Madame, my name is Chang Din. I need to speak with the head of your household."

"My husband is away for his work. I am in charge here."

"We belong to the People's Liberation Army of the Communist Party. We are here to help build up your town and restore order. We have come from far away and need a place to stay. You have a big house that can provide accommodation for us."

MayAnn suppressed her fear.

"Yes, I'm willing to help you," she answered, appearing unintimidated, "but I have my mother-in-law, who is advanced in age and not in good health. She has an ulcer and requires a quiet and less stressful environment. I also have two young girls and a baby and his wet nurse. I can make the south wing available for you and your troop."

"Ah, but that's not enough for us. We heard you have a large servants' quarter. All of you can fit in there."

The servants' quarter occupied the east wing. The west wing had been used for storage of tools and other odds and ends.

"We have two servant girls and also three menservants, who take care of maintaining the buildings and heavy chores. They need to have a place to sleep too."

"Menservants can stay with us. We will take both the south and north wings. The servants' quarter can put up your family and the two servant girls."

With that, MayAnn lost her house.

Most men in the group were peasants. They joined the Communist army with the singular expectation of owning farmland. Many were illiterate and undisciplined. They were not used to observing and maintaining the orderliness of their surroundings. The once pristine fruit orchard on the west end of the estate was soon spoiled with a pervasive putrid odor. The communists also conducted daily military drills, marches, and political classes for the soldiers; shouted propaganda slogans; and littered and destroyed the natural landscape of the neighborhood. The serene beauty of the town was quickly disturbed.

It was not long before the persecutions started. The targets were landowners, intellectuals, and anyone connected to the Kuomintang

Party. The first such occurrence MayAnn and her neighbors witnessed involved a man nicknamed Big Boss. Big Boss was a large man with an air of arrogance. He inherited some land that he leased out to the farmers. Although he charged them rather fairly, he was exceedingly unforgiving whenever payments were late. He was an obvious target for the communists in their bid to establish themselves as an ally of those who were less fortunate.

Pounding on the door, the leader of the group, Chang Din, shouted, "Big Boss, come out!"

Big Boss emerged, frightened and panicked. "Yes, my lord, I'm at your service. Please tell me what you want from me."

"You robbed from farmers who worked hard in the fields. Do you not agree?"

"But I only collect a fair share. The farmers keep most of their harvest to make a good living for themselves," murmured Big Boss.

A young uniformed soldier jumped out. With a baton, he hit Big Boss hard behind the knee, yelling, "You damned landlord!"

Big Boss fell, crying for mercy.

"Confess!" Chang shouted.

"I . . . I robbed the farmers. I was wrong. Forgive me, please!"

"Speak all your crimes." Chang was not satisfied.

"I don't know . . ." Big Boss was confused.

"Did you tell your neighbors you do not like communists?"

Big Boss never had such conversation with anyone. But looking at Chang's irritated face, he responded, "I told my neighbors I don't like communists. I was wrong. Please forgive me."

"You don't deserve to own land. Land should belong to the farmers. Now the land is no longer yours. We will take control," Chang ordered.

Most spectators were frightened and worried. But a few who had experienced harassment from Big Boss cheered inwardly.

As time went on, persecutions became more frequent and more brutal. One day, a middle-aged man was targeted. His brother was rumored to be a member of the Kuomintang, fighting underground against the communists in a neighboring province. Chang Din and his men dragged the man out of his home. Accusing him of a traitor, they pushed him around and began shouting out his crime.

"Lin, you are a lowly conspirator, a class enemy, a collaborator of the Kuomintang!"

"No, I am not! How can you charge me with those allegations?"

"You dare to talk back?" infuriated, Chang Din kicked him hard. Lin fell.

"I'm speaking the truth." Undaunted, Lin righted himself up. "Where is the proof of the crime you accuse me of?"

"What proof do I need? Your brother is a member of the Kuomintang."

"How would you know he is a kuomintang? Even if he is, what does that have to do with me?"

A soldier in the group raised his fists and began punching him, barking, "You still argue?"

A stream of blood flowed down the corner of Lin's mouth.

"I did not commit any of the crimes you accused me of," he insisted.

More punches and beatings followed.

"Confess!" Chang Din shouted.

"No, I will not!"

The group finally quit, leaving Lin on the ground. A couple of neighbors carried him back in his home. His wife tried to mend his physical wounds. With aches in her heart and tears on her face, she murmured, "You didn't have to be so stubborn."

"Yes, I did," he said, hiding his invisible wounds within.

The town was in a state of chaos and anxiety. No longer were there the comforting assurance of tranquility, the gentle chatter of adults, and the happy laughter of children. The quiet contentment of the life it had always known evaporated mercilessly.

Then the inevitable. A teacher was beaten. His students were forced to witness the humiliation.

MayAnn knew she would proceed with what she had to do.

II

MayAnn was a teacher. Like her husband, she grew up in a well-educated and well-to-do family. Being the only child, she had been the center of attention and affection. Her father was a school principal and a teacher who dedicated his life educating the young. Born a few years after imperial China's two-thousand-year dynasty rule finally gave way to the founding of the Republic of China in 1912, MayAnn enjoyed the opportunities bestowed by a progressively more open society. She met her husband Yang WayLee in high school. He was two years her senior. Frequent encounters at various school functions brought friendship that eventually blossomed into romance and marriage.

When his hometown XiangShan fell to Communist control, MayAnn's husband WayLee was a thousand miles away. He had joined the Kuomintang Air Force as a communications specialist, and the family had been living in Chungking, the provisional capital of the Republic of China at the time. But for decades, China had been at war. There was the civil war within China, and there was the war against the aggression of Japan. The war against Japan became part of World War II when Japan attacked Pearl Harbor. It ended in 1945 when Japan surrendered. As the country struggled to recover from the destruction, civil war resumed and continued on.

When the civil war intensified in 1948, WayLee decided to send MayAnn and their three young children back to their then untouched hometown XiangShan, while he stayed in Chungking to continue his work for the government.

By early 1949, connections became increasingly difficult, as the many battles being fought between the two parties across the country disrupted communications. Eventually, MayAnn lost contact with her husband.

Fully aware of the gravity of the circumstances, MayAnn had struggled with whether to stay in her hometown or to escape. She knew she was being closely watched. WayLee was a member of the Kuomintang Party, both WayLee's family and her family were landowners, and they were educated. She was among the classes of people considered enemies by the Communist Party. On the other hand, both their families had been generous and sympathetic to their less fortunate neighbors and had won the respect and love of the townspeople. Communists did not want to upset the entire town by persecuting her at this early stage of occupation. She could wait and see, she thought, hoping for the best. Yet intellectually, she could not ignore the signs. She knew she had to get out. *But how?* she asked herself. There was too much danger attempting to flee. She feverishly plotted strategies in her mind, delaying putting them into action, waiting anxiously to hear from her husband, and wishing against reason that things would one day return to normal.

The persecution of a teacher shocked her into action.

Two young soldiers in their late teens, Liu and Chong, had developed affection toward Lily and her younger sister Nan. They would play and joke with the sisters whenever they had a chance.

One morning, MayAnn told the group leader Chang Din she needed to visit her father-in-law's grave.

"My father-in-law passed away earlier this year. He was very kind to me. My husband is not here to pay respect regularly at his grave. I need to go visit and take care of it for him."

"How long will you be gone?" inquired Chang.

"About two hours. I will take the two girls with me."

"I will have a couple of my men escort you."

The two young soldiers, Liu and Chong, jumped at the opportunity and volunteered.

"You two keep your attention on them, and report to me when you get back," Chang told them.

As soon as they walked out of the front gate, Liu and Chong squatted down for Lily and Nan to climb on their backs. The girls were excited, so were the two young men.

"We are going on a field trip!" Lily yelled.

"Yay!" Nan concurred, throwing her arms up.

"Be careful! Hold on to Chong," her mother warned.

As they walked on, MayAnn began to make conversation with the two men. "Where have you come from?"

"My home is in Jiangsu, just north of your province. Liu's is farther north. He is from Shandong," Chong answered.

"What did you do before you joined the Communist Party?"

"We were both farmers. Life was very hard. I worked long days but could barely get enough to support my father, mother, and myself. My father tried to help me, but he is getting old and cannot do much. If only I had my own land and could keep all my harvests!"

"I'm in the same situation," Liu chimed in. "There's a girl in our town I like very much. She likes me too, but her father won't allow her to marry me. He said I'm too poor, and I can't support her."

"Ah, that's the misery of our lives," MayAnn lamented. She was born in a well-established family and had a sheltered life, but now she was struggling to find a way to escape.

An idea struck her. "Can you read?" she asked.

"I've never been in school. Chong here knows a few characters," replied Liu.

"Do you want to learn?"

"Yes, everyone knows it's important to be able to read, but we had to help our families around the house and on the farm. We couldn't afford to go to school."

"I noticed you have free time after dinner. Do you want to come over to the servants' quarter and I can teach you? We can use Lily's book."

"Really?" both men exclaimed in excitement.

"Yes, we can start today."

"Mama, look. The trees are bald!" Lily noted.

Many trees had lost their branches. The communists had been chopping down trees to use as fuels for cooking. Stoves were on all day long to feed the influx of the large number of soldiers.

The girls had gotten off the soldiers' backs and were chasing butterflies. The road began inclining uphill.

"I miss my parents, and I don't like this civil war. Why do we have to fight each other?" Chong said without thinking.

"That is unfortunate. There have always been times of peace and times of war in history. We are unfortunate that we live in this wartime." MayAnn sighed. "First, the long civil war between the two parties, then the war against Japan, and now this resumed civil war after Japan was defeated."

"Mrs. Yang, do you think Kuomintang is better than Communist?" Chong blurted out.

Carefully choosing her words, MayAnn replied, "I don't think it's a matter of better or worse. The principles of the two parties are different. The Kuomintang Party believes that people should have freedom to do what they desire, and they should have equal rights. The Communist Party believes that people should share their work and properties equally."

Pausing briefly, she continued, "I think both parties want to build a strong and prosperous China, but they both have made mistakes. Kuomintang, for one, tolerated too much corruption in the government."

"I wish there were no wars. How wonderful it would be if we all can just live without having to fight each other," Chong said.

"Yes, that would be ideal. Unfortunately, that's not what we have today. I hope we will see it in our lifetime."

"Mama, I'm tired," Nan whined. Chong immediately picked her up and carried her in his arms.

They were now approaching the grave site. It sat on top of a small hill with a commanding view of the town, deep blue sea on one side and endless rolling hills on the other.

"How peaceful!" Liu and Chong exclaimed simultaneously.

MayAnn's heart grieved. She knew she would soon leave her father-in-law's remains behind and flee the place that had nurtured her. She stared at the picture on the headstone. Her father-in-law's kind and loving eyes looked back at her.

"I am so sorry, Father. I promise I will get Mother and the children safely out of here." Choking back tears, she whispered, "We will be back to see you as soon as Kuomintang retakes XiangShan." As if on cue, a gust of wind tossed a perfectly heart-shaped leaf from a tall tree right onto her chest. She was startled and deeply moved. She perceived it as a sign of her father-in-law's approval. "Go, my child. I will be with you in spirit," she heard his voice in her heart.

The girls began playing hide-and-seek. "One, two, three, four, five," Lily counted. Nan ran to her mother and hid behind her. "Six, seven, eight, nine, ten. I'm coming," Lily shouted. She walked by her sister, pretending not to see her. "Where's Nan? Anyone see Nan? I can't find her." Nan giggled and moved out. "I'm here. I'm here."

With a heavy heart, MayAnn poured some oil onto a cloth and began to clean and polish the monument. Liu and Chong helped her. They also cleaned off bird droppings and fallen twigs and leaves. MayAnn thanked them, noting that was beyond their duty. The two men smiled and said awkwardly, "It's our privilege."

MayAnn made sure they got back within the two-hour period she had promised.

While they were out, a maternal cousin of MayAnn's visited their home. The guard at the gate stopped him.

"Who are you? What business do you have here?" he asked.

"I am Jon, Mrs. Yang's cousin. I am here to visit her and her mother-in-law."

"Mrs. Yang is not here now. She should be back within an hour."

"May I visit her mother-in-law for a little while? It has been a long time since I last saw her."

The guard did not think it would be of any harm. He let Jon in and asked a soldier nearby to take him to the servants' quarter.

MayAnn's mother-in-law greeted Jon happily. He came with a mission to deliver a letter. He took out the letter that was hidden in his inside pocket.

"A servant of MayAnn's father brought this letter to me this morning. It's from your son."

MayAnn's mother-in-law was overjoyed. "Finally! She will be so happy," she said, "Oh thank you, Buddha, the enlightened one!"

The letter had taken over a month to get to the right hands.

"I am in Taiwan, retreated with the government. I am in the process of obtaining the necessary documentation for all of you to come. Go to my brother WayGuo's home in ZhouShan Island and wait there for the documents. Please make arrangements and be very careful. Take care of yourself. I miss you." Elated, MayAnn read the letter over and over. Now she knew she could continue the journey she had already set in motion.

III

The reading class started the same evening. Liu and Chong brought another soldier with them. All three were excited and enthusiastic to learn how to read. MayAnn was torn, knowing how little she could do in the very limited time she had. She would teach them some basic commonly used characters, she thought, those related to daily living. She would explain how some stand-alone characters can be combined together and become new characters with different meanings. She would also show them the strokes used to form characters to give them some idea of how to write. She wanted to plant a foundation, and she hoped they would have a chance in the future to continue learning. All these were new to the three. They were mesmerized and ready to absorb whatever was taught to them. At the end of the two hours, they had learned to read half of the first lesson in Lily's first-grade school book and all three of their names. They were overjoyed and eager to learn more.

To get her captors used to their comings and goings, MayAnn began to make frequent short outings. She was stopped and questioned at the gate but was always allowed to leave. She sometimes went alone, sometimes with the children or her mother-in-law, twice with the baby and his wet nurse. She made multiple brief visits to her relatives and friends.

Her cousin Jon was the first person she visited.

"Where are you going, Mrs. Yang?" the guard asked as she was leaving.

"I am going to visit my cousin Jon. I missed him when he was here to visit me yesterday. It will not be long. I should be back in an hour."

"What do you have in your hand?"

"Only a small purse to hold my stuff," she opened it as she was talking and showed it to the guard. He glanced quickly and let her go.

MayAnn told her cousin what she intended to do.

"Are you sure it's necessary?" her cousin asked. "Your mother-in-law is already in her early seventies. She couldn't even walk far with her bound feet," he said, shaking his head. "It's too dangerous."

"I'm aware of that. But it would be more dangerous if we stayed."

"It doesn't seem so bad. Maybe everything will quiet down soon." Trying to convince himself, he added, "Maybe once the communists get full control, they will not need to torment people anymore."

"You have seen how they persecuted ordinary people. I'm in a more precarious situation since WayLee is a member of the Kuomintang. More importantly, it involves not only me but it involves also my mother-in-law and the children. I have to keep them safe and make my move quickly." MayAnn continued, "The situation is serious. Millions have died, many are innocent ordinary people." She pleaded, "Cousin Jon, please consider getting out yourself."

She had expected and understood there would be oppositions to her decision. But she also knew the grave consequences of inaction.

She continued to make brief visits to her friends and relatives, trying to persuade them to take action while they might still have a chance. Most people, though, were afraid of the danger and burden associated with fleeing and would rather remain in the comfort of status quo.

One of her good friends supported her decision, even though she too had some doubts. "It seems such a dangerous move. But I know you have the wisdom and always know what to do. We will all do whatever you need us to do to help you escape."

The nightly reading class continued on, and two additional soldiers joined in. The leader Chang Din did not object. It appeared he too had a soft spot.

The plot to escape was constantly on MayAnn's mind, and she tirelessly moved her plan forward. Then one evening, four weeks after she visited her father-in-law's grave, she went in her mother-in-law's bedroom after class.

"Mother, all preparations and arrangements are completed. The time has come," she said gently.

"Oh, you have shouldered such heavy burden." Deeply emotional, her mother-in-law struggled. "Just know that in case anything happens, you have done everything anybody can be expected to do. Do not ever blame yourself."

"I know, Mother, but nothing will happen." With great difficulty suppressing her own fear and anxiety, she continued, "We will tell the soldiers that you are going to the temple to pay your annual respect. In the morning, my cousin Jon will come to accompany you, Nan, the baby, and his wet nurse to my father's house instead. Lily and I will join you in two days."

I have to be very careful, she told herself. *I need to stay calm for Mother and the children. I am responsible for their lives.*

They packed luggage with items necessary for a few days' travel. MayAnn also prepared a couple of large baskets of rice. She contemplated hiding some valuable jewelry in the bottom of the baskets but abandoned the idea eventually.

It was a difficult night for both women. Neither slept well.

MayAnn got up early in the morning. When her cousin arrived with hired rickshaws, she and her family went out to meet them. The soldiers guarding at the front gate stopped them and asked where they were going.

"My mother-in-law goes to the temple regularly to make wishes and pay respect to Buddha," MayAnn calmly answered. "Once a year, she stays there for a few days to fulfill the promises she made to Buddha."

"What are the others going for?" one guard questioned.

"They always went on those yearly trips. My mother-in-law likes to take them for her company. Usually both girls went along. They like to play with other children around the temple. But Lily will not be able to go this year since she has started school. The wet nurse goes to take care of the children and also help with the cooking."

"What do you have in the baskets?"

"Rice. One basket is a contribution to nuns and monks, the other for themselves and neighbors around the temple. My mother-in-law always does this as part of her goodwill."

The guard waved his hand, signaling them to leave.

"Wait," the other guard called out, "let us take a look at the baskets and make sure it is just rice."

MayAnn sighed in relief. She was thankful for deciding against hiding jewelry in it.

Another sleepless night.

The next morning, MayAnn took a short trip to see her cousin.

"They got to your father's house safely without any trouble," her cousin said. "The laborers pulling the rickshaws knew they owed deeply to the kindness of both your parents and your parents-in-law. They were glad to have the opportunity to do something for your family. I am absolutely sure they will not tell anyone where they went."

MayAnn went home reassured.

The last reading class was excruciatingly trying. In the short four weeks, all her five highly motivated students had progressed beyond her expectation. Yet she knew this would be the last time she would be teaching them and, most likely, the last time she would ever see them. How she wished she could continue the classes. She struggled to hide her emotion.

"Teacher Yang." Out of the blue, Chong raised his hand.

"Yes?"

"I just want to tell you that we all very much appreciate your taking the time to teach us. Now we have confidence one day we will be able to read newspapers and books. We will be literate!"

MayAnn was moved. "My best reward as a teacher is to witness the progress of my students," she considered. "You all have shown your determination and have done better than I expected. I'm very proud of you."

"We just want to be able to read," Liu said.

MayAnn realized this was the perfect time for her to reveal what she had prepared.

"Since you are doing so well," she said, "I will give you some difficult and complicated words to study on your own."

She wrote down the characters for each of them. Pointing to each character, she read, "Be kind, forgiving, and compassionate. Love your country, and love your countrymen."

The students were delighted. Each one holding his own paper, "kind…forgiving…compassionate…love…country…countrymen…," they followed along.

"Watch how I write each character." She wrote slowly, stroke by stroke. "Try to study each character. Learn how to write them. It is not easy, but I know you can do it. Just be patient and be persistent."

Then with much effort suppressing her own emotion, she said, "Memorize this phrase: Be kind, forgiving, and compassionate. Love your country, and love your countrymen."

The students were overwhelmed with joy. They thanked her profusely.

When the class ended, MayAnn said calmly, "Remember to study how to read and write those words." Struggling to hide a tremendous amount of sorrow, she said, "Good night and see you tomorrow."

She gathered the two servant girls who had been with her family for years.

"We will be leaving tomorrow and flee to Taiwan. I have already talked with your parents, and you are free to return to your homes. You have been with my family for a long time, now it is coming to an end." Her eyes began to water. "May we meet again sometime in the future."

The two girls burst out crying. Lily joined in.

Sad lyrics crept in MayAnn's mind: *Farewell, my country. White mountaintops and Deep black waters. Bounteous land and Endless treasure. The Magnificent Yangtze River. The Mother Yellow River. China's pride and China's sorrow. Flee, drift, wander. Wander, drift, flee. Farewell, my country . . .*

She fell into a bottomless void of anguish and despair.

MayAnn did not inform the three menservants who took care of heavy chores around the mansion. She wanted to spare them with any knowledge of information that might jeopardize their lives later.

That night, her mother came to her in her dream. MayAnn was standing alone on the shore, waves racing gently onto the sand beneath her feet. The sun was setting, and she was amazed by the beauty of the sky. She turned around and saw her mother. She cried out, "Mama, you are alive! I have been so sad. I thought you were dead. Oh, I miss you so much!" Her mother smiled at her but said nothing. She tried to run to her mother, but her legs were very heavy. She could not lift them out of the sand and she was sinking deeper and deeper. In a desperate terror, she pleaded, "Mama, I am stuck. I can't move. I can't get out. Help me! Help me!" Her mother kept smiling at her but did not answer. "Please, Mama, don't go! Please! Please!" She cried as her mother faded away.

Startled, she woke up. It took her a few moments to understand what had happened. The gate that had kept her fear, worry, agony, and emotion tightly locked up for so long finally broke. For the first time, she let her tears flow.

IV

Lily went to school next morning as usual. Her mother reminded her, "Uncle Jon will pick you up from school today."

MayAnn walked into the courtyard. The mansion, named House of Pure Hearts, was built in a style called *sie-ho-yuan* or Chinese quadrangle. It consisted of four buildings arranged in a rectangle—the longer north and south wings and the slightly shorter east and west wings. The servants' quarter that MayAnn and her family now stayed in was within the east wing. In the center of the four buildings was the courtyard with plants, flowers, rocks, sculptures, a veranda, and a water lily pond. It had been her husband's family home for a few generations. She strolled slowly around, gently touching everything in sight, preparing herself emotionally to the likely forever loss of the place that had been her home. She greeted the soldier on duty and said, "It's lonely without my mother-in-law and the children around." He smiled in agreement. The other soldiers were exercising routine drills in the open space at the east end of the compound.

In the early afternoon, MayAnn walked out of her home for the last time. Other than a small purse she always carried whenever she went on her short outings, she took nothing. By now, the guards had been very used to her brief trips. They nodded at her. She said, "I'm going to visit my neighbor around the corner. Will be back soon."

She bid good-bye in her heart to her sheltered life and walked on without looking back, leaving behind all her possessions, tangible and intangible. She knew escape was her only option, and she was determined. She quickened her steps as soon as she turned the corner. When she reached the foothill toward the mountain road, her cousin and Lily were already waiting. They immediately walked on without exchanging any words. The road was uneven and at times difficult to pass. MayAnn had been on this road many times; it was the only way to her father's house. She had always sat in a sedan chair carried by laborers on those previous occasions. But on this day, she walked and crawled. Her cousin helped Lily, carrying her on his back at times.

It was near dusk when they arrived. Her mother-in-law grabbed and held her tightly. With tears and a trembling heart, she said, "I thought I might never see you again."

"I'm fine, Mother," MayAnn replied, swallowing tears and wondering how she had become so easily emotional. "I'm sorry I made you worry."

She turned and saw her father. "Pa!" She could no longer hold back her tears.

Her father patted her back lovingly. "Your luggage, a few valuables, and more baskets of rice have been prepared," he told her. "Everything is ready."

As one last effort to convince her father, MayAnn attempted. "Pa, you know there is now rumor you have been blacklisted by the communists for secretly aiding the Kuomintang underground force. It is extremely dangerous for you to stay. Please come with us."

By this time, the Communist Party leader Mao Zedong had announced the formation of the People's Republic of China and proclaimed it to be the legitimate government of China instead of the Republic of China that had been established in 1912.

"I'm already in my sixtieth. I don't have that many years of natural life left," her father said solemnly. "I want to spend what little time I have left to do what I can for our country," he continued. "This war is hurting so many innocent people, including many members of both political parties alike. A large number of peasants in the Communist Party are blinded by the promise of owning farmland if they fight and win the war." Saddened, he shook his head. "They don't know their party leader's personal agenda of absolute power and control. They will suffer from brutal atrocities by their own leader," he predicted.

MayAnn knew her father was right. She also knew he was determined to stay and fight for his country even though he foresaw the tragic fate of the country and of his own. There was nothing more she could say.

"Pa, I dreamed of Mama last night." MayAnn finally summoned her courage. "She just smiled at me and didn't say anything. I miss her very much."

With a hint of yearning, her father said, "I miss her too, every day for the last twenty years. It will not be long before I meet her again."

A year later, he was to be tortured and executed by the communists after being arrested under the pretense of "traitor of the people" and refusing to give up his contacts.

V

A messenger from the boat dock arrived with the news that water was too rough to cross safely that night. The home of MayAnn's brother-in-law WayGuo was on ZhouShan Island that was part of the ZhouShan archipelago just off the east coast of the mainland. The only means of getting to ZhouShan at the time was by boat.

Her father said, "All right, we will wait one day. You should be safe here; your captors will not be able to find out. I am sure no one in your town will lead them here."

This, she realized, was the fruit she was now reaping from the kindness her family sowed toward their countrymen all these years.

MayAnn treasured the gift of the extra day she had with her father. In his study, where she had spent a good portion of her childhood, she nostalgically thumbed through the bookshelf. "*Dream of the Red Chamber*," she pulled out and read the title. "One of my favorites."

"Indeed, one of the favorites of many. And one of the four classic literary greats in our history," her father resonated.

"Mama used to read to me before I could read myself. I can still hear her voice and feel my anxious anticipation. It seems like a century ago, yet it also seems like just yesterday." Her eyes began glistening again. She changed subject to control her emotion.

"Pa, I remember the days you taught us not only Chinese literature but also math. We all loved your class because you were so clear and so patient. You emphasized reasoning rather than memorizing." The picture of her class sitting with absolute concentration came in her mind. "I will never forget how you explained why the square of two numbers equals the sum of the square of each number *plus* twice the products of the two numbers. I can still see you showing us on the board, and we watched and listened, and suddenly, it made sense to all of us. You always dissected problems and presented to us in a clearly understandable manner. So many students have benefited tremendously."

"Those were the best days of my life—educating young people. It would be an ideal society if all young are educated, all old are respected, and all capable men and women are willing to contribute and serve."

"Yes, Pa, if everyone believes what you believe, we would be in a society of utopia."

"Such ideal society might not be possible, but a country without war should be achievable."

"Yes, it certainly should be."

"Daughter, you've done very well," her father praised. "I know how much it takes to get everyone here safely. It takes determination and wisdom. I'm proud of you."

"Oh, Pa, I've been so scared."

"I know, I know," her father said affectionately, patting the back of her hand. "It takes courage to overcome fear, and you did it."

The children enjoyed the love their grandfather showered on them.

"Grandpa, will you play hide-and-seek with us?"

"Of course. But I'm old, and I'm big. It's easier for you to find me. You must give me a leg up."

"Okay." Lily giggled, proud of having advantage over her grandfather. Nan ran around, following her sister. The baby watched and laughed.

MayAnn absorbed all these with a heavy but grateful heart. She knew this would most likely be the last images she was to have of her father.

"Grandpa, we are tired. Please tell us a story." The girls sat.

"Girls, you are wearing your grandpa out," their paternal grandmother interrupted with a smile.

"Let them, in-law. I'm having fun too."

Then he began one of the well-known stories from a compilation of twenty-four dutiful sons throughout Chinese history.

"Once upon a time, long ago, in the far northern China," he began, "there lived a poor family. The parents were getting old, and their only son worked very hard to support them. They did not have much, but they lived happily together. One day, his mother became sick. She craved for broth made with bamboo shoots. She said to herself, 'If only I can have some bamboo-shoot broth, it will make me well.' Her son heard her, and he went out with a shovel to look for it. It was deep in the winter. The ground was covered with snow and ice. There was nowhere to find bamboo shoots, which only appear in warm months. Discouraged and worried about his mother, he felt desperate and began to cry. As he walked on with blurry eyes, he tripped over a pile of dirt. It was very unusual to see this when everything else was white. He quickly stooped down and dug around the dirt. Underneath, he found a bed of fresh tender bamboo shoots! He brought them home and made broth for his mother, and his mother soon got well. From then on, the earth gave bamboo shoots in the winter every year so people can enjoy it even in cold weather."

Lily immediately thought of her mother and said, "Mama, when I grow up, I will get for you anything you want."

"Me too, me too!" echoed Nan reflexively.

"Good girls," their grandfather praised.

"Grandpa, tell us another story."

Their grandfather decided to tell a story that was depicted in a popular Chinese opera.

"Long ago, in a place not too far from here, a girl was getting married. She was from a very rich family. On her wedding day, she sat in a large beautifully decorated sedan chair carried by many laborers to her future husband's home. There were also many rickshaws full of expensive dowry. It happened that another girl was also on her way to be married. This girl was from a very poor family. Her parents could only afford a plain sedan chair and a single inexpensive dowry. It started to rain on their way to their respective destinations. They stopped at the same place to wait out the rain. Then the rich girl heard someone crying. She asked one of her servant girls to check it out. The servant came back and said, 'The poor bride is crying for her fate. Her future husband's family is also very poor, and she thinks her life will be miserable.' The rich girl's heart was filled with compassion. She removed from her neck a very expensive locket filled with expensive jewelries and told the servant girl to take it to the poor girl. Six years passed. There was a deadly flood in the rich girl's town, and she got separated from her husband and children. She ended up in another town and had to find work as a nanny to a little boy in a large mansion. One day, the little boy threw his ball onto a second-floor balcony, and she had to go up and try to retrieve the ball. She passed by a nicely decorated room. Looking through the window, she saw a beautiful table in the center. On top of the table was a locket placed inside a glass case. She immediately recognized the locket she gave away on her wedding day. Thinking of her own fate, tears flowed down her face. When the lady of the mansion heard that the new nanny was crying in front of the room with the locket, she asked the nanny be brought to her. After she heard the nanny's story, she held her and said, 'I was the poor bride to whom you gave the locket on my wedding day. My husband and I sold the jewelries inside and used the money to start a business that became very successful. I kept the locket to remind myself and to honor you.' So the lady elevated the rich girl's position from a nanny to be as her sister. With the lady and her husband's help, the rich girl and her lost family were able to be reunited."

"When I grow up and become rich, I will also give money to the poor," Lily said.

"Me too, me too!" echoed Nan.

"That's right, good girls!" MayAnn was satisfied.

Their grandmother smiled in approval.

The sea calmed down. MayAnn bid a heartbreaking good-bye to her father. By dusk, they were at the dock. The price for the trip was half the rice they brought for the journey.

"You will need two boats for all six of you and your luggage," the skipper commanded. "Distribute weight evenly, people and goods."

"We six will get on one boat. Luggage and rice will be on the other boat." MayAnn said.

"The weight will not be even. It can only be evened out by separating both people and rice between the two boats."

"I know this is a very treacherous undertaking. Besides communists, there is also the danger of the sea itself. I am not naive to expect a guaranteed safe passage. We will all sit in one boat. We live or die together." MayAnn was determined.

The skipper relented hesitantly.

They began the voyage.

"Be very quiet. Make sure the baby doesn't cry," the skipper told them. "After we pass the first communist stronghold along the shore, you can relax a little. There will be five more small ports guarded by communists. Once we pass all five, we will be on the open sea and will be safe from there on."

It was pitch-black where the boat was traveling, as far from the shore as possible. They could see occasional scattered lights in the distance. Everyone remained quiet, including the baby. He was not usually a hush baby, but somehow, he stayed still. MayAnn repeated silent prayers in her heart, asking for blessings. They passed the first major hurdle.

"Mother, we can relax for a little while now," MayAnn said quietly. They all stretched and moved around.

They again fell in silence as they approached the next communists guarded port. Twice they heard commotions on the distant shore. They held their breath; the noises died down. It was after midnight when they finally went through all the ports and onto the open sea. The skipper and his helper resumed their conversation and laughter.

The sea was rough and unforgiving; the boat rocked vigorously. Nan vomited first, followed by everyone else, except the baby.

By daybreak, they were approaching the Kuomintang-controlled ZhouShan archipelago, just off the east coast of the mainland. Kuomintang soldiers guarding the islands raised their guns. The skipper yelled, "Rice boat." They were allowed to dock.

Rice was scarce at the time. The soldiers took the portion that now belonged to the skipper and paid him market price.

Recovering from seasickness, they got off the boat. MayAnn realized they were now safe. She finally let go of her emotion. She held her mother-in-law tightly. "Mother, we made it."

MayAnn's only brother-in-law, Yang WayGuo, arrived to meet them. He was much older than his brother WayLee. There was a girl in between the two brothers who died of an unknown illness at age seven. WayGuo was a man of unflinching loyalty to his country. He was also very protective of his brother, and he loved MayAnn as a sister. He lost his own sister when he was ten.

"Ma, I am sorry you had to endure such trouble," he said. It had been many months since he saw his mother, and he had been quite worried that she might not make it out safe.

"It is your sister-in-law who did all the planning and arrangements. It was a huge burden on her. We are safe today because of her."

"Sister, no words can express my gratitude. My entire family owes you," WayGuo said.

WayGuo had been relocated by the government from his family home in XiangShan to ZhouShan Island nearly a year before to take upon new assignments. He had suggested that his mother and his brother's family move with him to be safer since WayLee was a thousand miles away from them, and the country was still in war. However, MayAnn had lost contact with her husband at the time and was afraid moving away would further jeopardize the process of reestablishing connection.

They went to WayGuo's home. There they waited for their visas to enter Taiwan.

WayGuo's wife, YeLin, took them to tour around ZhouShan Island, the largest among the more than thirteen hundred islands of the ZhouShan archipelago, most of which were uninhabited. The islands sat on the Yangtze River Delta, where the Yangtze River merged into the East China Sea. ZhouShan was a seaport blessed with stunning natural beauty and rich fishing grounds. They visited a number of famous attractions and popular destinations. Mount Putuo, in particular, was considered a sacred mountain in Chinese Buddhism. It was renowned for its unusually shaped peaks and rocks, cliffs and caves, combining the majestic beauty of land and sea. It saddened MayAnn to realize that she would soon have to leave behind this beautiful land with its picturesque seascape and plentiful natural resource. Still, she knew what lay ahead and would do whatever was necessary to get the family to safety.

WayGuo was a die-hard kuomintang. He believed it was his duty to protect his country, and he believed the ZhouShan Islands controlled by the Kuomintang Party would stay safe. He made his belief clear to MayAnn. MayAnn had to turn to his wife.

"Circumstances around the country are very serious. Our hometown XiangShan has fallen," she attempted. "ZhouShan may fall any day. Please, with five children, you have to be prepared to flee."

"I know that, and I understand very well. I wish WayGuo would agree to leave. But you know how he is. He is so completely loyal to the country. He will never give in. Live or die, we may have to face our fate with ZhouShan."

Knowing there was probably nothing they could do, the two women embraced in tears.

Less than six months later, in May of 1950, ZhouShan was to fall to Communist control.

Three weeks later, the authorization to enter Taiwan arrived. They were to take the air force plane for the one-hour flight.

WayGuo insisted that his mother stayed behind with them. "Mother is advanced in age. Even one-hour flight is too much for her. Those military planes are quite uncomfortable. She will be safe here."

"Brother, the country is in this struggle for the long haul. It may take more than five or ten years. Taiwan is the only safe place right now. Mother needs stability," MayAnn appealed in desperation.

WayGuo did not budge.

That night, MayAnn could not sleep. Tossing and turning, she needed to find a way to convince her brother-in-law to let his mother go. *WayGuo is the older son. I am the younger daughter-in-law,* she thought. *We both want the best for Mother, but I can't win this by myself.*

She got up and quietly walked to her mother-in-law's bedside. "Mother, I and the children will be leaving tomorrow," she began. "WayGuo wants you to stay because he thinks the travel is too hard for you, and he believes it will be safe in ZhouShan. But it is too chaotic here. With your ulcer, Taiwan will be a better place for you as a temporary home at this time," she continued. "If you decide to go with us, he will not oppose."

Early in the morning, her mother-in-law got up and started packing.

"Ma, you really want to go?"

"WayGuo, let me go. You all come soon too."

That afternoon, they boarded the plane. WayGuo was given special permission to get on board to see his mother off. There were no real seats. The other passengers, mostly air force servicemen, made a makeshift bed for his mother. WayGuo was at last moved.

"Blessed is your family," he said to MayAnn. Deep down, he realized MayAnn might be right that ZhouShan could fall.

Tears in her eyes, she made a final plea, "Please consider, for your wife and children."

WayGuo mumbled some words unintelligibly. With a heart filled with sorrow and sadness, he said good-bye reluctantly.

At three thirty on December 20, 1949, they stepped out of the plane at the Taipei Airport in Taiwan. Mother and son, husband and wife, father and children were at last reunited. The five-month precarious journey finally ended.

A family portrait was taken. On the back, MayAnn inscribed:

"Out of the Lion's Mouth"

PART TWO

Taiwan, the Beautiful Island

I

Taiwan. Formosa. The beautiful island.

The family started their new life in Taipei, the capital city of the province of Taiwan. Taiwan was a small island off the southeast coast of mainland China. The air force allotted WayLee a small apartment in a cluster of nearly identical one-story buildings, each consisted of six to ten units in a row. This was one of the many villages built hurriedly across the island as temporary housings to accommodate the mass exodus from mainland China. Nearly all residents in this village were air force families. Many had young children. They came from different parts of China, and many had their own distinct dialects that made verbal communications difficult for those who did not speak Mandarin, the official language of China. Nevertheless, they quickly assimilated. Resources were limited, but the camaraderie among all was immediate. A melting pot indeed, unexpectedly united together by fate.

Lily continued first grade at the Taipei Elementary School for Children of Air Force Personnel like all other young children in her village. Nan started kindergarten when she turned five. They were not used to having so many playmates, both in their village and at school. They took full advantage of this newfound opportunity and made many friends. Arguments and fights were common among the children, but hostility toward one another was always short lived.

MayAnn was able to find a part-time desk job at a local police station to help support the family. She also tutored reading and math to neighborhood children who needed additional help. At times, she thought of the reading class she had in her hometown. She wondered how her students were and if the class had made any impact on their lives. Then she would be invariably overtaken by an overwhelming feeling of sorrow for not being able to complete what she had desired.

WayLee was grateful for being able to reunite with his family. He remained in the air force and was gradually promoted through the ranks to that of colonel. He would spend as much time as possible with the children. They walked to the nearby railroad station to watch trains go by, took buses to the airport to see planes take off and land, visited botanic gardens and the zoo, and went to the children's playground and occasionally to the movies. When weather was not cooperating, they stayed home, and WayLee would tell them stories. Later, the baby joined in when he was old enough. His wet nurse stayed with the family until she remarried to an acquaintance of WayLee's three years later.

MayAnn's mother-in-law settled in. She was unusually active for her age, and her ulcer rarely flared up, if ever. She made friends in the neighborhood, and they visited one another often. Whenever she could, she helped around the house to allow MayAnn to concentrate on her work. Her mind, though, was always on going back to the mainland and to reunite with WayGuo and his family.

Thus, after losing everything material, they tried to rebuild their lives together in this beautiful island of Taiwan.

In this meager yet nurturing environment, the children grew up.

II

A small white church with a wooden cross on its door stood on the roadside of the narrow street that MayAnn passed everyday on her way to and from work. It was quiet most of the time. Some days, she saw people going in and out. Occasionally, she heard music played on the organ. She would unfailingly stop to listen. It reminded her of her teaching days of what seemed like a lifetime ago. She taught a class of sixth-graders. She had them for an entire year and for all subjects, including music. The school had one small organ. She would take her students to the organ room twice a week for music, and she would play the organ. There was one musically talented girl who always led the class in singing. *What was her name?* she searched her memory.

"Excuse me. Do you need help?" a friendly voice interrupted her thought.

"Ah, sorry. I was listening to the music. It was so peaceful."

"I was practicing hymns for Sunday service. Are you from around here?" the woman in her early thirties asked.

"I live in the village just beyond the other side of the street." She pointed to her right. "We moved here about four months ago."

"Oh, the Military Dependents' Village. We are getting so many new neighbors. I am RoSie, and I am a third-generation Taiwanese. Hope to see you again."

"I am MayAnn. Nice meeting you."

When she got home, her mother-in-law had food prepared ready for cooking. "Thank you, Mother," she said gratefully as always.

She told her husband of the encounter. "I miss playing organ," she blurted out.

After considerable thought, WayLee responded, "Perhaps someday we can get one."

"Madame Yang, are you busy?" knocking on the door, the couple in their fifties called out.

"Come in, come in, Mr. and Mrs. Su," MayAnn's mother-in-law answered, letting her neighbors in.

"Is everyone at work or at school?"

"Nan is playing with her little friend next door. Only the baby and the wet nurse are here, keeping me company. Good to have neighbors visiting," replied MayAnn's mother-in-law. "Mr. Su, when do you think we can go back home? WayLee always says soon, but it is now nearly five months since we fled mainland China."

Mr. Su expected this question. In fact, this was the first question many asked right after they greeted each other.

"My son gives me the same answer whenever I ask him. Soon, he always says. I told him, 'You are in Intelligence, you should know. Do not just say soon, soon.' But he has not given me any other answer," Mr. Su said.

"WayLee's brother WayGuo and his family are still in ZhouShan. At least it is safe in Kuomintang hands. We just got a letter from him a month ago."

"That is good. At least we still have those islands off the coast of your province."

"Well, I hope we can reclaim the mainland soon," ventured MayAnn's mother-in-law. "After all, we are the rightful government of the Republic of China."

"That's right," Mr. Su said. "It is too bad we lost the civil war to the Communist."

"Our poor neighbor, Mr. Chen, his family could not get out in time," Mrs. Su sighed.

"I heard about it. How did it happen?"

"It was chaotic when two million people around the country were trying to flee all at once. Mr. Chen, whose home was in northern China, was going to leave with his family on a large ship headed for Taiwan. He wanted to go and say good-bye to his best friend who had decided not to leave. His wife and three children were to meet him at the seaport. But he could not find them when he got to the dock after he visited his friend. People were pushing, and he was not able to get out of the big crowd. As he was being pushed up the gangway, he saw his wife and children running, trying to get to the ship. He tried to push his way back down, but he could not get off. That was the last he saw them," Mr. Su said sadly.

"It has been four months, and there has been no news of them whatsoever." Mrs. Su shook her head.

"That's very sad. My family is luckier. My daughter-in-law took all of us safely out, all six of us. WayLee was already in Taiwan at that time. I just hope WayGuo and his family will stay safe." MayAnn's mother-in-law repeated the details of the journey they took to get out of the mainland. The Sus listened attentively; they could not get enough of the tale.

Unbeknownst to them then, the ZhouShan Islands were soon to be taken by the Communist.

Passing by the small church weeks later, MayAnn ran into the organist RoSie.

"Hello, RoSie."

"Ah, MayAnn. I was hoping to see you again. Do you by chance play the organ?"

"Yes, I was a teacher in mainland China. I taught all subjects to sixth-graders, including music."

"I thought so. You had that nostalgic look when you said you were listening to the music when we first met," RoSie said. "Would you like to come to the church sometime and practice on the organ? I am the only organist here. Perhaps you can fill in when I cannot make it some Sundays."

"Really?" enthralled, MayAnn could not comprehend her good fortune.

"Of course, it will be good for both of us. I will be here Friday evening. Can you come at seven? I will set you up then."

MayAnn was in a state of bliss. WalyLee sensed his wife's excitement when he got home from work.

"Well, what is it?" he asked, looking at MayAnn's face of unsuppressed eagerness.

"RoSie wants me to practice the organ in case she needs me to fill in for Sunday services!"

"Unbelievable! I'm so happy for you," he exclaimed.

In May of 1950, news arrived that the ZhouShan Islands had fallen.

Although it was not unexpected to WayLee and MayAnn, the report nonetheless was shocking, and they were filled with a sense of enormous pain and sorrow.

"WayGuo being a kuomintang, I fear his life will be in serious jeopardy," WayLee said in private.

"We can only hope for the best. Miracles do happen," MayAnn struggled.

No words could possibly describe the devastation and anguish of WayLee's mother when she was given the news delivered by WayLee as gently as he could. She cried out, "Buddha, why did you let this happen? Please save them. I will give you anything you want. I will go to the temple and burn incense for you. Please just save them."

She stayed in bed for two days, not able to do anything. Then she got up and burned incense. MayAnn took her to a temple not too far from their home, and there she burned more incense and prayed to

Buddha for the safety of her older son and his family. She tried to hold on to a slim hope that WayGuo and his family would somehow be able to escape.

MayAnn had been practicing organ whenever possible at the church. She practiced hymns mainly. Occasionally, she would play the songs she used to play in her music classes. Most of those songs were unknown to RoSie. "Those are lovely songs. I will use them for my private students," she told MayAnn.

MayAnn's opportunity to play for Sunday services finally came two months later.

"My husband's parents live in KaoHsiung. We haven't seen them for a long time and would like to take some time and go visit them. Would you be able to play for the next two Sunday services?"

"Of course. I'll do my best not to disappoint the congregation."

"I know. You're good. You'll do well."

Somewhat nervous but confident, MayAnn perfected her accompaniments the following Sunday. Afterward, she sat and listened to the sermon.

"Thank you, Mrs. Yang. That's a beautiful job you did." The pastor approached her after the service. "It's nice to have a second organist."

"Thank you, Pastor. I appreciate the opportunity."

A number of the congregation came to MayAnn and introduced themselves to her. They congratulated her and welcomed her to the church.

This was the first sermon MayAnn had ever heard. Prior to that, the only religion to which she had any reasonable exposure was Buddhism. She knew this was a Christian church but did not quite understand what it represented. The sermon had raised questions in her mind.

MayAnn was eager to get the answers from RoSie. As soon as she welcomed RoSie back, she asked, "I haven't had any exposure to Christianity. Would you be able to help me?"

"I've been waiting for you to ask." RoSie smiled.

"The pastor said that there are two kinds of love that we can experience—the finite love we were born with that is limited to our own ability to love ourselves and others, and the God-given love that gives us the capacity beyond our own finite ability to love even those who have wronged us." Rather bewildered, MayAnn continued, "It seems almost impossible to love our enemies."

"Indeed it seems," RoSie said. "But this is what Christianity is. It's the self-sacrificing love of God for us. It was shown by Jesus Christ when he went to the Cross to die for all of us. Likewise, we are to have the same kind of love for God and for our fellow human beings. This is what Jesus said:

> You have heard that it was said, 'You shall love your neighbor and hate your enemy.' But I say to you, Love your enemies and pray for those who persecute you, so that you may be children of your Father in heaven; for he makes his sun rise on the evil and on the good, and sends rain on the righteous and on the unrighteous. For if you love those who love you, what reward do you have? . . . Be perfect, therefore, as your heavenly Father is perfect."

"Ah, I've never thought of it that way. What a wonderful teaching!" MayAnn was moved.

"Let me give you a Bible, and you can read it when you can."

Direct communication between mainland China and Taiwan had been largely abolished after Kuomintang retreated to Taiwan. It took nearly six months for a letter written by a close friend of WayGuo to reach WayLee. It had been relayed through a few hands and with great care and secrecy.

The letter was dated February 19, 1951, more than a year after WayLee's family fled the mainland.

"WayGuo maintained his loyalty to his country till the end. He was executed a month ago on January 15, eight months after the fall of ZhouShan. He withstood interrogations and persecutions without yielding," the letter read. "He achieved what he said he would do: 'to succeed or to die for my country.'

"Like many families here, his children are scattered," it continued. "His wife had to give up two of them to childless couples because she had no means to raise them. Their oldest son was sent to hard labor for being the son of a 'traitor.' The two other girls were married off to farmers.

"The communists turned the society upside down. The educated are persecuted as the class enemy. The uneducated are elevated as having 'good family background.' We cannot even speak what we think or believe," it concluded. "We are in deep waters and burning fire, waiting to be rescued."

It would take another twenty-some years before the terror and oppression forced on its own people began to slowly relax.

The tragedy was too great to bear. WayLee was not able to control his emotion. MayAnn held him, trying to comfort him, but she was crying intractably herself. She recalled the first time she met WayGuo. WayLee took her to his home to meet his parents. The Yangs asked her about her family. The two families lived in the same town; they knew of each other but had not yet been acquainted. MayAnn was somewhat nervous, being in front of her prospective future parents-in-law for the first time. After a while, WayGuo came home from work, and WayLee introduced them. WayGuo went straight to the point. "My brother said you are the only child. You must have been the center of all the attention in your family."

"Yes, I have been," she had answered, not knowing what he was leading to.

"My brother has also been the center of our family. He is much younger than I am, and I try to protect him any way I can. Do you think you will be able to respect him and not put yourself in the center?"

WayLee was worried. He was afraid his brother might voice opposition, and MayAnn might be deterred.

"I've been in the center of my family. But that doesn't mean I don't know right from wrong," she had answered. "I believe all humans are equal. I'm fortunate to have parents who keep their attentions on me. That only taught me to respect and value others."

That first encounter had set a firm foundation for their everlasting close relationship. They appreciated and regarded each other. WayLee told her later that WayGuo was quite satisfied with her answer that day.

"We will not be able to hide our grief from Mother," WayLee finally spoke. "We need to formulate a way to break it to her."

This time, the effect on his mother was beyond monumental. The slim hope she had tried to hold on to was mercilessly robbed away. She fell ill in a serious depression and was not able to get out of bed. Her ulcer that had only very rarely bothered her aggravated and required medication.

"When did it happen?" she finally asked on the fifth day.

"January 15 this year, Mother," MayAnn answered.

"What day is it today?"

"August 19."

She fell back to silence.

MayAnn took some time off from work to tend to her mother-in-law and to heal her own wounds. When she got married, she also gained a big brother she never had. She wondered if there were something else she could have done to convince him to flee to Taiwan. She could not shake off her regret.

A voice rose in her head. "He achieved what he said he would do: to succeed or to die for my country." Her eyes began to water, but she was comforted.

"Mother, WayGuo maintained his unwavering loyalty to our country. He was determined to succeed or to die for the country. He had fulfilled his wish." MayAnn struggled to complete what she wanted to say.

Tears flowed from her mother-in-law's anguished eyes.

Three days later, she got out of bed.

Healing was a long and challenging process. There were good days, and there were bad days. Slowly, MayAnn's mother-in-law was able to carry some conversation. She kept reminding herself, "He had achieved what he wanted to do. He had fulfilled his wish." That knowledge gave her strength and consolation. Neighbors gradually resumed their visits. Eventually, the question "when do you think we can go back home?" was once again the usual greetings.

The news of execution of MayAnn's father by the communists took longer to arrive than that of WayGuo's. It took place in his hometown XiangShan on December 29, 1950, seventeen days before WayGuo was martyred. The message was verbally relayed through people in Hong Kong and finally reached MayAnn in November 1951. She had been prepared for the news, but the heartache was nevertheless unbearable. Her mother-in-law held her and mourned with her, so did WayLee. Some days, MayAnn felt so troubled she wanted revenge. When she was at last able to think, voices came in her heart:

"I want to spend what little time I have left to do what I can for our country."

"He achieved what he said he would do."

"Love your enemies and pray for those who persecute you so that you may be children of your Father in heaven . . ."

By this time, she had been reading the Bible, attending Sunday services regularly, and conferring with RoSie and the pastor for passages she had difficulty understanding. She drew strength from those voices, knowing her father had no regret for his resolution.

"Mr. Chen, are you there? May we come in?" the Sus knocked on their neighbor's door. They had been worried about him. He seemed more depressed lately.

There was no answer. They knocked again and again. Finally, they heard some incoherent sound coming from within. Mr. Su said to his wife, "I think he is drinking again."

They pushed the door open and walked in. Chen was slumbered in his chair, apparently drunk. He opened his eyes slowly and said, slurring his words, "Are you bringing my wife and my children back to me?"

"They will come sometime. Right now, you need some rest." They helped him to his bed.

"Where are they? Bring them back to me," Chen mumbled. "Why? Tell me why I had to go see Mo. Did he force me? Did you force me? Why did you force me? Give them back to me, please!" he stammered and begged.

Mrs. Su wiped her tears. "Three years, still no news," she agonized.

They straightened up some of the disarray in Chen's apartment and then closed the door behind them as they left.

This torment of the heart lasted much longer than three years.

In 1970, some twenty years after Chen was separated from his family, he received a letter that had been traveling from friend to friend around the United States and Hong Kong then finally to Taiwan. Direct communication between the two sides of the Taiwan Strait, a body of water one hundred ten miles wide separating mainland China and Taiwan, was still not possible at the time.

Holding the letter, Chen rushed into his neighbor's home. He was laughing and crying, crying and laughing, simultaneously.

"They are alive!" he declared triumphantly.

He had been waiting for this day for twenty years, twenty years of not knowing the fate of the ones closest to him in this world. He had imagined in his mind over and over what this day might bring him. He never anticipated an emotion so overwhelming that made him both laugh and cry.

The Sus laughed and cried with him.

Yet Chen was among the lucky. There were countless families separated from their loved ones during the exodus from mainland China. Many were still in uncertainty. And many more lives had been lost during and after the Communist takeover.

Such was the tragedy of their generation.

III

The children grew and continued their education in Taiwan. They excelled in school, especially Nan. She was always at the top of her class. The baby, being the only boy, was the favorite of their grandmother. Under her protection, he was sometimes able to get away with playing mischief on his sisters. But he loved them, and he was always kept in check by his parents.

"Shane!" Nan jumped up, waving away a dragonfly from the back of her neck. Her now six-year-old brother ran out of the apartment, laughing.

"Mama, Shane did it again!"

"Papa and I will have a talk with him tonight."

"Boys are boys. Don't be too hard on him," MayAnn's mother-in-law chimed in.

"I know, Mother. We will just let him see how he was disturbing the girls when they are trying to do their homework. Besides, they don't like the feel of insects on them."

After dinner, the adults brought chairs outside to sit and chat, and the children in the village ran around, playing various games as usual. After a while, WayLee gathered his children and asked if they wanted to hear a story. They were excited; they always liked listening to stories. A group of their playmates also joined them. They sat on the ground and waited expectantly.

"Far away from the earth, up in the sky, hundreds of thousands years ago, there were two moons. They were joined together by many stars in between so people who lived on each moon could walk on the stars and visit back and forth. The moon and star kept the sky lighted after the sun went down to rest. Everyone on the moon was assigned a job. Two brothers, one on each moon, were both given the work of keeping the moon clean and shiny. The two brothers loved each other. Their personalities, though, were quite different. One was more serious, while the other was rather mischievous. One day, the mischievous brother finished his cleaning early and was bored. He said to himself, I will go play a trick on my brother. So he quickly walked on the stars and went to his brother's moon. A large mass of fluffy stuff was forming and obscured part of his brother's moon, and the moon looked like a crescent shape instead of the usual round. He saw his brother at the tip of the crescent, rubbing and cleaning. *What a perfect chance,* he thought. *I will scare him so he will slide to the edge, holding on the tip like a hook. That would be very funny to watch.* He made a sudden loud and scary noise. His brother startled so violently that the moon shook and tumbled with his brother holding on to the tip like a hook, just as he had imagined. But the moon did not stop. It continued tumbling until it disappeared forever. The mischievous brother was heartbroken. He never laughed again since that night. His moon mourned with him and began changing shapes night after night, repeating itself month after month, in search of the lost moon."

The children were sad for both brothers; one who was lost and the other in everlasting misery. They looked up and watched the night sky. WayLee explained that the shape of the moon that night was called waxing crescent. They imagined a boy on the moon crying for his brother.

"We want to hear more stories!" they chanted.

"Maybe another day," replied WayLee.

"Shane, do not play tricks on me again, or you may regret and be sad forever." Nan grabbed the opportunity.

The children went back to their games: hide-and-seek, catching bandits, eagle and chick, skipping rope, and the like.

Even after five years of exile, the conversation among adults turned invariably to "when do you think we can go back home?"

"We are fortunate to have been able to flee from the communists. So many people could not get out," one said.

"That's right. Although most of us lost our possessions, we are free at least," said another.

"Those remained behind the iron curtain are treated cruelly by the communists. They don't have any freedom, and many people lost their properties," echoed someone else.

"I heard a funny propaganda by the Communist," said Mr. Su. "'Liberate Taiwan, save the people in Taiwan from their misery.'"

"They thought the people in mainland China were naive enough to not realize that they themselves are the ones living in misery," WayLee commented. "They ignored the fact that people had experienced freedom and peaceful life before China changed hands."

"Mr. Su, has your son said anything about when we can go home?" WayLee's mother had to ask.

"Still the same. 'Soon, soon.' I can't get anything out of him."

"But the brutality, the lack of basic human rights, the seizing of people's personal belongings without any cause; this kind of regime has to fall eventually," someone reflected.

"Yes, I agree," MayAnn spoke up. "I realized this struggle between the two sides of the Strait was going to be a long drag," she continued pensively. "The mainland is so vast, and Taiwan is so tiny. Taiwan is not even half of 1 percent the size of the mainland. Taiwan's population is less than 2 percent of that of the mainland. By logic, Taiwan should have fallen to the Communist. But we are still here five years later." She thought of her father and her brother-in-law and fell in silence. Again, she wanted revenge, for her country lost to the Communist and for her loved ones viciously executed. A voice rose, "Love your enemies and pray for those who persecute you." She murmured, "Oh Lord. It's hard!"

Time moved on relentlessly. Months turned to years, years turned to decades. Those who fled to Taiwan were still in Taiwan. The hope to reclaim mainland China dwindled gradually then extinguished. People ceased to ask "when do you think we can go back home?" They finally realized Taiwan was home. The Communist, in the meantime, had changed the leadership several times and had eventually relaxed the grip on ordinary citizens. The efforts to link postal service, transportation, and trade between the two populations began slowly in the 1980s. The two governments on the two sides of the Taiwan Strait remained separate politically.

IV

WayLee did not forget his promise. As soon as they had saved enough, he shopped for an organ. Organs had become less popular. After much searching, he decided to get an upright piano instead. It was delivered on a Sunday before MayAnn and the children came back from church.

"My!" MayAnn was completely astounded.

"Piano, piano!" The children jumped up and down.

WayLee apologized, "I looked and looked but cannot find a suitable organ."

"It's perfect." MayAnn was very pleased. "I had long realized piano would be a better choice. The children can learn and enjoy too."

Although MayAnn was much more experienced in organ, she had learned piano years before when they were in the mainland. She practiced and was able to pick up after a while. Lily and Nan began taking lessons from her. Shane played for a while but eventually quit.

They had now been in Taiwan for more than ten years. Economic growth in Taiwan had begun. Like many of their neighbors, they had done some remodeling and added two rooms in the back. Living conditions were improving. The camaraderie among all villagers remained the same, although some personality clashes were unavoidable.

There were two women next door to each other in their village who did not get along. They argued often. One was quite good-looking but not too crazy about keeping her household neat. The other was the opposite; she was fanatical about keeping her household immaculate.

The good-looking woman nicknamed her neighbor 'headless fly', and the fanatic woman nicknamed her neighbor 'lazy bug'. One day while cleaning, headless fly swept dusts out to the walkway outside. Some got on lazy bug's property, and an altercation ensued that quickly escalated into a physical fight. Other neighbors tried to stop them, but they continued yelling at each other. One of the onlookers said, "Let's get Mrs. Yang."

Sociable, kind, and intelligent, MayAnn had unintentionally established herself as the 'sage' of the village, and people listened to her. So MayAnn came, Lily and Nan in tow.

"Mrs. Lau, Mrs. Chu, did either of you get hurt?" she asked.

"Just some scratches." The two women had already relaxed themselves, rather hurriedly, in anticipation of MayAnn's disapproval.

"Was there something so serious that cannot be resolved without hurting each other?"

"No."

"That's good. Would you forgive each other then?"

"Yes."

The show was over.

Nan was proud of her mother. *I want to be as wise and as helpful as my mother when I grow up,* she decided.

After television became available, WayLee suggested they try to buy one.

"Television seems to be an impractical luxury." MayAnn was hesitant. "Perhaps we should consider refrigerator instead."

"Television is not pure entertainment. Educational programs can broaden children's knowledge," WayLee expressed his thoughts. "More importantly, although neighbors come and visit Ma often, she rarely goes out now. There is not much else to occupy her time, and we are not always here to keep her company. I think she will like watching television."

"You are right. You always know how to analyze." MayAnn looked at her husband in agreement. "Please try to get it as soon as possible. We will consider getting a refrigerator later when we can."

This was the second television set in the village. The excited neighborhood children surrounded the delivery men when it arrived. Now they had another home to congregate in after school.

WayLee's mother was very pleased. She watched whenever she had nothing else to do. Her favorite was Chinese opera. The program usually started later at night. Sometimes she would take a short nap after dinner and ask MayAnn to wake her up before it came on. MayAnn would watch with her mother-in-law. She treasured those moments.

"I always enjoyed Chinese opera," her mother-in-law would reminisce. "Back in those days, we had no television. Operas were sung and played live on stage. It was a big deal. We had a stage in our neighborhood for the performances, but the stage was not regularly maintained. Whenever a show was planned, they would fix it up, and we would know to expect a show to be on soon." Her eyes brightened. "Oh, those beautiful costumes and headgears, painted faces, magnificent singings, and intricate stories. What a treat!

"WayGuo and WayLee were not too crazy about it," she continued. "But WayGuo's wife, YeLin, enjoyed as much as I did. She always accompanied me to the performances." She became quiet. "I miss WayGuo very much. And I am left without knowing what happened to YeLin and their children."

MayAnn could only put her hand over her mother-in-law's and grieve with her. "Lord, please bless them and keep them under your care," she said silent prayers.

Although WayLee's mother had stopped asking "when can we go home?" the question was always on her mind, and she still wished for that day to come. From time to time, she would tell MayAnn, "I may not be able to be buried in the same grave as your father-in-law." MayAnn would invariably respond, "Mother, you are very healthy. You have a long way yet. We should reclaim the mainland, and you will go home alive." In her heart, she did believe her mother-in-law would live to see that day. *How can such a warm, kind, and loving person die in a foreign land?*

One morning in late summer of 1967, WayLee's mother did not get up at the usual time. MayAnn went to her and asked gently, "Are you not feeling well, Mother?"

"I feel all strength has gone out of me. Maybe I just need some rest. Don't worry. I will be fine."

She was still in bed half an hour later. MayAnn was worried and decided to stay home to take care of her. At noon, her mother-in-law got up. MayAnn brought food to her and said, "Mother, you didn't have any breakfast. Please eat some. You need it."

"It's not Sunday, is it?" she asked. "Do you not have to go to work?"

"I asked for the day off," MayAnn answered. She had anticipated disapproval. "It's all right, Mother. It gives me a chance to rest too." She helped her mother-in-law with some food.

"You and WayLee had a marriage by choice without a matchmaker. My marriage was the traditionally arranged kind."

Whenever MayAnn was home alone with her, her mother-in-law would tell stories about her life back home in mainland China; those complex relations among the extended families, the various events in the family and among neighbors; events large and small, good and bad. She described everything in vivid detail. MayAnn would listen as if she were a small child listening to exotic stories, never tired no matter how many times she had already heard.

The topic that day, though, had never come up before.

"Almost all marriages in my time were arranged. In fact, a good proportion of marriages in your time were arranged too. I remember the day when two matchmakers brought your father-in-law to my home," she continued. "I was sixteen, and he was nineteen. The matchmakers emphasized that my family and his family were both prominent and respected in the community. The marriage would be a perfect match, they said. They added that this young man was well educated and was known in the neighborhood to be a devoted son." She was lost in her thoughts. MayAnn waited. "In those days, girls were not supposed to show themselves to strangers. I hid behind a screen and listened. My servant girl standing next to me nudged me to peep through the side of the screen. I finally summoned up my courage and looked." She was now talking to herself, "How handsome!" Her eyes lit up but soon dimmed.

"Mother, do you want to rest now?" MayAnn asked softly after a few minutes of silence.

Her mother-in-law returned to reality.

"You have a good marriage by choice, and I had a good marriage by arrangement. We both are very fortunate. Not everyone is as lucky," she said. "I miss your father-in-law very much. He died too soon. People said the gods were jealous of our marriage, and they took him from me early to make me pay." Wrinkles on her face deepened; a drop of tear fell from the corner of her right eye. "I want to be buried with him."

MayAnn's heart was trembling. With a quivering voice, she said, "Mother, we shall go back to our hometown soon."

"Ah, I am very tired," her mother-in-law said. MayAnn helped her to bed.

She did not get better. WayLee and MayAnn took her to the hospital, and she was admitted. Three days later, she died from complications of a flu-like illness. She was eighty-nine. It was nearly eighteen years after they fled their hometown XiangShan.

MayAnn could not be consoled. She had nightmares night after night. She would find herself awoken in WayLee's arms. Mourning the loss of his own mother yet trying to shoulder the pain of his wife, WayLee whispered in MayAnn's ear, "This will pass." Verses appeared in her mind: *Look not at what can be seen but at what cannot be seen; for what can be seen is temporary, but what cannot be seen is eternal...*

It was drizzling the day of the funeral. The cemetery was high up on the hill accessible only by foot. With family and friends following, the twelve pallbearers struggled as the coffin seemed to become very heavy all of a sudden. The procession was forced to stop. The pallbearers set the coffin down. The family knelt on the ground.

The head of the procession pleaded, "Esteemed madam; your son, daughter-in-law, and grandchildren are all kneeling. Please have mercy on them. Accept this temporary resting place. They will move you back to be with your husband as soon as we reclaim your hometown."

The pallbearers took hold of the coffin and, with a "go!", lifted it up miraculously without much effort and carried it all the way up to the gravesite.

MayAnn lost her mother when she was fifteen. She could still hear her mother's spasmodic cough, aggravated in the winter and at night. Whenever she was awoken by the sound of cough, she would realize her father was up, helping her mother with medicine and rubbing her back until the cough stopped and her mother fell back asleep. Asthma eventually took her mother's life at age forty-two. Her father remained a widower despite multiple advices from his friends to remarry. He took up the role of both father and mother in raising her. When MayAnn married into the Yangs, she regained a mother's love bestowed by her mother-in-law. In fact, many of their neighbors thought they were mother and daughter, seeing them so close and loving with each other. MayAnn reflected on all the treasured moments they had together and played them out in her mind one by one. She recalled the day of her wedding. WayLee and she wanted a simple and relatively modern ceremony. There were no loaded dowry, no red and gold embroidered wedding dress, no weeklong banquets. Neither her father-in-law nor her mother-in-law objected. Rather, her new mother-in-law was overjoyed. She embraced MayAnn and told her, "You are now my daughter." She remembered how touched she was, being embraced and loved by a mother. Those were beautiful memories, but they were also hauntingly aching to recall, memories that could never be realized again. Her mind knew she should accept the tragedy that life dealt her, but her heart was weak and was filled with grief. She realized, like the rainbow, she could no longer hold her mother-in-law in her arms; she could only hold her in her heart. She waited for healing that time might mercifully bring.

Two weeks later, MayAnn returned to church for Sunday service. RoSie and the congregation embraced her and welcomed her back.

"We are very sorry for your loss," RoSie said. "We know how close you were to your mother-in-law. But we are sure you will be able to take her back to her husband, one way or another." She added, "Recovery can be a long journey, but time does heal. Have faith!"

V

Lily followed her mother's footsteps and pursued a career in teaching after she graduated from college. She secured a position as a high school Chinese literature teacher. The school provided her a living quarter, but she came home as much as she could to keep her mother's company, especially after her grandmother died. She sometimes played the piano, but most of the time, she talked with her mother and listened to her recounting the memory of her grandmother.

"I really enjoyed watching Chinese opera with her," MayAnn told Lily. "Sometimes she got tired after dinner and needed to take a nap. She asked me to wake her up when the program started. I did. The next day, your father questioned me in private. 'Why did you have to wake up Ma? It is not like the end of the world to miss an episode. You should let her sleep,' he said. He didn't know, for a Chinese opera fan, missing an episode is a big deal. It is tantamount to losing something of utmost importance that can never be replaced," she continued with a wink. "From then on, I tried to be very quiet waking her and made it seem she woke up herself." She added, "Oh, how I miss those days! I would give anything to get them back."

"Your grandma was such a storyteller. I never got tired of it," MayAnn would say. "She told me all the comings and goings of her relatives back in mainland China, the gossips among her extended families and neighbors. It was like listening to the *One Thousand and One Nights* and better.

"One of the stories your grandma told was about a distant niece of hers, CinCin. She was plain, but she had a very attractive personality, always bubbly and agreeable. She had been promised to the son of one of her father's good friends. Both families were rather well to do, and the arranged marriage was accordingly a good match. But CinCin fell in love with a young farmhand of her father's. She fought vigorously against her father. CinCin's mother came to your grandma crying.

'I don't know what happened to this girl. Where did her good nature go? What did I do in my previous life to deserve this punishment?' she said.

'Is this farmhand a good boy?' your grandma asked her.

'I don't know. I have never even seen him.'

'Then how can you be so exacerbated? It may not be a good match by wealth, but it can be a good match by love,' your grandma told her.

Her distant cousin abhorred what she heard—'good match by love'. *How could a lady say such a thing?* It was incomprehensible for her cousin to hear the word 'love' from the mouth of a lady. She left in a hurry, never again returned to ask for another advice from your grandma. Shortly after, the young couple eloped. People said they both joined the Communist Party and were sent to Sichuan. Then there were rumors that CinCin was not able to endure the harsh treatment by the communists, and her husband could not help her. She jumped in the Yangtze River and drowned herself. 'It was not a good match after all,' your grandma exclaimed sadly."

MayAnn was silent for a while. Then she continued, "I can see your grandma was ahead of her time. Even though she never had formal education, she learned to read from her father, which was not common for a girl of her generation. That reminds me of another story she told."

Lily waited eagerly.

"She had a beautiful jewelry box made of expensive wood and decorated with exquisite carvings and paintings. It was part of her dowry when she was married to your grandfather. Her father, your great-grandfather, inscribed her name with gold paint on the top of the box among the original works of art. One day, not too long after she was married, two of her female cousins on her mother's side came to visit her. They wanted to see her dowry. So she showed them the jewelry box. They were fascinated, especially by the gold decoration on top, not knowing those were Chinese characters of your grandma's name. They copied the gold decoration on a piece of paper and took home the sample drawing. Then they had an artisan in their neighborhood add the drawings on their own jewelry boxes. Their copies were not quite accurate, and the artisan was illiterate. One box ended up with the symbols of characters meaning 'Too Fat,' the other 'No Good.'"

Lily could not stop laughing. She found herself mesmerized by the stories her mother retold, just like her mother had once sitting by her mother-in-law captivated by everything she was saying. Retelling those stories was bittersweet for MayAnn. But RoSie was right. Time did heal, very slowly. Gradually, there was more sweetness than bitterness. Nonetheless, MayAnn never forgot her promise: to bring her mother-in-law back to her husband in the mainland. She waited longingly for that day to come. And she would find herself asking her children the same question her mother-in-law had repeatedly asked: "When do you think we can go back home?"

VI

Lily did not marry until she was twenty-nine, five years after her grandmother died. She spent years keeping her mother company. Her vague memory of the journey out of the mainland had been reinforced by the detailed recounting of the events by her mother and her grandmother. She knew she and the family owed their lives to her mother. Subconsciously and consciously, she believed it was now her responsibility to support and care for her parents.

"My parents had suffered an extremely arduous journey in life. The trial of their generation was so much harder than ours. I now realize how wise and courageous my mother was, bringing the whole family to safety from the communists," she told her boyfriend, pleading her case for delaying the wedding. "I am the oldest, and it is my responsibility to take care of my parents. I want to spend more time with them before I plunge into the endless responsibilities of my own family."

Shane graduated from college when he was twenty-two. After mandatory military service, he joined a start-up electronics company. With his outgoing personality, he had been very popular in school and had attracted quite a few admirers. He finally married the girl from a neighboring college whom he met at a dance party. They had been dating on and off for three years. By the time his older sister Lily ultimately married, he and Sue already had a one-year-old son. He had lost his mischievousness but remained gregarious.

Time continued moving forward. In a blink, they had been rooted in Taiwan some thirty years, an excruciatingly painful length of time none of those who fled the mainland had ever expected to have to endure. The Military Dependents' Villages, originally built as temporary housing, had suffered repeated assault from nature and needed constant attention. The government was in the very early stage of planning to eventually replace these villages with high-rises. Shane took the opportunity and persuaded his parents to move in with them while waiting for the new constructions to take place. By that time, in 1982, WayLee and MayAnn had both been retired for a number of years.

This move proved to be a good design for all of them. Shane was relieved that they were able to have his parents under their care constantly. It was now easier for the entire family to see one another. Lily, her husband, and their two sons visited them as often as they could. MayAnn, in particular, cherished those occasions. Now a grandmother of five, three boys and two girls, all under the age of ten, she was content. They never moved back to the newly constructed high-rise building after it was completed many years later. Shane's home became their permanent home.

Except Nan. She had decided to pursue postgraduate studies abroad after college.

PART THREE

Cornell Days

I

A year after her grandmother died, Nan left her home in Taiwan and journeyed to the United States, leaving her parents and siblings. It was 1968.

She flew to San Francisco, and from there to Syracuse. Her advisor to be, Dr. Thompson, at Cornell University had arranged for one of his colleague's graduate students to pick her up and drive her to Ithaca, New York.

"Nan Yang?" A tall and rather thin young man with hair covering his ears approached her after she walked into the terminal.

"Yes." She was tired, arriving in a foreign land after a long and exhausting journey. *He's got a somewhat unusual-looking face*, was her initial impression.

"I'm ShiMin Lin. Welcome to the States."

"Thank you."

They had corresponded by mail. ShiMin was also from Taiwan and graduated from the same National Taiwan University. Dr. Thompson had asked him to write to Nan and assist in her preparation of traveling to Cornell.

They picked up her luggage, a single gigantic red suitcase her father and she shopped together for. She recalled her father's comment as the two of them spent hours walking from store to store looking for the perfect suitcase. "It must be strong and it must be large enough to hold everything," her father had said. A mood of unexplained melancholy fell upon her.

"It's not too far. An hour and a half at the most," ShiMin said as they approached his car.

The radio was playing Mendelssohn's *Violin Concerto in E minor* when he started the engine.

"Ah, this is one of my favorites." Nan was happy it was the very first music that greeted her in this faraway land from home.

"You like classical music too?" ShiMin asked.

"Yes, absolutely."

They were silent until the music ended.

"I think you'll like Professor Thompson," he said after they had driven further for a while. "He's very popular among students, and his classes are usually difficult to get in."

"Is it hard?" Nan was rather apprehensive of what she was to face.

"Nothing to worry about. Just from Thompson's description of your academic achievements, I'm sure you'll do well."

"How far are you now?"

"I'll be starting my third year. I should be getting my degree in two years."

"Are you working on your thesis now?" Nan wanted to get a sense of the time line.

"Yes, have been for almost a year. It's going all right, sometimes better than others, as expected."

"What's your research on?"

"Glutamine metabolism."

"Awesome! I can't wait to start my research."

Nan was tired after the long flights. She dozed off and was somewhat embarrassed when she woke up. "Sorry, I fell asleep," she said.

"No problem. It's quite understandable," he replied.

She looked out of the window and saw the unfamiliar but beautiful landscape. *I will get used to this.*

ShiMin took her to the dorm where she had registered in advance and helped her check in. "I'll take you to do some shopping for necessities tomorrow," he said before leaving.

She went to bed, spending her first night in an entirely foreign and unknown country far away from home, all by herself. That realization hit her all at once. She cried.

Nan was amazed by the enormous variety of items the store carried. It had practically everything. "Ah, needles and threads!" she exclaimed. "That's what my mother scrambled to get for me at the last minute because we had forgotten it," she told him.

"Your suitcase was so huge. I thought you brought your entire life's worth with you," he joked.

She remembered how the whole family had helped her with the packing, in a way as if she were going to a completely barren land. "Toothbrush, toothpaste, comb, soap, razor . . . Oh, you don't need it . . . towel, gauze . . ." She heard her father commanding. A rush of warmth and longing stirred inside. Her eyes began to blur.

"You'll need lotion. The weather here is much drier than in Taiwan. People always complain of the itchiness when they first arrive in the States."

"That's what it is then. I was wondering why I felt prickly all over. I don't think I've seen lotion in Taiwan."

As soon as she got back to her dorm, she sat and started writing.

Dear Papa and Mama,

I arrived in Ithaca safe and sound. I am now writing from my dorm room. This will be my home away from home, possibly for the next four years.

My trip was very smooth. I did not encounter any problem. Only it was exhausting because of the long flight and the wait for changing flights. The luggage survived well and remained intact. Papa, you can be rest assured now. I have unpacked everything and stored it under my bed. It barely fits!

It took me quite some time before I fell asleep last night. I knew I had many dreams but could not remember any when I finally woke up late this morning.

This afternoon, ShiMin Lin took me shopping. Guess what, they have *everything* here, including needles and threads!

It is very different here from home. The weather is much more comfortable, only it is drier, but ShiMin told me I will get used to it. Best of all is the landscape, lots of green and open land, with patches of flowers, fruit trees, and gentle hills here and there that I saw on our way here yesterday. I even saw cattle and sheep grazing on the fields! I imagine it is more like our homeland in the mainland as I have heard you describe many times.

There will be an English proficiency test for all new foreign graduate students this Friday before classes start. The school wants to find out if anyone may need to take a special English course to help preparing them for classes. I got a notice in my mailbox informing me I am exempt from taking the test because I scored very high in the TOEFL exam.

I want to get this letter in the mail as soon as possible. I love you and miss you already.

My love to Lily and Shane too.

Nan

ShiMin lived off campus. He took Nan and introduced her to his all-male housemates. There were five of them in this old large grayish-blue house four miles from campus. Nan noted the house number was 12, the same as that of her home in Taiwan. All five were graduate students majoring in various subjects. One engineering student from Taiwan who came to Cornell the year before was from a Military Dependents' Village in the city of TaiChung, approximately one hundred miles south of Taipei. He was generally a man of few words and had rarely talked about his life back home. But the "Village" struck a chord. He and Nan connected immediately.

"There were so many kids in our village. We always congregated after dinner at the large open field in the middle of the village, running around, shouting, and playing all sorts of games. Every night, our parents had to call out repeatedly, 'Bedtime, bedtime,' to get us back to our apartments. We had so much fun. We just didn't want to quit," JeFu said.

"We did the same," Nan said. "It seemed we were always outdoors. One Sunday afternoon, a group of us wanted to play in the woods at the back of our village. To get to it, we first had to cross a small stream. Usually, my older sister, Lily, carried my little brother to cross. That day, I decided to carry him despite Lily's objection. I was not even seven. I slid. We both fell in the water, and Lily had to pull my brother out." Nan had forgotten this incident all these years, and she had never told anyone other than her family. She wondered why it resurfaced then and what made her share it with virtually total strangers.

Fortunately, her audience just laughed without making any comments.

"Once, the village was playing a movie in the open field and these three troublemaking boys played a prank." JeFu was quite animated by now. "They sneaked near the projector, waited for the part just before the most guarded secret was to be revealed, and unplugged the power. Everyone was fired up with anger. They yelled and chased after them to get the power cord back. It took a good twenty minutes to settle down and return to the movie."

Another bout of laughter erupted.

"JeFu, that's the most words I've ever heard you speak," ShiMin joked.

"Ah, that's right." Nan remembered. "We didn't have an open field large enough for movies. So we went to our neighboring village not too far from us to watch. The kids from that village would let us know. 'They are putting up the screen today,' they would say; and we all tried to finish our dinner early and went to watch."

"Sounds like fun, to have so many playmates around," said Larry, a chemistry student from Baltimore who would be in his last year at Cornell.

"Yes, I think it was a unique experience with so many children coming from all over mainland China gathered together," Nan said.

"How big is Taiwan?" Ethan, a red wavy-haired physics major from Boston, asked.

"It's almost fourteen thousand square miles," Nan answered.

"That small? That's not even twice that of Massachusetts."

"It's a small island," JeFu said.

"What about the population?"

"Just about fourteen millions now, and it's growing, I think."

"Wow, that crowded?" Ethan said.

"Yes, Taiwan is very crowded, especially Taipei, my city," Nan said.

"So what made you come to Cornell?" Eric, an economics student from Columbus, Ohio, asked.

"When I was applying, I got accepted by three schools—UC Berkeley, Purdue, and Cornell. 'Berkeley is too liberal, Purdue is too conservative. Cornell maybe just right for you,' someone told me. I wasn't sure if that analysis was accurate, but it might have been a toss-up anyway. So, here I am."

"Swell!" Eric said. Nan understood the word 'swell' to mean 'to expand', so she was not sure what Eric meant. Self-conscious about her ignorance, she did not ask.

"Good choice. Whatever the reason is," Ethan said, "I hope you'll like Cornell. You're in for at least four years."

"Is this your first time in the States?" Eric asked.

"Yes, I've never even been outside of Taiwan."

"This must be a cultural shock for you then," Larry commented.

"It's very different from Taiwan. I was born in mainland China. From my parents' description, it seems the landscape here is more like that in the mainland."

"Well, welcome to Cornell," Larry said.

Nan liked the group. And, somehow, her appearance made this group of five men closer.

II

Nan wrote again as soon as she got back to her dorm.

Dear Papa and Mama,

I met ShiMin's housemates today. There are five of them including him, all graduate students, living in an old large house off campus. The number of the house is 12, same as our home in Taiwan, a coincidence. The names of the other four are Larry, Eric, Ethan, and JeFu. JeFu is from the Military Dependents' Village in TaiChung, so we have something in common, and we shared our memories of life in the villages. The other three are Americans. Larry is from Baltimore. He is a chemistry major. Eric is from Ohio. He is an economics major. Ethan is from Boston, and he is a physics major. They all seemed very nice. I know you worry about me. But I really know how to take care of myself, and now I already have some friends.

Ithaca is a beautiful and quiet college town. The city itself is only about six square miles, which is fifteen some square kilometer. I have not seen much of it yet. It is now late August, and I am looking forward to the fall foliage, something we do not have in Taipei. It should begin in late September, they told me.

Last night, I dreamed I was in Taiwan. I was playing with AnLing and her sister MeiMei next door. We were arguing about something. Then Mama came and said, "The truck is here, we have to go." But I was still arguing with AnLing. I told Mama I did not want to leave until I win. "You don't have to win all the time," Mama said. I turned back, but everyone was gone. No AnLing, no MeiMei, no Mama, no truck. I was scared, and I kept yelling come back, come back, come back. Finally, I woke up and was very relieved it was only a dream.

ShiMin and perhaps some of his housemates will take me around and show me the campus tomorrow.

I am looking forward to the start of school, with just a bit of apprehension.

How are Lily and Shane? I miss them too.

Love you all,
Nan

She went to the mailroom to put the letter in the mail and was pleasantly surprised that a letter from home was sitting in her mailbox. Excited, she opened it without returning to her room.

Dear Nan,

When this letter reaches you, you should have already settled in your dorm. Coming back from the airport after your plane took off, we all felt at a loss. Even Shane was quiet.

I miss you already. You are the one never making your father and me worry. You have always been self-sufficient and have never got into any kind of trouble, in or out of school. From grade school through college, we never had to worry about your schoolwork or whether you will be able to get in the best high school and college. But now I must admit I am very worried. I worry about your going to a place so far, so unknown, all by yourself. Can you handle it? Are your wings firm enough yet? I know you are almost twenty-two, but you are always my child in my eyes. How I wish I could hold you, protect you, and always have you by my side. Silly me!

After your grandma died, it took me a while to get used to hearing 'Mama, I am home' instead of 'Grandma, I am home. Mama, I am home.' Now I will have to get used to not having you coming home every day and call out to me 'Mama, I am home.'

We know you will do well in school. But remember you do not need to always be perfect; it is not possible and we do not expect it from you. Just relax and enjoy your graduate school experience.

We love you very much.

Mama

It was dated August 26, 1968, the day she left Taiwan.

Nan could not hold back her tears. She rushed into her room, threw herself on the bed, and cried.

In Taiwan, the family soon fell into a routine. The first question asked when anyone came home was "is there a letter from Nan today?"

ShiMin came to pick her up the next day as arranged. JeFu and Eric came along.

"Larry and Ethan wanted to come too, but they had to go in to do some preparation for their lab duties," ShiMin told her. "Can you walk?" he asked.

"Sure."

They strolled out of her dorm. It was a clear day, deep blue sky with a gentle and tenderly caressing breeze. Two squirrels were chasing each other around a tree.

"Squirrels!" Nan exclaimed. She had never seen a squirrel back home in the busy and crowded city of Taipei. She stopped and observed intensely. Her companions smiled in amazement, watching and waiting.

"Hello, guys," a voluptuous blond girl walking by called out, her eyes fixed on Nan.

"Hi, Melissa," Eric said. "This is Nan. She just arrived from Taiwan, brand new. She will be in the same department as ShiMin, biochemistry."

Melissa greeted Nan. She never took her eyes off her.

Eric whispered to Nan after Melissa walked away, "She's interested in Ethan."

Nan had never dated. Sure there had been suitors, but she never felt any yearning for a boyfriend. Studying and learning were her only interests. She treated everyone the same, male and female. A classmate, in particular, persistently pursued her over the last three years of college. He even went to the airport when she was leaving Taiwan, wishing for an all-too-slim chance of getting a response from her. She very politely greeted him and then went back to talk with her family.

They walked on. Nan took in everything around her and felt blissful within. *What a beautifully tranquil place!*

"Here's our building," ShiMin told her. "Dr. Thompson's lab is on the second floor. My advisor is on the first floor."

She looked at the building gratefully. *Thank you for taking me in,* she said in her mind, *I will work hard.*

They walked around the beautiful hilly campus. The men introduced various buildings to Nan. The Big Red Barn, "It's a student center", ShiMin told her; the Arts Quad, with the three 'Old Stone Row' buildings defining the west side of the quadrangle, and the statues of Ezra Cornell and Andrew White at the western and eastern edges of the Quad facing each other; the iconic McGraw bell tower that housed the Cornell Chimes; the Sage Chapel; the Uris, Olin and many other libraries; the Engineering Quad and the Sundial.

"Ezra Cornell and Andrew White were the cofounders of Cornell. White was the first president of the university," ShiMin explained. "They founded the university in 1865, and Cornell opened its door for students in 1868, one hundred years ago."

There were footprints painted on the ground, stretching between the two statues.

"Legend had it," Eric said, "if a virgin crossed the Quad at midnight and the chimes at the bell tower rang, the two statues would walk off their pedestals to meet in the center and shook hands to celebrate students' virtuousness. Then they would switch places."

"We are still waiting for the bell to ring at midnight," ShiMin said jokingly.

"And a virgin to walk by," JeFu added.

The two statues had stayed where they were since they were first erected.

JeFu pointed further to his right. "That's where my office and lab is."

They were now standing at the top of the Libe Slope. The weather was inviting, and the sight was intoxicating. Nan took in the images of the countless buildings that had been built with various materials and architectural designs, the magnificent McGraw bell tower that marked hours and chimed concerts, the lake with deep blue water, and the gentle hills filled with lush green trees as far as the eye could see. For a moment, she felt utterly free. Oblivious of her companions and without any inhibition, she stretched out her arms and turned around in ecstasy, embracing the beauty of nature and the ingenuity of human mind.

Her three friends were astounded. They stood speechless.

Years later, she would be told, "That day we took you to tour the campus when you first came to Cornell. At the top of the Libe Slope, all of a sudden, you spread your arms and turned around and around. You were radiant. You were glorious!"

After getting back to her dorm, Nan sat and wrote. She described everything she experienced that day, touching her deep feelings. She recounted how, standing at the top of a large grassy hill called Libe Slope, witnessing the wonders of God made her utterly joyful. She wanted to share all the beautiful things with her parents and her siblings, and she wished they were there to enjoy with her. "I will work hard to not betray the trust you and the school invested in me." She closed with the promise and mailed the letter.

III

It was Friday. Since Nan did not have to take the English proficiency exam, ShiMin and his housemates except Larry came to take her to see other parts of the campus and the college town Ithaca. Larry had gone to Baltimore to visit his girlfriend for the Labor Day long weekend.

"Have you heard of Finger Lakes?" ShiMin asked.

"No."

"They are long and narrow lakes north of us, all in the state of New York. Because they are shaped somewhat like fingers, they are known as Finger Lakes," he explained. "They are in a more or less north-south direction. Ithaca is on the southern end of the longest lake called Cayuga Lake. You'll see the word Cayuga around here as in Cayuga Street."

"Oh, that's the lake you saw yesterday when we were on top of the Libe Slope," ShiMin added.

"Are there five lakes then?" Nan wondered.

"More like ten or eleven."

The day was as nice as the previous day; clear, calm, and inviting.

"Ithaca is blessed by the many waterfalls and gorges. They add so much charm and splendor to the landscape. We are blessed by Cornell being built in Ithaca," ShiMin said. *And blessed by fate that brought us here together. She could have gone to Berkeley or Purdue.*

They walked around and passed by Woolworth. "That's where you discovered needles and threads." ShiMin smiled at Nan.

"What about needles and threads?" Eric questioned.

"I just thought I might not be able to find them here, and I had to bring them with me from Taiwan. At least they didn't take up much space." Nan laughed at herself to cover up the embarrassment she was feeling.

"Here's the Cayuga Street," Ethan said.

Nan looked up and saw the street sign "Cayuga Street." Reality was beginning to set in. She was now in the United States, and she was starting to connect with this foreign land.

After pizza at Pirro's for lunch, they went to the picturesque Beebe Lake. It was a man-made lake on campus originally created in 1828 to capture the hydropower and later completed in 1898 by raising the dam higher.

"Shall we walk around the lake and the trail? The entire perimeter is about one mile," ShiMin asked.

"Sure." Nan did not hesitate. So the group strolled around the lake.

The lake was lavishly and abundantly adorned by nature with waterfalls, bridges, trees, flowers, shrubs, herbs, and a diverse species of birds. The scenery was magical. Nan was touched, "I am so fortunate to be here," she said with gratitude.

They sat on the grass by the lake, enjoying the spectacular surroundings. It was late afternoon. The sun was gentle, the breeze caressing.

"Oh, I think existence is a blessing." Nan was overcome with appreciation and, in a moment of epiphany, she declared, "The past is no more, the future not yet, only now! We should live our life intensely, feelingly, and passionately."

Ethan spoke after a noticeable moment of silence that was among the group. "Are you sure literature or philosophy is not your major?"

"Yes, I'm sure. When I was trying to decide what to major in college, my high school Chinese literature teacher suggested for me to study literature, my math teacher said math, my chemistry teacher said chemistry, and my biology teacher said biology. You know what I ended up with."

"No one suggested physics?" Ethan, the physics major asked.

"Physics was my weakest subject. I could only get 80s and 90s, never 100." It had taken a very long time for Nan to accept the fact that, on this subject, she was not the top student in her class.

The image of her high school physics teacher appeared in Nan's mind. She was very pretty and very smart. She married her college classmate who later became an accomplished physicist. Their marriage began to deteriorate after the birth of their only daughter. A birth defect causing severe developmental delay was diagnosed when the baby was one-year old. Her husband was not able to handle the pressure of having a disabled child, the marriage became strained, and they eventually divorced. Nan had seen the child who was always in a wheelchair. People would talk about the tragedy and lament, "The beautiful and talented are unfortunately doomed with a tragic life."

"For me, it was easy," JeFu was saying. "I listed my wishes rather randomly and was assigned to mechanical engineering by my test scores."

"What do you mean 'assigned by test scores'?" Eric and Ethan questioned.

"That's the college admissions process in Taiwan. It is by exam, not by application as is here in the States. You list your wishes by school and department. Graduates from all schools around the entire island take the exam simultaneously. Test score results are sorted, highest first, lowest last. If you are lucky, you get in the school and department of your first choice," JeFu tried to explain. He added, "Except for a very limited number of top graduates from a very limited number of top schools, they are guaranteed a place of their choice without having to take the exam." He suddenly realized and turned to Nan. "You're one of those, aren't you?"

"Yes," Nan answered.

"In fact, I just remembered, the process is the same for junior high and senior high admissions, not only college. They are all by examination," JeFu added.

"Your system is quite different from ours. I learned something," Ethan said.

"That's right. Nan, I bet you are one of those who didn't have to take the high school admissions examination either. You just went straight ahead all the way to college," JeFu said enviously and admiringly.

Nan just smiled.

"No wonder so many students here from Taiwan are graduates of the National Taiwan University. It must be the best university there then." Eric said.

"Good observation. Nearly one hundred percent of all students list it as their first choice," JeFu said.

ShiMin was still mulling over Nan's comment of existence.

"Do you regret not pursuing literature?" he finally asked.

"No, I'm satisfied and happy with what I've done so far. Literature and writing will always be my first love. But since I've chosen biochemistry, I'll try to do my best. I want to live my life to the fullest of my capacity."

The sun was beginning to display its brilliance before it had to give way to darkness. Yellow, orange, gold, red, every color in between and beyond. The sky became deep red, and then darkness began to creep in.

They bid good night to that remarkable day.

Back in her dorm, Nan read the letter from home that had been waiting for her in her mailbox. They were fine, trying to adjust life without her around. Shane's school had started. This was his third year in college. "I remember how worried I was when he was taking the college admissions examination, whether he could get in one of the good universities." Her mother wrote. "You had spared me of that worry. That was a blessing."

"Yes, all the blessings! Full of blessings!" Nan declared to herself.

In her letter to her family, she eagerly depicted in detail her astonishing encounters with nature that day, including her interpretation of existence. "I was so touched. God was everywhere. Yes, I am blessed."

Then she wrote again.

My friends at No. 12,

These few days gave me a chance to examine myself and search my soul. The beauty and grandeur of Cornell and Ithaca are touchingly exhilarating. I am privileged to be part of it.

I have only just met you. Forgive me if I revealed myself too much. But you made me feel easy, and I have that impulse to share it with you.

Soon the last golden rays of the day,
Will give way to dusk.
Then darkness will take over,
Until the sun rises again.

It will be repeated faithfully,
Day after day,
Season after season,
Year after year.

But each moment is unique and unrepeatable,
We live through it,
Then it is gone.

Except in our hearts.
Those wonderful moments once captured,
Forever they are ours.

Thank you for your friendship. I am blessed.

Nan

IV

The men of No. 12 invited Nan for a Labor Day barbecue in the park. They were not used to doing things as a group, and none of them had been involved in planning or executing a barbecue party before. But they were all enthusiastic to have an opportunity to introduce to Nan one of America's traditions. After some glitches, they finally sat down on the benches. The table looked pretty good.

With some hesitation, Ethan, chosen as the spokesperson for the group, began, "We wanted to reply but we didn't know how to rival your letter. That was the most beautiful and poetic letter any of us ever received. Thank you for sharing with us."

"It made me think how everything moves forward regardless of whether we want it or not," he added.

"I was speaking my heart," Nan responded.

"True. 'The eyes are blind, one must look with the heart,'" ShiMin quoted.

"You read *The Little Prince* too!" Nan was delighted. "I like the book. It taught me what is truly important in life." She recollected. "I once made a bookmark. On it I drew the fox and wheat fields. It was a beautiful story of friendship." Suddenly a revelation, she added, "Friendship, you cannot buy it, you can only develop it."

ShiMin was moved. *She is so sensitive.*

"What other books do you like?" JeFu wanted to know.

"I like many. *Long Day's Journey into Night, Les Misérables*, for example." Nan thought of them with nostalgia. A feeling of sadness enveloped her as she recalled the miseries of the Tyrones.

Melissa, the girl Eric said had an interest in Ethan, came over to their table.

"Ethan, I can't believe you guys really did it." She glanced at the table, and her eyes were on Nan again. "I thought you only said that to make me not force you to join us."

"Hi, Melissa," Nan greeted her politely.

"You two have met?" Ethan was surprised.

"Yes, the first day we took Nan to tour the campus. You were busy with the lab. You missed it," Eric said.

Melissa stood for a while and then went back to her own group dispiritedly.

JeFu tried to resume the conversation.

"*Les Misérables* is such a gigantic book. I could never finish it," he said. "Where did you find the time to read?"

"I love reading. I used to read all the time. When I was in high school, sometimes I would put a book on my lap. Not *Les Misérables*, obviously, it was too big, and I tried to steal a few passages when teacher was not looking in my direction," she added, "when teaching was going too slow, of course."

"Swell," Eric said again. Nan finally figured out what it meant.

"You, Nan, of all people? I don't believe it!" JeFu protested.

"Oh yes." She was now letting it go. "One afternoon, our class was cancelled because the teacher had an unexpected emergency. Two other girls and I decided to take advantage of the free time. We sneaked out of school and went to watch the movie *Giant*. It was worth the risk. But I felt so guilty; I never did it again."

The house of No. 12 laughed.

"That's the one thing I never told my mother," Nan admitted.

"I thought that sort of stuff is reserved for people like me. Good student like you don't do things like that," JeFu said.

"With all that, you were still at the top of your class," Eric said admiringly. "Amazing!"

"Those books and movies, are they in Chinese or English?" Ethan wondered.

"Books are translated to Chinese. Movies have Chinese subtitle," Nan said.

"Okay, that makes sense. How did you learn English?"

"English language is a standard subject taught in junior and senior high schools. In fact, curriculum of secondary schools in Taiwan is the same across the board. There are no electives."

"There are advantages and disadvantages with that, I suppose." Ethan gathered.

It was a perfect day for a barbecue. The park was quite crowded. All tables and benches were occupied. Children running and playing, squirrels chasing here and there, Frisbees trying to fly wherever they could. The air was filled with a delicious aroma that made one hungry, for food and for nurturing of the mind.

"How perfect!" Nan exclaimed.

The men felt flattered. They were very happy they could pull off this gathering successfully.

"Too bad Larry has to miss this," Eric commented.

"Don't feel sorry for him. I'm sure he's having fun with Amy in Baltimore," Ethan said.

"It's been only a few days, but I feel I've known you for a long time," Nan blurted out.

"I think we feel the same," Eric agreed. "And some of us here are generally not very easy to make friends with."

Eric was thinking of the long dark period after he broke up with his girlfriend. They were high school sweethearts. She stayed in Ohio for college at the Case Western Reserve University, and Eric went to U Penn. Even though it was more than four hundred miles apart, he went back to see her as often as possible, and they wrote each other constantly in the beginning. When the second year rolled around, letters from his girlfriend became less frequent, and she stopped mentioning their plans for their future together. When he went home during the winter break, she broke the news to him that she had met someone else. Eric was so wounded that he closed himself up for years.

ShiMin admitted, "I'm glad you came to Cornell."

Like any day, this perfect day must end.

By the time Nan got back to her room, she had a roommate.

"I'm Lauren. This will be my second year of grad school," the friendly-looking girl introduced herself.

"I'm Nan. I just came from Taiwan."

"Welcome! Was your trip okay?"

"Not too bad, just tiring."

"It must be very difficult for you to come so far. Let me know if you need anything."

"Sure. Thank you."

Lauren went back to what she had been doing. Nan sat at her desk and began her letter home.

V

"Professor Thompson?" Knocking on the open office door, Nan waited.

"Ah, Nan?"

"Yes."

Thompson walked toward Nan and warmly welcomed her.

"How was your travel?"

"It was not bad. Just a bit exhausting."

"Of course, it's a long trip. Did ShiMin pick you up all right?"

"Yes, he helped me settle in."

"Perfect. Let me introduce you to other graduate students."

They walked around the building. She was introduced to many people, both students and faculty, from Thompson's group and other groups.

"Ah, there's ShiMin," Thompson said. "He doesn't need introduction."

"Indeed." Nan was glad to see him. They greeted each other.

After the tour, Thompson sat with Nan. He explained the workings of the department in general and his group in particular. He went over the courses she was going to take and the possible research areas she would be involved in.

"As you are on a research assistant scholarship, you don't have teaching responsibilities like the TAs, teaching assistants, do. You just need to work on research. You'll start by helping one or two postdocs with their research, but eventually, you'll have your own for your thesis."

A girl stuck her head in the door.

"Ah, Jennifer, right on time." Thompson waved her in.

"This is Nan." He turned to Nan. "Jennifer is in her second year. She'll show you your 'territory' and get you oriented."

"Well, welcome to your four years ahead," he concluded.

Jennifer was happy to see Nan, as the majority of Thompson's group were males. She was glad to have another female on board.

Her "territory" was in one of Thompson's labs. There were desks and file cabinets in various corners of the lab that were designated for graduate students.

"Here you are, next to me, but we are on different projects," Jennifer said with a smile. She was a petite girl. With her dimples, she appeared quite attractive when she smiled. "Use it however you like, neat or messy or anywhere in between. No open food, though. This is a lab after all."

Nan looked at Jennifer's messy desk and smiled.

With that, they began their lifelong friendship.

That night, the letter home was all about the excitement she felt of the opportunity and prospect of her new life. "I will begin going to church with Eric. He is the only one at No. 12 regularly attending church. There are many churches here, both on and off campus. Eric will pick me up on Sundays and take me to his church near where they live." She added.

Within two weeks, the school was in full swing.

VI

The men at No. 12 decided they might try to cook on weekends and eat together rather than going their separate ways for quick bites. They invited Nan, of course, and Nan accepted, naturally. She had not done much cooking in the past. MayAnn never encouraged her or her sister Lily. "Your job is studying," she would say, even though she knew Nan needed no additional time to study. In fact, Nan never stayed up past nine o'clock, even when she was in college. She did her homework as soon as she returned home, and she usually did not need much time studying. "Then go to play with your friends or read your novels," her mother would tell her.

Nan picked up the art of cooking rather quickly and was able to help the men in the kitchen.

"Certainly beats McDonald's," they would say.

"Or Elba's pizza."

"Or Curly's Chicken House."

"Or George's beef."

"Or Johnny's Grill."

"Even Joe's Italian."

They enjoyed the food, the camaraderie, and the conversation.

"How was church?" well satisfied with his dinner, Larry asked.

"Swell." Eric replied.

Nan tried to envision a picture in her mind. She said, "I like the pastor. He seems very genuine and truly believes what he preaches."

"How do you know?" challenged Ethan.

"He was consistent, to the point. Never said anything about himself, never had a hint of trying to glorify himself. Everything was about God." Nan pondered. "We go to church to be fed by spiritual words. I got it in this church."

"What makes you believe there is God?" Ethan pushed.

"That is a difficult question. Otherwise, the world would be all believers." Nan fell in a deep muse. "My mother sometimes played the organ in a church near our home. She took us with her. I had no understanding in the beginning. As I grew older, I began to challenge it. It took me ten years to find him."

"How?" ShiMin was curious and wanted the answer.

"By listening, by reading, by experiencing, by reasoning. Like many people, I needed proof before I could accept. I have since realized that it's easier to prove God exists than to prove God doesn't." Nan paused, thinking. "For example, do you think if you put all the necessary parts of a car—engine, brakes, lights, screws, and all—together in a pile and let it sit, after millions or billions of years, big bang or not, it will somehow assemble itself perfectly and becomes a car that can run? No, I don't think so. There has to be a maker to make the car. Humans are infinitely more complex than cars. They cannot evolve from a number of atoms and molecules, no matter how long you wait. It is mathematically improbable that humans evolved spontaneously from inanimate matters. There must be a maker of humanity. The problem with accepting religion is that there needs to be an element of faith, as we cannot see God as a concrete being, standing before us. On the other hand, we all believe oxygen exists, even though we can't see it."

Nan felt burdened. It was a very difficult subject, and she was not sure she would be able to present her thoughts convincingly. She continued, "I don't think creation and evolution are necessarily mutually exclusive. There can be evolution, after humans have been created first. Small changes or 'evolutions' occur in our genes that make it easier and better for us to adapt to the environment, and we become smarter, generation after generation."

Then she added, "I admit I waver and have doubts sometimes, and I have to resort to faith. I was told, though, that doubt is part of the journey of faith. Even his disciple doubted Jesus' resurrection. Jesus had to show his wounds before Thomas would believe. Jesus said, 'You believe because you have seen me. Blessed are those who have not seen and yet believed'".

No one spoke. They were trying to digest what they heard. Finally, Eric broke the silence.

"I remember a joke the pastor once told. It was bedtime for a little boy. His mother sent him upstairs to bed, reminding him not to forget to say his prayers. When he passed by his sister's bedroom, he looked in and saw she was kneeling besides her bed, saying her prayers. He rushed to his room and jumped right in bed. His mother came up shortly to make sure he was getting ready for bed. When she saw he was already in bed, she asked, 'Did you say your prayers?' 'No,' he answered. 'Why?' his mother asked. To that, he said, 'Well, I came by Jenny's room and saw that the line was busy.'"

Laughter erupted, Nan included. Then she summoned her courage and spoke again.

"The line to God is always open," she reasoned. "The Bible says, 'Behold, I stand at the door, and knock: if any man hears my voice, and opens the door, I will come in to him, and will sup with him, and he with me.' But he can't open the door for you. This you must do yourself."

That night, Nan described the emotionally draining conversation in her letter. "Afterward, I felt closer to them," she concluded.

Soon, the group was known as 5+1 around campus.

VII

Nan liked her postgraduate work. It opened a new horizon for her. The news that one of their biochemistry professors had just won the Nobel Prize thrilled her, even though he was then taking leave from Cornell and was at the Salk Institute in California. *This is an exciting field and an exciting place.*

ShiMin took her shopping when she received her first paycheck as a research assistant.

"I want to get things for my family," she told him.

He was amused by her purchases: dish pads, dish detergent, dishcloth, laundry detergent, paper towel, lotion, shampoo, conditioner, and the like. She also got a blouse for her mother, an overcoat for her father, a dress for Lily, a shirt for Shane, and cookies and candies; spending nearly her entire paycheck. She gave her mother directions. "Squeeze a few drops of dish detergent on the dish pad. That's all you need. It works wonders, and you will like it. Send with love."

The season had turned, and fall foliage was in its utmost. The brilliant colors of all shades were dancing everywhere, on and off campus.

One Saturday, both Nan and ShiMin were working in their labs. They ran into each other in the stairwell.

"Are you almost done?" he asked.

"In about half an hour."

"Want go for a walk and see the foliage when you are done?"

"I'd love to."

They went to Beebe Lake.

The air was crisp, the colors dazzling. The surface of the lake was smooth as a mirror, reflecting all the brilliance in the water. Then there was also the sound of waterfall!

Nan could not help but let out a cry, "The magic of nature!"

"The wonders of life," ShiMin added.

"Indeed!" Nan was ecstatic, realizing his capacity to relate.

A tug at his heart, he almost embraced her.

Instead, he said, "I'm glad to see you happy."

They sat on the grass, watching the magic of nature and pondering the wonders of life.

"My heart is overflowing with gratitude." Nan opened herself up. "I was born in mainland China. My mother brought my grandmother, my sister, my brother, and me out of the Communist-controlled homeland. I grew up in a family filled with love and now I'm here, among friends, in a place I never dreamed of only a year ago."

"I wish with all my heart that you'll have this happiness all your life," ShiMin said in wholehearted sincerity.

Nan felt so comfortable that she began pouring out her life story, or rather, her mother's life story. How against all odds, her mother was able to flee the mainland. "Between freedom and the seemingly safer option of inaction, she chose the lesser-traveled road at the time, giving up all her worldly treasures." She took out a small photograph protected by clear plastic coverings from her handbag.

"This was taken the day we arrived in Taiwan, escaping from the communists," she said.

"Your mother appeared as thin as a stick in this picture."

"Yes, that was a testimony of how much pressure and burden she had been under," she said. "On the original picture, she had written on the back these words: Out of the Lion's Mouth."

"How true!" he said. "It's hard for me to imagine what you had to endure. I didn't have to go through the terrifying journey you described. My family had been in Taiwan for generations. We didn't have exposure to communism."

Taiwan, originally part of China, had been under Japanese rule for fifty years since 1895 when the last imperial dynasty of China lost its war to Japan and had to cede Taiwan. It was returned to the Republic of China in 1945 after Japan surrendered and World War II ended. People who had been in Taiwan had therefore been shielded from the influence of communism.

ShiMin listened to Nan's tragic stories. He was silent, trying to overcome his own emotion.

"I was the only child," he said at long last. "I was weak and was often sick during my first year of life. My parents were not sure if I would survive." Pausing and searching for strength, ShiMin told Nan the one secret he had never before, nor since, told anyone else, "My father finally left us when I was three. My mother has been the sole caretaker and breadwinner ever since. Like your mother, she is a strong woman."

With a rush of compassion, Nan reached and squeezed his hand. "We all have our own battles to fight."

They sat in silence for a long time. Nan realized ShiMin had just confided in her the one thing he had never intended to disclose to anyone.

"Shall we walk?" Nan suggested.

They got up and walked around the lake. Birds were flying and singing amongst the trees. They watched the luxuriant foliage, close-up and from afar. Nan felt richly rewarded.

"Cornell has some legends about relationships. The one about Beebe Lake is that if a couple walk all the way around the lake holding hands, they are destined to be engaged," ShiMin told her.

"Says nothing about marriage?"

"No, just engagement."

"That's convenient, to leave an easy way out for the ones who might just be in a temporary romantic mood." Nan smiled.

It was already dark when they got back. Nan found her roommate lying in bed crying.

"What happened, Lauren?" Nan asked gently.

"We had a big fight. Tom and I. It's over. I know this time he won't come back."

"Oh, Lauren!" Nan sat beside her, feeling her desperation.

Lauren gradually calmed down.

Nan waited until Lauren was able to listen. "Remember what the Bible tells us. 'Love is patient, love is kind, love is not jealous . . . Love rejoices with the truth, bears all things, believes all things, hopes all things, endures all things.' Be patient, Lauren. Talk it over. Examine your feelings for each other. You'll be back together if you truly love each other."

VIII

Classes were going well. Nan's lab assignment was to help a postdoc with his research project. She prepared chemical and culture reagents, maintained cell lines, helped compile experimental results, analyzed data, and sometimes went to the library to do literature search for references related to the research. She did so well that when the research paper was eventually published, her name was included in the authorship.

Christmas rolled around, and winter break began. Other than the foreign students, most went home. Jennifer, Nan's lab mate, the girl with dimples, stayed behind too. Her parents were trying to sort through their marital problems and preferred she did not come home. Nan had by then developed a close friendship with Jennifer. Jennifer confided in her.

"Oh, Nan, I'm so scared."

"Do you have any idea how or why?"

"Not really. Last time I was home, I heard them fight once. I heard my mother shouting a woman's name. My father was quiet most of the time. He just stood there, looking very sad. I don't think my mother really loved him."

"What makes you think that?"

"I've never seen her showing any affection toward my father. Sometimes my father tried to get close to her, she just walked away, pretending she didn't notice."

"Do you have any explanation?"

"I don't know. It was always like that since I can remember. For whatever reason, she married him. Now they are both suffering." Jennifer began to cry.

Searching her own soul, Nan said, "If there is no longer love between them, it might be better that they suffer the pain of separation now than to prolong the agony."

"Oh!" Jennifer was heartbroken.

"They both will be happier," Nan said sorrowfully. She wondered why relationships needed to be so complicated. *The bondage humans put on themselves!* she thought helplessly.

Nan invited Jennifer to visit No. 12 with her and introduced her to JeFu and Ethan. Jennifer already knew ShiMin as they were in the same department. Larry and Eric had gone home for the holidays. Ethan had to finish some work in the lab and was going to stay for a few more days before he headed home.

It was a blanket of white outside, warm and inviting inside. The luscious smell of food further complemented the tempting atmosphere. Even Jennifer was able to forget the burden on her heart for the moment.

"How wonderful it would be if this moment could be frozen," she said.

"Yes, but there will be many moments like this in life. We just need to be willing to experience it and accept it," Nan responded.

"That is so true," JeFu echoed. "Like the village I grew up in. We were completely ignorant of how materially poor we were. But we played with one another and shared with one another. I have nothing but happy memories of those days."

"I too agree," Ethan interjected.

"What do you know? You have no idea what poor means," JeFu retorted. He had been much more certain of himself since his first conversation with Nan and after he became closer to his housemates.

"I do know. My parents may be rich, but I want to stand on my own two feet. You don't see me driving an expensive car or wearing expensive clothes, do you? I'm going to look for happiness by myself, not in money but in life." Ethan was adamant.

"Well said. That wasn't my intention. My apology," JeFu said.

"Apology accepted." Confident about himself, Ethan continued, "But what I agreed was that, rich or poor, we need to be willing to experience and accept the things around us, find those jewels, and embrace them."

ShiMin finally spoke, "I'm not so naive as to think there is only good in this world. But while there is ugliness, there is also beauty, where there is cruelty, there is also kindness. The world is filled with beautiful things waiting for us to explore and accept."

"Wow, this house is becoming a house of philosophical thinking!" JeFu joked.

"These are just facts," ShiMin concluded.

"I like you guys," Jennifer said.

"I like the conversation," Nan said. She was touched by Ethan's comment, "Find those jewels and embrace them," and ShiMin's comment, "The world is filled with beautiful things waiting for us to explore and accept." She recalled what ShiMin told her of his childhood, and she hoped he would indeed be able to forget the wound and search for beautiful things instead.

Jennifer, on the other hand, was very impressed with Nan's friends at No. 12. This encounter and the stimulating exchanges also made her wonder if Nan was right after all, that her parents might be happier if they were set free to pursue their separate destinies.

So Jennifer went with Nan and visited the house of No. 12 regularly. She soon became one of the group. Some people on campus began calling them 5+2.

Jennifer's parents separated and filed for divorce a month after the winter break. Jennifer broke down and cried.

"It's okay to be sad," Nan told her, "but I hope you'll be comforted by knowing your parents are no longer caged. They are free from the bondage they put on themselves and on each other."

"Yes, they should find themselves happier," Jennifer reassured herself.

IX

When Larry returned to campus after the holidays, he brought back the exciting news that Amy had accepted his proposal, and they were engaged. The wedding was planned for the summer at Amy's hometown, Towson in Maryland.

Winter finally gave way to spring in Ithaca. Although Nan loved the snow, and appreciated the season of solitude and austerity, she was also happy she no longer needed to put on heavy coats, gloves, boots, scarves, and all. Suddenly, everything was in bloom. The earth revived.

This was Nan's first spring in her newly adopted country. The day was so appealing that she decided to go for an early-morning walk before class. The air was crisp, and birds were singing. She closed her eyes and drank in the sweet air along with all nature's beauty. When she opened her eyes, Ethan was standing not too far from her, smiling. She smiled back. The rays of the gentle morning sun bouncing on his red hair, his five-feet-eleven stature looked quite handsome.

"Didn't expect to see you this early, especially around here." Nan was pleasantly surprised.

"I got on campus too early and decided to take a walk. Want to walk with me?"

"Sure."

They walked in silence for a while.

"How's your research going?" Ethan spoke first.

"Good, I think. At least I have my topic identified."

"That's not bad. Some sort of metabolism?"

"Yes." Nan smiled. *They can't tell one amino acid from another or one enzyme from another. No need to bother with the complicated scientific names.*

"Are you still getting letters from home often?" Ethan changed topic.

"Yes, at least twice a week, and I write as often. I know they want to read mine as much as I want to read theirs. I guess you didn't have the experience of anxiously waiting for letters from home."

"Come to think of it, I did, during my first year in college and first time away from home. But it didn't last too long. There were too much activities and too much fun going on in school without my parents watching over me."

"I think it's easier for boys than for girls."

"I don't understand how you can have so much to talk about," Ethan attempted.

"We talk about everything."

"Including me?"

"Including you." Nan laughed. *He's going to wonder what I say about him.*

"Really! What sorts?"

"I won't tell. All facts though." She laughed again, tossing her hair back.

Ethan watched her with adoration. "Looks like I need to be nice to you."

"Sure you do. See you Sunday, if not sooner." They parted.

On Sunday, the group gathered at No. 12 as usual. The topic of the conversation somehow landed on relationships.

"Nan, you must have had many boyfriends in the past." Eric turned to Nan.

"No, never."

"That's surprising. Why?"

"Why not? I haven't had any interest. I was perfectly happy with all my friends, women and men. I don't believe in having a boyfriend just because everyone else has."

Jennifer was thinking if her mother married her father because she felt she had to have a partner as all her friends did.

"My mother used to tell me the story of one of her friends," JeFu said. "Her friend was fair, but somehow, no men had shown much interest in her. She became anxious when most of her friends were married. Then she met a man who fell in love with her. She did not have real feelings for him, but he was good to her, and she was willing to marry him even though there were warning signs. She had realized he was very particular and rigid in many ways. To him, everything was black and white. There were no shades in between. She had to be very careful with what she said and how she acted. Otherwise, he would accuse her of not having her heart in him. That perception made him feel so helpless that he reacted by violence. In the beginning, she tried to cover up the purple and blue marks on her arms and made up stories of accidents for those on her face that she could not hide. Eventually, she ignored it, and people stopped asking her questions. The marriage fell apart, but they stayed together, unhappily." JeFu's mother had warned him, "Don't ever marry someone just because you think you have to marry. You will have to pay the price later if you did."

"Wouldn't her friends have reported the abuse?" Eric asked.

"That was in the old days in China. Those things were hushed. There was no such thing as spousal abuse," JeFu said.

"In a relationship, there are always at least two people involved. Both will have to take responsibility," Nan said.

"Is this why you are not interested in having a boyfriend?" JeFu asked.

"No, and I didn't say I'll never date. I just haven't so far."

"At least we are in a modern society, and we can choose our own partners without interference from our parents. Otherwise, tragedies like Romeo and Juliet would be bound to happen," Larry concluded.

Nan and Jennifer sat on the lawn outside of their lab. The weather was nice, in the upper sixties, quite comfortable for them to enjoy their lunch. It was a Friday in the second week of April.

Jennifer started after some hesitation, "What's your opinion of the guys at No. 12?"

"Their personalities are quite diverse. But I think they are all good people," Nan answered.

"What do you mean by diverse?"

Nan thought for a while. "Eric, for example, is very easygoing and kind. He seems to like everyone and does not know how to dislike. JeFu is rather introverted. It takes time for him to make friends, but he also has a sense of humor and is not afraid to speak up when he feels necessary. Larry is the most mature, more of a protective type. Ethan is fully confident of himself, knows and usually gets what he wants. He seems to have a clear goal in life. And ShiMin . . . I can't quite read him. He seems to be sure of himself, but then, there are times he seems so quiet and withdrawn. I think there is something he can't let go . . . beyond I can understand. He hides his emotion. I wish I knew what it is."

Jennifer was mainly concentrated on JeFu. "I think I'm attracted to him," she blurted out.

"Who?" Pulled back from her own thoughts about ShiMin, Nan asked.

"JeFu."

"Oh, Jennifer, I'm happy for you. He'll take good care of you. I can tell."

"I'm also afraid. I don't want to fall in the same situation as my parents."

"I think your mother might have married your father for the wrong reason. That was a tragedy. Just make sure you are true to your heart; you'll be fine." Nan tried to assure her.

"But I don't know what his feelings are. He wouldn't know my feelings either."

"I'll drop him a hint," Nan said happily.

On Sunday, Nan made good of her promise. As they were cleaning up in the kitchen after dinner, Nan found herself alone with JeFu.

"JeFu, how is it that you don't have a girlfriend?"

JeFu was caught unprepared.

"I . . . don't know. I never feel comfortable approaching girls. What if they don't like me?" he faltered.

"Well, girls are generally hesitant to show their interest in a man. Someone has to take the first step, and it's usually expected that the man be the one. You know this is true for Chinese, but I know it is true for some American girls too."

Not too long after that conversation, Jennifer was going out on dates with JeFu. The other men in the house were happy for them.

"It's also good that we didn't lose the romance to an outsider," they said.

X

Larry was nearing the end of his graduate studies. He defended his thesis in the spring and left Cornell and No. 12 in May after he received his PhD degree. It was the first disruption of the group since they became one coherent body with the arrival of Nan the year before. A sentiment of loss befell them all.

In July, the group drove down to attend the wedding ceremony. This was the first time they met Amy. She was in her last year of medical school at Johns Hopkins. Amy welcomed and thanked them for being in Larry's life. She had heard so much about them from Larry that she was able to put their names and faces together quickly.

Larry introduced them to his parents. His father was in the Navy and had been in the United States Seventh Fleet that operated out of Japan twenty years before. Mr. Clark was very happy to have an audience, including the three young people from Asia, to hear the tale of his tour during the Korean War.

"I was only nineteen when I enlisted in the Navy, shortly after I graduated from high school. They put me on training and on various assignments." He was quite chatty. "I didn't realize it but I had problem with seasickness, and I couldn't get out of bed for days in the beginning. They almost kicked me out of the Navy, but I survived. I was moved around, sometimes back on land in the States that allowed me to continue my relationship with Larry's mother. My big break came when I was finally assigned to the USS *Hollister* in 1950. She was a beautiful ship, and I loved that assignment. What I remembered most was the evacuation of Tachen Island. Our ship *Hollister* provided protection and assistance for that evacuation in 1955."

"Ah, I remember that evacuation," Nan said. "We saw refugees pouring into Taiwan, and we were told they were from Tachen Island. I remember how sad my grandmother and my parents were when they realized Tachen finally fell to the Communist. They told me Tachen was off the coast of our hometown XiangShan, it belonged to our province Zhejiang. I was about ten then."

Tachen Island was located just south of the ZhouShan Islands, the home of Nan's uncle WayGuo. It was the last stronghold of Kuomintang's Republic of China.

"Were you born in Taiwan?" Mr. Clark asked.

"No, I was born in mainland China; my mother brought us to Taiwan when the communists came to our hometown."

"You're lucky. I witnessed the Tachen evacuation; it was very sad. So many people waited on the beach in the cold to be taken by boat to our *Hollister* and many other Seventh Fleet ships waiting off shore. I can still remember that overwhelming emotion I had when I held the frightened children handed to me by soldiers on the boats. I was happy I was able to get them to safety one by one; in the mean time I felt so sorry for them having to leave their innocent lives behind and going into a new and unfamiliar place. After the entire island was evacuated, the soldiers dynamited the underground military installations; they didn't want to leave anything for the communists. We then took the refugees to Taiwan about two hundred miles southwest of Tachen Island."

"I too remember the refugees arriving in Taiwan," JeFu said. "I think they said there were around twenty thousand; men, women, and children all together."

"That was a sad history. My mother was quite disturbed by that news also, even though we had been in Taiwan for generations," ShiMin said, recalling.

Mr. Clark was excited to discover this connection to his son's friends.

"You are dominating the conversation," Mrs. Clark said to her husband. "You should let Larry's friends talk."

Mr. Clark still wanted to continue the conversation, so he asked questions. "What do your fathers do?"

"My father and Nan's father are both in the military," JeFu answered.

"Did you know each other before?"

"No, we were in different cities. We met at Cornell."

"How nice," Mr. Clark said. "What about you, ShiMin?"

Nan startled. She worried if ShiMin would be stuck.

"He's no longer with us." ShiMin had been asked about his father before. He had already formulated his answer.

"I'm sorry," Mr. Clark said. Yet he was not finished, he continued, "How did he die?"

"It's been so long. My mother didn't want to talk about it."

"Oh, I understand," Mr. Clark said and then turned his attention to Ethan, Jennifer, and Eric.

The wedding was small but meticulously planned to the smallest detail. Nan and Jennifer helped decorate the church, and the men were charged with odds and ends and final touch-ups.

Although wedding ceremonies in Taiwan had been modernized and most brides wore Western-style white gowns and grooms wore suits, instead of the traditional elaborately embroidered red dress for women and dark blue or black robe usually embroidered with a dragon for men, the customs remained quite different. Nan took note of everything at this first wedding she attended in the still not-so-familiar land.

They toasted the newlyweds at the reception. "May your life together be filled with happiness, and may the friendship of No. 12 be everlasting!"

"Friendship is a wonderful thing," Nan said impulsively.

Larry raised his glass to Nan. "We were like scattered sand until you came. Like glue, you put us together."

On their way back to Cornell, Nan could not stop going over the wedding in her mind—the beautiful music, the touching vows, and the holiness of a union between two people truly in love.

She thought of her roommate Lauren. One day, after Lauren returned from the holidays, she came to Nan in ecstasy. "Thank you, Nan, for your advice. Tom and I are back together. After scrutinizing myself thoroughly, I knew my feelings for him were true. I admitted to him and asked him to examine his feelings for me. We came to the conclusion we love each other too much to waste our lives dwelling on the little things that we don't agree on. We don't have to be always in agreement. There can be compromises, and we don't have to fight. We haven't fought since. I think we should be okay."

Laruen and Tom became Nan's good friends.

XI

ShiMin's mother was thirty when her husband left her. She met him when she joined an analytical laboratory right after she graduated from a two-year college with an associate degree. He was her boss. Life together was good during the first four years of marriage, especially when they were finally expecting their first child. But their excitement with the birth of ShiMin was short lived.

"Mr. and Mrs. Lin, I'm afraid I have some not so pleasant news," the doctor told the couple. "Your baby has a feeding problem. We'll need to keep him in the nursery for a few more days. Also, his face seems slightly asymmetric, one side is smaller, and one of his ears appears different. It didn't form as well as his other ear."

"What does that mean?"

"We don't quite know yet. We just need to see how he grows. He may get better, stay the same, or may get worse. Right now, we should be concentrating on his feeding, making sure he can take in enough nutrient."

The couple was devastated, but they tried to comfort themselves. "Don't all babies look asymmetric when they are just born? Probably most babies don't feed well in the beginning either," they told each other. They did not want to believe that their baby was different from the norm.

It was quite difficult for ShiMin's parents. It took a long time to feed him, and he required constant care for his frequent bouts of colds. The asymmetry, although relatively mild, became apparent to his parents gradually.

His mother quit her job. But the strain on the marriage was too grave. His father finally left when he was three. ShiMin blamed himself when he was old enough to understand.

It would take another seventeen years before a medical term was introduced for the condition: hemifacial microsomia. The structure of one side of the face is smaller than the other.

They had seen a specialist a year after the diagnosis was known. "Surgery could be attempted but hardly seemed worthwhile. The risk would outweigh the benefit," they were told. "What about the cause?" "Not clear. Might just be a fluke." "Could it be passed on to his children?" "Probably not, but families with both affected parent and child have been reported in the literature occasionally."

This was the battle ShiMin had been fighting against, his unjustified guilt because of his father's departure, his injured self-esteem because of his appearance, and the possibility of transmitting it to his children, no matter how small the chance might be.

The only concern ShiMin's mother had in this world was his happiness. She brought up the subject again in her most recent letter. "Have you found that someone yet? You are getting older, not younger. You know this is the one wish I have, your living a happily married life."

He was not able to answer.

"The name Nan came up in a number of your letters," his mother continued. "It seems you like her. If she is the one, go for it. You will have to show her."

He put his mother's letter aside.

But the letter touched the depth of his heart. After a few days, he wrote. "Yes, I do like her, a lot. But she is too perfect. She is unreachable."

"What do you mean 'too perfect' and 'unreachable'?" his mother repudiated immediately. "Do not let your condition get in the way, my son. It did not affect your intelligence, and it did not affect your ability to live and enjoy life. Plus, you have a mild form of it. If she is really as good as you described, she will look beyond it."

ShiMin was hesitant. Although he believed his mother, he did not have the confidence. He was afraid any move would destroy the friendship he so treasured. So he kept his feelings to himself.

XII

Nan decided to take three weeks in August and go home to her family. The whole family met her at the airport. It was like old times right away.

MayAnn and WayLee managed to take some time off from work to spend time with Nan. Lily did not have to teach since school was on summer break. Shane too was home from his college. He had been accepted three years before to an engineering program based on his scores on the college admissions examination. It was not his first choice, neither the school nor the specialty. Still, it was quite desirable. Shane was happy, and his parents were satisfied.

The family walked around their neighborhood with Nan. Nothing had really changed in the year she was away from home, except perhaps a little more marks of aging on the buildings. They went to the back of the village, and there it was, the small stream flowing gently. Nan recalled the first meeting she had with her friends at No. 12, when she somehow volunteered the story of falling in it carrying Shane. Now Larry had graduated, moved away, and married. The rest of them were all one year further in graduate school. *Things did change fast. I hope our friendship will last forever.*

"Ah, Nan, how nice you are back!" An old neighbor ran into them.

"Huang Ma-Ma, nice to see you. I'm visiting my parents for three weeks."

"Come, come to our home for a while. Mr. Huang will be happy to see you." She started to pull on Nan's arm. A feeling of warmth came over Nan. After a year in the States, she had forgotten this uninhibited gesture of friendliness that was common among her fellow villagers.

They went to Mrs. Huang's home.

"Old companion, look whom I brought home to see you," she called out to her husband.

"Huang Pa-Pa, how are you?" Nan said happily.

"Ah, Nan, what a pleasant surprise! Sit, sit, please, Mr. and Mrs. Yang, Lily and Shane."

Mrs. Huang was hurriedly serving tea and sweets. Nan immersed herself in this enthusiastic treatment she had been used to growing up in the village.

"Our son would have been happy to see you," Mrs. Huang said, winking at her husband. "He is doing his last three months of military reserve training in TaiChung."

He was one of many who had an eye for Nan and was quite disturbed when she left for the States.

"We encouraged him to look elsewhere, but he was fixated on you. Good thing the training does to him. It takes his mind off. His letters are much more upbeat lately," Mr. Huang said.

"Nan, you have not changed a bit." Mrs. Huang looked over Nan carefully.

"It's only been a year, Huang Ma-Ma."

"Yes, I guess it is true for most Chinese. We usually look younger than our age. Have you found a boyfriend there yet?"

"No, not really."

"You should begin to pay attention. You know we all need a partner in our life. Do not keep your standard too high, or it will be too late when you realize." Mrs. Huang gave Nan a motherly talk.

"You are right, Mrs. Huang," MayAnn said. "I had a colleague back home when I was a teacher. She was smart and quite good-looking. One of our male teaching staff chased after her diligently, but she did not give him a chance. She told me he was not as handsome as she would have liked. I felt sorry for them. He was a good person. Later, he married. She was still alone by the time I left the mainland."

A week later, a postcard with images of Boston came for Nan. It read, "Greetings from Boston. Hope this finds you happy and content." Signed Ethan.

This was a pleasing surprise for Nan. She had indeed been happy and content.

Like ShiMin's mother, MayAnn was anxious to know her daughter's male friends. She had been waiting for Nan to come home so they could talk face to face.

"Have you found someone yet?" she asked as the two sat near the window by the small upright piano. It was a lazy afternoon, light breeze flowed in gently.

"No one in particular, and I'm not in a hurry. I have to finish my studies first."

"That is true. But studying and dating are not necessarily in conflict with each other if you find the right person and you are sure of your heart. I will feel much more at ease if I know you have someone taking care of you. You are so far away. I worry all the time."

"I know, Mama. But I'm good friends with all the boys at No. 12. They take good care of me."

"Yes, I got that from your letters. But that's not the same as two people committed to each other, willing to spend their life together. On the other hand, what is most important is not to get in a relationship until you are absolutely sure you have found the right person. It has to be mutual, and it has to be true to the heart. A good marriage is not by luck. It is your own choice. You are responsible for it."

"I know. I'll remember."

Aside from being so far away, MayAnn was not without other worries about Nan. She and WayLee had been having conversations about their children.

"Our three children are so different from one another." She had told her husband. "I am not too worried about Lily and Shane. Lily, even though she seems weak and soft in her heart, she is capable to adapt and she should have her own luck. Shane, even though he didn't get in the best university, his warm and easy-going personality makes it easier for him to succeed in life. Nan, though, she worries me. She has all the gifts and virtues, but I worry about her pride and stubbornness. She wants to be on top in everything. She's too used to success. But in life, it's not possible to always succeed. I worry that she will not be able to handle failure."

"Yes, that's Nan's biggest flaw. She's very kind-hearted but she's prone to develop envy toward people better than her, like the girl in her class who almost always gets better grades in physics. She's too competitive. I think deep down, she has this insecurity; she cares too much about what people think of her. We need to continuously remind her." WayLee had said.

"How's your school work going?" MayAnn asked, now that Nan is sitting in front of her.

"It's not easy. I realized there are many smart people. I have to work hard."

"It's good you realized. Don't forget it's not possible to always be the best. You have to accept when others are better than you are. Don't be too competitive, admit your weakness and acknowledge other people's merits."

"Yes, Mama. I am trying."

"Now tell me more about your friends."

"Let me see," Nan began. "JeFu is very dedicated to Jennifer, very protective too. They both will be in their third year when school starts in September. They looked so good and so happy together. Jennifer went to see her mother right after semester ended. She said her mother looked calmer and indeed happier. So was her father. He now has a girlfriend. Jennifer said she was happy for him, having gone through a painful marriage and divorce."

"I am glad you gave Jennifer support when she needed it." MayAnn said.

"Yes, I'm glad everything worked out well," Nan continued. "It will be Eric's last year when school starts. He is the nicest person, very kind. People said he was once hurt by his first girlfriend. Perhaps that's why he doesn't show any interest in girls anymore. He never said anything about it, and I didn't ask."

"That's unfortunate. But we all have our own destiny. He'll find the right person someday."

"I certainly hope so," Nan said, then continued, "Ethan, he is very confident of himself. I think he'll succeed in whatever he wants to achieve. He's one year ahead of me, like JeFu and Jennifer."

"What about ShiMin?"

"I don't know . . . I think something is bothering him, and he's unwilling, or unable to let it go. Sometimes he's very quiet when everyone else is excited about some topic that was being discussed. He hides his emotion. I wish I knew what it is."

"Did you ask him?"

"No." That was only half true. ShiMin had shared with her in confidence his father's abandonment of them. But Nan was determined to treat it as if something almost sacred. She would not reveal it even to her own mother, not if she did not have his permission. She could understand how his father's departure might have affected his ability to connect with people, but it was more than that. There was something else. *What was it?*

"Then ask him, if it helps," MayAnn said.

Nan almost startled. "Sorry, I was thinking."

"Trying to figure him out?" MayAnn smiled.

"I'm not sure I can," Nan lamented. "He is the most sensitive among them all," she added.

"What about your roommate Lauren?"

"She and Tom have been very happy together. I can tell they have put aside the unimportant disagreements."

"That's very good. Sometimes a little reminding and direction can make a big difference," MayAnn said.

Nan was glad she had these conversations with her mother. She treasured those interchanges. *How nurturing. I'm so glad I came home.*

On Sunday, the family, including WayLee, went to their church. The little white church in their neighborhood had been rebuilt years ago when Nan was still in high school. The congregation had grown greatly, and a church large enough to hold all congregants had been needed. The pastor who first introduced Christ to MayAnn nineteen years before had retired, while RoSie continued to be the church musician. She approached Nan after the service.

"Your mother has been very excited about your visit. I'm sure you know how much she misses you," RoSie said.

"Yes, I know. And I'm glad I came home. It's especially good to see my father is finally willing to explore Christianity."

"Truly it is. We were all very happy when we saw him here. He will accept when he is ready."

Studying abroad was not yet very common at that time. Many of Nan's high school and college classmates stayed in Taiwan. They organized a welcome home get-together dinner for her. Many came, including the one who had pursued Nan for three years in college. He brought his girlfriend and introduced her to Nan. Nan was very happy to see that he had moved on. His girlfriend had just graduated from the same university as theirs. She majored in literature.

"It's a good subject. I had contemplated literature too," Nan said.

"Really? It seems biochemistry and literature are two completely different fields."

"That might be true. On the other hand, all disciplines could be interconnected in some way. There is crossover in the most basic sense. Human minds are so amazingly ingenious. They have the incredible ability to learn and absorb vastly different types of knowledge." Nan had never thought this through before, but as she was talking, it just made sense to herself.

A few others joined in the discussion. The subject eventually changed to politics, and the group swelled. Finally, everyone was in the discussion. Most of them, like Nan, were transplanted from mainland China to Taiwan at the time of the Communist takeover. Some had been Taiwanese for generations. Opinions were divided about what the political future of Taiwan should be; whether it should be reunited with mainland China or whether it should be independent. Sadly, to everyone's disappointment, two years after that discussion among friends, in October of 1971, a United Nations General Assembly Resolution was passed that recognized the delegation of the People's Republic of China in the mainland as the legitimate representative to the United Nations, in place of the delegation of the Republic of China in Taiwan that had been one of the five founding members of the United Nations and the first to sign its Charter.

The party continued late into the night. The restaurant was going to close, and they had to call quits. Nan reluctantly said good-bye to all her friends.

As the time of departure from Taiwan came nearer, Nan's lingering sadness mounted. To her surprise, this was much harder than a year ago when she left home for the first time to be on her own. It was the excitement of exploring a new horizon then. It was now back to the place once unknown, not sure when she would be able to see her family again.

XIII

ShiMin picked up Nan at the airport. He was obviously happy to see her.

"I'm glad you are back," he said, relieved. "Tell me what you did in Taiwan." ShiMin prodded as they got in his car. The radio was playing the second movement of Bach's *Double Violin Concerto in D minor*.

"Oh, may we finish listening to this movement?" Nan asked.

"Sure." It happened to be one of ShiMin's favorites too. He thought the second movement was more romantic than Beethoven's *Romance*. He turned up the volume. They sat there and listened.

"Music, so beautiful. Yet you cannot see it and you cannot touch it," Nan reflected when it ended.

"But you can see it in your mind, and you can touch it in your heart," ShiMin said.

Nan's heart fluttered.

"I took violin lessons when I was in junior high, senior high, and the first two years of college," he said.

"How nice! Have you played this?" she asked.

"Yes, it's one of my favorites. I think it's very romantic."

"More romantic than the two Beethoven's *Romance*," she said. "The two violins following, chasing, and answering each other. It's as if two people so connected with each other that they are naturally in sync in all their movements."

"Exactly!" ShiMin exclaimed. "I used to have a recording by David and Igor Oistrakh, father and son, of this music. I was always moved when I listened to this second movement."

"Now back to your Taiwan experience." ShiMin said as he started the car.

Nan began detailed accounts of her three weeks, the things she and her family did, the conversations they had, the places they went, the reminiscence of old times, and the reunion she had with her high school and college classmates, including their heated discussion of politics. She chattered on, leaving out only the exchange she had with her mother about her friends at No. 12.

He listened intendedly.

"Ah, I got a postcard from Ethan." Nan just remembered.

"What did he say?" with a start, he asked.

"Only 'Greetings from Boston. Hope this finds you happy and content.'"

He was silent.

It was late August. The weather was nice, in the low seventies. They saw a sign off road pointing to an orchard. "Apple Picking," it said.

"Are you tired? Do you want to go walk around?" he asked.

She was tired. But she also wanted the opportunity. So they veered off.

They parked the car and walked into the rows of trees laden with fruits. The sight of the overflowing abundance almost made Nan giddy.

They walked around the field and sat on the grass.

"I'm so blessed in this world full of beauty and riches," she stated.

"There are ugly things too."

"Sure, but I think in the end, beauty trumps ugliness."

"Do you truly believe it?" he questioned.

"Yes, I do. You said yourself, while there is ugliness, there is also beauty, where there is cruelty, there is also kindness. You do mean it, don't you?"

"Of course I do. I didn't think you'd remember."

"Why not? And are you exploring and accepting the beautiful things in this world?"

He could not answer.

After some struggle, Nan spoke, "It was not your fault that your father left you and your mother. I'm sure he loved you. Only the burden was too heavy for him, and he chose to avoid it rather than to face it. It's unfortunate it happened this way. But the world goes on, with or without our consent." Her eyes glistening, her forehead unknowingly frowning in deep muse, "You have to move on. Let it go, ShiMin. Find and accept the beautiful things life has to offer."

He felt helpless. He wished his life had been different. He wished he were able to love her freely.

"I hope you'll seek and find God," she finally said.

They left without picking any apples.

ShiMin did not go home after he dropped off Nan. He drove around trying to make sense of his emotions. He felt inundated with conflicting thoughts. "Why does God, if there is a God, put her in my life, knowing she is unreachable to me?" he asked. "Then maybe mother is right. Maybe she will look beyond my birth defect." He changed his mind immediately. He wondered whether she was just being a good friend. Moreover, he was worried that the birth defect would be passed on to his children.

But his desire for Nan was overpowering. "Maybe I should have a talk with her. Maybe mother is right," he concluded.

When he finally got back, his housemates asked anxiously, "Did you get her?"

"Yes," he said. Then he saw Ethan's fine blue eyes beamed brightly. He recalled the postcard Nan mentioned. It immediately extinguished the courage he tried so hard to gather.

XIV

A new academic year began. The composition at No. 12 changed. A second year graduate student, Mark, moved in to take up the opening left by Larry. Mark was quickly assimilated.

ShiMin harbored no resentment toward Ethan. He was strong enough to know it was his own predicament, Ethan was not to be blamed. But a slight feeling of jealousy was present, nonetheless.

Nan and Jennifer continued to visit the house on Sundays.

"Ethan, thanks for the postcard. I like it," Nan told Ethan as soon as she saw him.

"I'm glad." Ethan appeared satisfied. "Tell us all about Taiwan."

"It's very different from here. My hometown Taipei is the most crowded city in Taiwan. Cars, tricycles, bicycles, and pedestrians were everywhere, fighting one another to find a space to go. Small shops and homes were piled on top of one another, and I rarely saw a green space. But it's home, and as they say, there is no place like home."

"Taipei is notoriously crowded," JeFu said. "My hometown, TaiChung, is more spacious. There are parks in the city."

"I was thinking of taking a trip to TaiChung to visit your village but didn't get around to doing it," Nan said.

"That would have been nice. I know my parents would have liked to meet you."

"I hope you didn't say anything bad about me," Nan kidded.

"Is there anything bad to say about you?"

"We all have our own strengths and weaknesses."

"What's your weakness? Let's hear it." JeFu was curious.

"More like what are my weaknesses. For one, I don't accept failure well. My mother had to remind me, 'You don't have to win all the time. There are going to be failures in your life for sure. The sooner you learn, the better it will be for you,' she says. I know she's right, and I'm trying."

"So, did you talk your mother's ears off? You wrote to each other so much when you were here," Ethan asked.

"It's more like she talked my ears off," Nan joked.

"Giving you advice?" Ethan asserted.

"Yes, all kinds!" Nan laughed.

"You are just joking, aren't you?" Jennifer asked naively.

Nan just smiled. She was now thinking about the conversation she had with her mother regarding ShiMin. A hint of melancholy arose.

ShiMin had been observing Nan and Ethan. He was convinced Ethan was serious about Nan. *I have nothing to compete with.*

"Mark, what's your major?" Jennifer changed topic.

"History."

"Good subject. History was my minor in my undergraduate years." Jennifer was excited.

"Really? What was your concentration?"

"Civil war."

The two carried on their conversation.

Nan walked over and sat next to ShiMin.

"I haven't seen you around in the lab this whole week," she said rather longingly.

"I've been working hard on my research."

"How is it going?"

"Very well. I'm getting some good results. I should be able to finish this semester." ShiMin had thrown himself into his work and was determined to finish his thesis and to graduate by the end of the school year.

Ethan came over. "So, Nan, was it easier to leave home this time?"

"Actually, no. It was much harder. I didn't cry the first time I left. I think at the time, I was looking forward to the opportunity of advanced studies here. I didn't realize then that homesickness could be so heart-wrenching."

"You still feel homesick?" Ethan was rather surprised.

"Yes, I don't think I'll ever completely get over it. But it'll get better like everything else."

"Nan, come. Let's cook," Jennifer was calling.

"Call if you need help," JeFu shouted after them.

They went in the kitchen.

"I feel bad for that Melissa," Jennifer told Nan. "She has such a crush on Ethan. But he doesn't seem to have any feelings for her."

"The ones who love each other are the blessed," Nan said. "Now you know how fortunate you and JeFu both are."

"I always know. After witnessing the tragic marriage of my parents, I treasure him more."

"I can see that. He's very dedicated to you too. I'm happy for you," Nan said.

Three days later, Nan went to ShiMin's lab after everyone else had gone home.

"Are you in the middle?" she asked.

"I can stop."

"Want to go for a walk?"

They walked out of the building.

The night was still young. They walked further to Libe Slope. ShiMin took off his jacket, laid it on the grass, and they sat. It was getting darker, and millions of stars were twinkling in the sky. Nan broke the silence.

"My father once told us a story about moon and star. There were two moons in the beginning, he said. They were connected by many stars in between so people from the two moons could visit each other. But one moon vanished because one of the two brothers living on separate moons played a prank on his brother, causing his brother's moon, together with his brother, to tumble and fall. It was lost forever." She was stuck by the image of the group of her playmates sitting on the ground, circling around her father and listening earnestly. ShiMin patted her hand lightly. "My father made up the story to teach my brother Shane not to play tricks on me," Nan continued. "Shane liked insects. He used to catch them and let them free inside the home; butterflies, dragonflies, and fireflies. I didn't like the feel of insects on my body, so Shane would deliberately put them on my neck as I was doing my homework. It seemed so long ago." She paused. "Afterward, whenever the night sky is as crowded as tonight, I would look for a bright trail of stars near the moon, imagining walking on it to find my friend at the other end."

They looked up at the busy night sky, trying to find their trails of stars. It was again a waxing crescent moon that night.

"Did you have many friends back home?" ShiMin asked.

"Yes, I always had. I was used to having many playmates growing up in the Dependents' Village. That might have something to do with my making friends easily later on."

"I'm the opposite. My mother was so protective of me that she didn't just let me go out and play. She always wanted to know whom I was with, and she would go and find me if I was only out a little longer than she thought I ought to be."

"It's understandable why she did that."

"Yes, I know. But sometimes I wished she didn't."

"One of my friends in high school was a year older than I was." Nan thought of her friend in Taiwan. "She had to repeat fifth grade because of a bus accident that took her father's life and put her in the hospital for more than a month with multiple injuries. Later, her mother remarried, and her stepfather didn't particularly like the idea of having to care for her and her older brother, so she sent them to live with their grandmother. I met her the first day of school. We were both looking for our classrooms and realized we were in the same class. She was very quiet, and some of our classmates made fun of her because she was older and somewhat slower. One day, I found her crying in the restroom, and I decided to defend her. Gradually, she opened up to me, and we became good friends. Her brother was five years older and was in college. When his girlfriend met her and realized she was slower than other people, she became greatly concerned and told him not to bring her along to any of their functions. She didn't want people to know that her boyfriend's sister was slow. My friend's brother broke off with his girlfriend."

ShiMin was quiet.

"It was such a flawed presumption people back home had at that time, that somehow the defect of our relatives would shame us," Nan said. "I think it's getting better now. People are more accepting and more understanding. We certainly shouldn't see this here in the States."

"I don't have any brothers or sisters. I'm the only child," ShiMin said after a long while, pushing back what he was really thinking. *I am sure Mother would have wanted more children, but her dream ended tragically with my birth.*

"You have friends, friends who care about you," he heard Nan's desperate plea.

"Yes, I think so. I'm grateful," was all he could utter.

XV

Ethan showed up outside of Nan's lab. She was surprised.

"Oh, hi, didn't expect to see you here."

"I had to stop by the Mann Library and decided to come and walk you back to your dorm."

"A nice surprise. Have you waited long?"

"Yes, a long time!" He laughed.

Nan liked his openness and his confidence.

They walked, in a direction opposite to her dorm. Nan did not object.

It was late September. Some leaves had already raced ahead of the others, winning autumn's first gift of colors.

"This beautiful fall foliage. I can never be tired of it."

"What kind of weather do you have in Taiwan?"

"The Tropic of Cancer runs through the middle of the island. Taipei, my hometown, is toward the northern end. With the ocean, I think it's more subtropical, but it's very humid most of the time. There are fall colors, but only in the mountains."

"Did you get to go hiking in the mountains?"

"Only very rarely. Life in Taiwan is very different from what you see here. Most people are middle class, which means they have enough to support a simple lifestyle. To do anything else is a luxury." Then she remembered her school days back home. "Every school year, there would be one so-called Day of Outing. There was so much excitement when the day approached. A week or two before, the whole class voted for a destination, usually one of the famous vacation spots. Then everyone began counting days, excitedly waiting for the day to arrive. We brought our own lunches, much better than what we usually had. I can remember my mother and my grandmother preparing my bag. It not only had lunch but it also had snacks, drinks, fruits, and desserts; things we didn't routinely have. Then the whole class got on a bus that had been arranged by the school for the trip. Oh, I miss that!"

Ethan was fascinated. He watched Nan's fervent and yearning face with admiration. *I am so glad she came to Cornell,* he too told himself.

"It's hard to comprehend that I'm here, now, far away from the place I grew up in," Nan said, "in a foreign land, talking to you."

"Are you happy here?"

There was a moment of pause. "Yes."

"But?"

"Ah, I don't know. I just have this melancholy that I can't pinpoint, every now and then."

"Is it homesick?"

"Maybe." Nan brushed it away.

"I wish you could share with me. I want to see you happy." Ethan was sincere.

Nan was moved. She smiled and said, "Everything will be fine." Then added, more to herself, "Things happen for a reason."

"Let's go have ice cream," Ethan suggested.

"In this weather?"

"Why not? It's probably low sixties. You can have ice cream even if it's snowing."

They went to Baskin-Robbins 31 Ice Cream. Not many customers were in the shop.

"What's your goal at Cornell?" Ethan asked, holding his huge three-scoop cone.

"Finish up the degree as soon as possible."

"Then?"

"Get a job in the field, either here or back home if I'm needed. I want to be able to contribute to science, to give something back to the society."

"Have you been to Boston?"

"No, Baltimore was the only other place I've been to, that time for Larry's wedding."

"You'll like Boston. It's such a vibrant place, full of life, full of culture."

"My undergraduate thesis advisor spent a year as a visiting scholar at Harvard. He told me about the city, Harvard, MIT, Charles River, Museum of Fine Arts, Boston Symphony Orchestra, on and on. He said it was the Charles River that helped him curb his homesickness in the faraway land. He would walk along the bank, watching sailboats go by and counting the number of days before he would return home."

"That's quite touching. I guess I'm lucky my home isn't so far away. I don't have to go across continents."

"We are grateful nevertheless for having the opportunity to advance our studies here," Nan said.

"I'm glad you are here," Ethan said without thinking. Then he added, "I didn't know you have to do thesis as part of undergraduate study."

"It wasn't required. Very few students did it."

"What was your topic?"

"The Effect of Stress on Protein Metabolism." Nan recalled the summer she spent in the lab working on the project. An image came up.

"Want to know the subtitle?" she asked.

"Sure."

"Urinary hydroxyproline excretion in rats after fever-induced stress." Nan smiled, waiting to see the reaction.

"Wow." He had to think it through in his mind. Then he realized. "Rats? Did you have to handle rats?"

"Of course!"

Ethan stopped eating his ice cream. Nan laughed.

As he walked her home, he told himself, *I have found my jewel.*

XVI

On October 15, 1969, a Vietnam War Moratorium was held around the country, which was followed by a massive demonstration a month later in Washington, D.C. The Cornell community was actively involved, and the campus was filled with anti-Vietnam War sentiment. Nan and her friends attended several speeches, including those given by the Cornell president and a New York senator. Afterward, they gathered together to discuss.

"I hope we will get out of this war soon. The casualties are too high. I wish we never got involved," Jennifer voiced her opinion, and Eric echoed.

"It seems that if the Communist government of North Vietnam wants to reunify the country by taking over the Republic government of South Vietnam, it's their civil war. Unless there are obvious violence and cruelty imposed on human life, we shouldn't get involved," Ethan ventured.

ShiMin, not having direct knowledge of what the Communist regime was like, agreed with Ethan. "War is destructive. It needs to be reserved for truly justifiable causes," he said.

JeFu and Nan had experienced the effects of the Communist takeover, although they were too young to understand at the time their families had to flee from the communists. But they knew their childhood growing up in the "Villages" and saw their parents struggling to start over their lives afresh in Taiwan. Nan also knew how devastated her parents were by the brutal murders of her uncle and her grandfather. *And poor Grandma. She died two years ago without seeing the day of returning to her home XiangShan she so longed for.*

"I'm against war too," JeFu started, "but in this case, I have mixed feelings. The Communist Party, at least the one in mainland China, exercised total control of its people. Just look at the 'Cultural Revolution.' It has been going on three years and still has no end in sight. Mao, their party chairman, using the pretense of 'preserving true Communist ideology,' called for persecution and purging of the 'impure' and anyone he perceived as against him or disloyal to him. The death toll was horrendous. I'm afraid the South Vietnam people may fall into the same fate if the North Vietnam communists win."

"My opinion is similar to JeFu's," Nan said. "My mother took my family to Taiwan when I was four. She knew we would be persecuted and maybe even murdered if we didn't flee from the communists."

"Children too?" Jennifer asked in disbelief.

"Yes, children too. Like JeFu, we were the lucky ones. We got out. Many of those left behind lost their lives because they were considered to have 'bad' personal or family background. My uncle and my grandfather were among them. People with the 'good' class background also suffered—"

"What are the 'bad class' and the 'good class'?" Jennifer interrupted.

"—the bad class are the intellectuals, landowners, and people who have relatives belonged to the Kuomintang Party. The good class are the workers, peasants, and communist soldiers."

"How strange the way they define the two classes."

"Right," Nan agreed. "Mao pushed his personal agenda without regard for the population. As an example, his disastrous 'Great Leap Forward' policy destroyed the economy and was the main cause of the great famine that resulted in millions of deaths," she continued. "Taiwan is a tiny island compared to the vast expanse of mainland China. But Taiwan survived, due in part to the protection provided by the U.S. Navy in the Taiwan Strait. We don't know what the North

Vietnam Communist regime is like and what will happen to the South Vietnam people if the North wins. But the president of South Vietnam has pleaded that the United States continue its support and remain in Vietnam. So I'm not sure. I can't say if I'm for or against this call for ending the involvement in Vietnam."

"You have a good argument. I didn't think of that," ShiMin said. He recalled that Saturday afternoon a year ago at Beebe Lake. They went to see the foliage; they ended up sharing their life stories. Nan told him her mother's journey fleeing Communist-controlled homeland. He told her his deep secret of being abandoned by his father in his early childhood.

"We need to learn from history," Mark, the history major, said. "Like many situations in life, there is always more than one side of a story. We shouldn't jump to the conclusion without having all the necessary information," he reflected and added. "The war has been going on for fourteen years. Whether it could have been won by now if our involvement were strategically different is not for us to judge, but the tragically heavy toll so far is undeniable."

"Unfortunately, that's beyond our limit and understanding," Eric said.

It would take another three and a half years before the United States finally ended its involvement in the Vietnam War. Two years later, on April 30, 1975, Saigon fell to North Vietnam. The colossal tragedy associated with the evacuation of Saigon after the unexpectedly rapid collapse of South Vietnam and the struggle of hundreds of thousands 'Boat People' who fled Saigon in the following years left a painful mark in history.

XVII

In late February of his last year at Cornell, ShiMin completed the draft of his PhD thesis. As he put down his last sentence, an uncontrollable desire to share with Nan overcame him. He went to her lab.

Nan smiled at him, noticing the rare sparkles in his eyes.

"Can you leave?" he asked.

"Yes."

The sky was clear, and the sun was shining. The day would easily be perceived as warm and welcoming. But it was too cold to walk. They drove to Beebe Lake, sat in the heated car, and watched the frozen lake—large patches of snow scattered on the ice, tall tree trunks with their barren branches, fully foliaged evergreens ornamented with snow, a partial rainbow across half of the sky. There was not another soul around. Radio was playing Beethoven's *Violin Concerto in D Major*. They were silent, listening.

Nan said passionately when it ended, "I love this hauntingly beautiful music and the solitary landscape in this deep chill of winter. I feel so indebted to the marvel of the great minds and the splendor of nature."

"You are a poem," ShiMin said before he could think.

Then he said, "I'm done."

"I know, congratulations!" Nan smiled through her tears. "What's next?"

"Review, revise, get it approved, then defend."

"And?"

"Find a postdoc position somewhere."

"Will you consider staying in Cornell?"

"I don't think so."

Nan was silent.

"At the Labor Day barbecue, almost a year and half ago, JeFu asked you what books you liked," ShiMin asked the question he had long wanted to confirm the answer. "*Long Day's Journey into Night* was your answer. You looked sad then, just like now."

"I was thinking of the tragedy of the Tyrones. You can feel the despair O'Neill must have felt when he was writing his own family story, those four deeply troubled souls." The feeling of sadness and helplessness came back to her. She was deeply moved. "He wrote it in tears and blood as he said in his letter to his wife. I don't think there is much more a writer can give to his book and his audience. Such a powerful play, dug deeply into the souls."

"I thought that's why you looked sad. That is a great play. One of my favorites too."

"You didn't say anything then at the park. You are not saying anything now of your true emotion either. You are evading." Blunt and forceful, Nan tried to reach him.

ShiMin was silent. He thought about the letter from his mother a week ago and the struggle he had within himself. He looked at Nan's face in veneration, the girl he so longed for. Then he was reminded of his fear. *I cannot do this to her.* So he repressed his heart and said nothing.

In desperation, Nan pleaded, "Couldn't you share with me what you are really thinking?"

ShiMin was crying on the inside. He opened his mouth then closed it in dejection.

Nan realized she would not get her answer. Hopelessly, she said, "I only wish you could let it go. Whatever it is."

She concluded they were close friends but not close enough for him to let her in the depth of his soul.

The music came on again. It was Mozart's *Requiem*.

"I just finished my draft thesis today," ShiMin replied to his mother's letter. "I should be able to finish by June. I cannot be sure what lies ahead for me, but I will face it whatever it might be." Realizing the day of separation from Nan was rapidly approaching, he was struck by an emotion of tremendous loss that might never heal. He got up and put on the recording of Beethoven's *Violin Concerto in D Major*. "Nan and I went to Beebe Lake and listened to music in the car. She had tears in her eyes. She is easily touched by beautiful things, and she herself is like a poem. You reminded me again that my birth defect is mild. I know that. I am also aware in most cases it is not hereditary. But the specialist also said there were cases of transmission in families, and if it did, the child could be much more severely affected than the parent. There is no guarantee. I also know Ethan is crazed for Nan. She deserves a good life without any worry. I cannot take that away from her." He stopped. With his eyes closed, he immersed himself in the music, allowing the hauntingly beautiful sound of violin and orchestra to torment his heart with a love he could not have. He ended his letter with enormous ache in his soul. "I will begin applying for postdoc positions in universities not too close to Cornell. Hopefully that will make Nan's life a little easier."

His mother read the letter over and over. She knew the heavy burden of despair and sorrow her son was carrying. And her own unjustified guilt for his birth defect was excruciating. Her heart bled.

XVIII

But life had to go on.

ShiMin successfully defended his thesis. It was now time to begin his next journey.

He had decided to join the Los Angeles County Harbor General Hospital, affiliated with UCLA Medical School, as a postdoctoral research fellow. Eric also graduated; he was going back to his hometown in Ohio to work in a financial company.

The group had their last Sunday meal together.

"The experience at No. 12 turned out to be the most valuable of my years," Eric said. "Nan, you brought friendship to the whole house. I shall never forget."

Mark, the newest member of the house, resonated, "I didn't anticipate such strong friendship when I moved in. I thought this was just going to be a place to sleep and study by myself. It proved to be an experience even better than my undergraduate days."

"I didn't expect this cohesiveness either," Nan said, recalling. "I didn't know what would be ahead of me when I first left Taiwan. But I landed here and met you all. You took me in and accepted me immediately without any reservation. I'm the fortunate one. I feel so blessed."

"We can't stop the clock and wish time would stand still. When the moment comes, we have to let it go," ShiMin said helplessly.

Nan fought back her tears.

"It's hard to say good-bye. But we all have our own bright futures to look forward to." Ethan tried to stay positive.

"There is always an end to everything, unfortunately," Nan said with crushing emotions.

"I'm so glad I'm part of this group," JeFu said.

Looking at JeFu, Jennifer said, "Thank you, Nan, for bringing me into the equation."

Tears were shed, even among the men. After all, for so long, they were like siblings.

ShiMin drove Nan back to her dorm.

"Let's go watch the stars," Nan said.

They passed her dorm and went to Beebe Lake for the last time, the place Nan was introduced to in the early days of her arrival at Cornell, the place where she declared "existence is a blessing." It had become their favorite.

"Have you been back to visit your mother since you came?" She asked.

"Once. My mother cried so hard when I had to leave as if she would never see me again."

"Could you take sometime and go see her before you start your work?"

"I don't think so."

He had gone home the first summer after he came to Cornell. His mother was very excited and invited a few of their friends and neighbors for dinner. One of ShiMin's classmates in college was among the guests. Mimi lived in their neighborhood and had always been hoping to attract ShiMin's attention. His mother liked Mimi and considered her a potential daughter-in-law.

"Why didn't you spend more time talking with Mimi?" his mother asked disappointedly after guests left.

"I was polite to her. What more would you like me to do?"

"Mimi is a good girl and quite good-looking too. I just want to see you married and settled down. You need a life partner."

Besides not wanting to see his mother cry, he also did not want to have to confront the pressure of marriage.

"What are you thinking?" Nan asked.

"Oh, just some of the conversations my mother and I had when I went home last time."

"Care to share any?"

"Nothing really of substance or importance."

The night sky was busy. The moon was again crescent.

"I can picture exactly where I was sitting, listening to my father telling us the story of the two moons and the stars. I was only nine then," Nan said despairingly. "Oh, I wish time would stand still."

"But time does go on. And we all grow older, hopefully wiser," ShiMin reflected.

"I know, but it's so hard to accept."

"That's not like you, Nan. I always thought of you as very sensitive but incredibly strong and courageous. You are able to face with determination whatever life throws at you."

"But I also have difficulty with letting go of certain emotional possessions, good or bad. That's another of my weaknesses."

"You know change is *the* constant in our lives, some gradual, some abrupt. But it always happens. We have to acknowledge; there is no other way."

Nan understood what he was conveying. She knew this chapter of life she so cherished was closing, and there was nothing she could do.

They looked up at the sky. Millions of stars blinking down back at them.

"I did have a good friend."

Nan was astonished by what she heard. ShiMin had told her that he did not have many friends, and he had professed to her what she thought was the deepest secret of his life. *Could there be such a thing more unspeakable than being abandoned by his father?*

"I was in my first year of junior high. She was two years older than I was and one class higher. We were in the same choral group. We practiced three times a week after school. She had a very good voice. One day, at the end of practice, the teacher singled her out and said in front of the group, 'Your math teacher told me that you cannot be in the choral group if your math does not improve.' Her face turned red, and some people made not-so-kind joking remarks." His voice trailed off . . .

ShiMin knew how it felt. He had the experience. He had been posed with such unwelcome comments as "what's wrong with your face and ear?" Those questions were not necessarily raised out of maliciousness. They might have been asked merely out of curiosity. But it bothered him, and it wounded his self-esteem, especially when people studied him purposefully and critically with a look of superiority on their faces. He had since let his hair grow to cover his ears.

He had waited until only he and the girl were left in the music room.

"I can help you with math, if you want."

"How? You are one year behind me, aren't you?"

"I'm quite advanced in math, even though I have to stay in the same class as everyone else. My mother has bought some math books for me. I know what is being taught in your class now."

He looked over her textbook and was confident he would be able to handle the material. It took some time, but the tutoring was able to get her math back on track to her grade level. They became good friends.

The choral group represented their school in a citywide junior high competition. She sang her solo passages beautifully and perfectly. It probably contributed to their taking the second place in the competition. Everyone was elated, especially the music teacher, and he began keeping her after practices to groom her for a future in music. Those sessions gradually became personal. She felt trapped but was not able to escape. Students were used to teacher's absolute authority in those days. She became reticent and less interested in her surroundings. ShiMin sensed those changes in her.

"I know something is not right. What is it?" he asked.

She was quiet.

"Tell me. Don't you trust me?"

She began to cry. ShiMin was anxious for her. He did not know what to say or do.

"I'm having a baby," she cried.

He was stunned. It was inconceivable to him. He had his own identity crisis, and he was not even thirteen. He knew the gravity of the situation, but he did not know what he could do. He thought of asking his mother, but how can you speak such unspeakable matter to your mother? It was unheard of in the Chinese society at the time as far as he knew. And to report it was out of the question. She was the victim, but she was the one who was ashamed. So he sat next to her, watching her cry and sharing her desperation.

Two days later, she was hit by a car at a busy intersection. She died along with her unutterable secret. People thought it was an accident. Other than the music teacher, ShiMin was the only person who knew the truth.

"Besides mourning for the loss of my good friend, I also had to deal with this excruciating guilt. For a long time, I couldn't forgive myself. It still bothers me now for not having done something to prevent it," he said with profound regret.

"I'm so sorry for the tragedy, but I'm not sure there was much you could have done at the time. It was so long ago, and the culture you were in was very different from here today." Nan tried to console him. "We all have our regrets. They are difficult to shake off, and many of us hold onto them, unwilling to let go."

The time of departure was drawing near. Nan recalled what ShiMin had quoted from *The Little Prince*. "The eyes are blind, one must look with the heart." She thought of the true friendship between the fox and the little prince. *There is always an end to everything*, she heard herself.

"Write to me," she said.

"I will."

Nan stretched out her arms. ShiMin embraced her. Then they parted.

She watched him leave with an overwhelming emotion of loss. She wept.

He is a mirage I cannot hold, an enigma I cannot realize. She decided.

So she stowed away her feelings for him in the deepest recess of her heart, not to be touched or revealed.

PART FOUR

Tragedy in the Gorge

I

Ethan showed up at Nan's lab the next day.

"I just want to be sure you are okay," he said.

"I'm fine." Her eyes were still red. She corrected herself immediately, "No, I'm not. I feel a part of my limb has been cut off." But it was not her limb, it was her heart.

"I know. I feel at a loss too. You two were so close."

"Tell me, Ethan, why do we, humans, put bondage on ourselves?"

"Because we have emotion, and we develop friendship and attachment to each other," Ethan said, not quite understanding Nan's true feelings.

"Sometimes I wonder if it would be better if we don't have this emotion."

"No, you don't want a bland world, do you? I don't think your God intended that way either." Ethan smiled.

"You know you are right," Nan had to agree. *But it is so painful!* She cried internally.

"You need to be cheered up. I'll pick you up when you are free. We can go watch a funny movie or something."

Jennifer came in. She was glad to see Ethan.

"It's difficult to see ShiMin and Eric leave," she said. "Cheer Nan up, will you?"

Ethan called later. "The Cinema Society is playing double feature comedy, *Dr. Strangelove* and *The Apartment*. We can watch one or the other, or both. It starts at seven thirty. I'll be over around six. We can have dinner first," he told her without asking. "Just as well," she thought, "I would probably say no if he asked, but it may be good for me."

The movies did make Nan laugh and momentarily pushed behind her nagging sadness.

And life went on, regardless of how one dealt with it.

Nan spent most of her time in the lab, working on her research during the summer. The postdoc she assisted during her first year and the first half of her second year had completed his postdoctoral training, published his paper, and moved on to Washington University in St. Louis as a junior faculty. He had invited Nan for dinner and movies before his departure, but Nan excused herself. She was now concentrating on her project and hoping to be able to complete her thesis on time.

In the meantime, Ethan had been spending as much time as he could with Nan. He had found his jewel, and he would embrace her.

Two weeks after ShiMin departed, the house of No. 12 received a postcard from him.

"Dear friends," it read, "I am sort of settled in and have started my work here in sunny California. The environment seems good, and people appear friendly. Nevertheless, it will take time to adjust. Mostly, I don't think I will ever have the same group of friends as close as you all are to me. I have cherished it, and will forever cherish it."

Nan kept the card and eagerly waited for the letter he promised. It finally arrived a week later.

Dear Nan,

I found this small apartment not far from work. The landscape here is very different from that in Ithaca. The charm and beauty are missing. But about seven miles farther south from my apartment is the Palos Verdes Peninsula, and that is a gem on the Pacific Ocean. It protrudes into the ocean at the southwest corner of Los Angeles. Standing on the beach, you can see the shore with its rich cityscape curving around in a semicircle, and the Catalina Island on the south in the distance. The sea is always deep blue, the sky almost always clear. Some days there are sail boats on the water. Then there are the hills and trails. Standing on top of the hills, you have the commanding view of the ocean and city all around. I go there after work often. When it is late at night, after all the commotion of humanity has ceased, you can hear the unrelenting heartbeats of the ocean, so tranquil yet so vibrant. I too sometimes wish time would stand still.

The sky is very busy most nights. I always look for my trail of stars, wondering if you have found your friend at the other end.

I know you are well taken care of by the house of No. 12, especially Ethan. That makes me feel reassured and less worried. Still, I miss our days together at Cornell. But we all have to do what we need to do. We can only hope our choices will be proven right eventually.

ShiMin

"Dear ShiMin," choking, Nan wrote. "I am glad you are settled, in a place close to the nature you so love. I can imagine you, alone on the beach, with the shore your stage and the sea your foreground, listening to the heartbeat of the ocean and perhaps looking to find your friend at the end of your stars. I truly hope you will find the one you are looking for. As for me, I am trying to concentrate on my research, hoping that will help carry me through my two more years at Cornell."

Unable to write further, she mailed the letter.

Then, with tears, she stored his letter in the tenderness of her heart.

II

Two more graduate students moved into No. 12 after Eric and ShiMin left. Bob, a business management major, and Rodney, a medieval studies major. They both had heard of No. 12 and were happy to have the opportunity to be part of the group. Nan and Jennifer continued to visit the house, and the Sunday dinners were uninterrupted.

Among the incoming undergraduate freshmen class was Mark's little sister Allison. Mark was charged by his parents to watch and take good care of her. He introduced Allison to No. 12 as soon as she was settled in. She was a petite and vivacious girl. She came to their Sunday dinner a few times but soon became involved with her own peers and would rather hang out with them instead. The house of No. 12 rarely saw her. Mark called on his sister once in a while.

"I met Allison's new boyfriend today," Mark told the group one Saturday after he visited his sister.

"Is he a freshman too?" JeFu asked.

"Yes, actually he is also from Arizona. Tempe to be exact."

"What city are you from again?"

"Scottsdale, not far from Tempe at all."

"That's convenient," said Ethan.

"Yes, I'd say. Scott seems to be a nice boy, quiet, not like Allison."

"Opposites attract, I suppose," JeFu concluded.

Everyone went home during Christmas except Nan and JeFu. It was now Nan's third year and JeFu's fourth and likely last year.

Jennifer saw her mother, who was much more relaxed and not as irritable as she used to be. Her father had remarried but stayed in the same town. Jennifer was surprised to see how different he looked. The sparks and love between him and his new wife were palpable, something Jennifer never imagined to witness of her father. She was thankful to know he was finally able to have someone who loved him.

Ethan did not want to leave Nan alone for too long. He returned in four days.

"Ethan, you are back so soon?" Nan was surprised when Ethan showed up in her lab.

"I don't want to leave you alone too long."

"I'm not alone. JeFu is here."

"I miss you, then," Ethan admitted. "Besides, I need to work on my thesis. This is going to be my last year."

Mark and his sister Allison also went back to their home in Arizona. Their parents checked their only daughter closely and were satisfied that she had not changed, and she appeared very happy. A few days later, Allison brought her new boyfriend to meet her parents.

"Allison told us you live in Tempe. Did you grow up there?" her father asked.

"Yes, sir."

"Why did you choose Cornell?"

"My father wanted me to."

"Do you know why?"

"It was his alma mater."

"Was there any other reason?"

"He liked his experience there. He said it has the most beautiful campus."

"Do you like it so far?"

"Yes."

"Is it as beautiful as you imagined?"

"Yes."

"What other schools did you consider?"

"Princeton and Johns Hopkins."

"Have you thought of what you want to do for your life?"

"Let him alone. Don't keep on interrogating him." Mrs. Cooper tried to rescue Scott.

"Come, let me show you my doll collection," Allison pulled Scott away. Soon there were voices and laughter from behind the door, mostly Allison's.

"Well, he doesn't have too many words," Mr. Cooper commented.

"Maybe he's just shy. You are too inquisitive. He is only Allison's boyfriend; it's not like they are getting married," his wife said.

"I don't know. He seemed almost depressed," was his conclusion.

Scott was from a strict family. His father was the absolute and dominant figure. His mother was never able to contradict him. Scott had seen his mother wiping her tears in devastation. She met her husband outside a movie theater in Ithaca when she and her classmate at Ithaca College were waiting to get in. They struck up a conversation, and the two were immediately attracted to each other. She was very popular at her school, so was he at Cornell. The wedding that took place at the most beautiful campus of Cornell was envied by many, not only for the ceremony but also for the union of two of the most admired people.

Scott did not come back with Mark and Allison when they returned to Cornell after the holidays. He did not feel well, he told Allison, and would make the trip a few days later.

There had been a confrontation, or rather, Scott was disciplined severely by his father. He had gotten up that morning feeling happy. He was going to leave home and return to Cornell. His father stopped him.

"You better watch out. I send you to study and to get good grades. You can't get anywhere in life if your grades are poor."

Scott was in a good mood. He reacted without thinking, "Grade is not everything. No one is going to deny me a job if I have a *B* on my college transcript."

He instantly realized he just said something he knew he should never have said.

His father was enraged. "Whom do you think you are talking to? Who pays your tuition and expenses? You don't have to go back to school if you think grade is not important."

Scott was terrified. He immediately admitted his mistake and asked for forgiveness. His mother was frightened. She held her breath, not able to say anything.

"You don't need to come home if your grades don't improve," his father said angrily. "You think it over seriously."

Scott knew full well the only thing he could do at that point was to wait for his father to tell him to leave. He waited.

Once, when Scott was eight, the family took a ski trip to Arizona Snowbowl during winter break. He and his brother were excited. Perhaps too excited, they unfastened the usual restraint they maintained whenever their father was around. As they were waiting for a table in a restaurant, the two brothers began joking with each other. "That's enough," their father said. "We are too happy to stop," he had replied heedlessly. He regretted as soon as he said it, but it was too late. Their father turned and walked out of the restaurant. Mother and sons followed timidly and miserably, agonizing over the punishment that was to follow. The anticipation of a happy family outing forsaken instantaneously.

"I'm not paying your tuition and all the expenses for you to have these kinds of grades. I don't want to see any Bs again. Don't come home until your grades improve." His father finally released him.

He missed his flight.

Scott got back to Cornell two days later. He appeared fine. Allison was relieved. She took Scott to No. 12 for Sunday dinner and introduced him to the group.

"What did you have?" Mark asked him.

"Just a cold and weakness. I couldn't get out of bed."

Nan noticed Scott was rather reserved. She tried to bring him into the conversation.

"Do you have brothers or sisters, or are you the only child?" she asked.

"I have one older brother. He works in the aerospace industry in Phoenix."

Ethan was interested. "Where did he go for college?" he asked.

"MIT."

"No wonder."

"Actually, my father wanted him to go to graduate school and get at least a master's degree, if not a PhD."

"I guess your father relented," Ethan said.

"My brother insisted that he accept the offer right away. He said the opportunity was too good to pass. He could handle the job well without further education, and he said he can go back to school later if necessary. It seems he was right. He is doing very well." Scott was opening up.

"What about you? Do you like it here so far?" Nan asked.

"It's okay. I just worry about my grades."

"You know, college is not like high school. Your main focus should be learning and understanding the material. It's not just what the textbook says. Grades are important, but it's not the most important thing, and it doesn't necessarily always reflect how much you know." Nan realized she had relaxed her own competitiveness, if only a little.

"Tell that to my father," Scott said. He looked dejected.

"I'm sure your father understands grades are not everything," Bob, the business management major, said.

"He's serious about my getting better grades." Scott appeared worried.

"That's unfortunate. What about your mother?" JeFu asked.

"My mother understands. But she's as afraid of my father as I am. I know she tries to protect me, but she couldn't do much." He was very sad.

"I don't know what we can do to help you," Ethan said sympathetically. "But if any of us here can help with academic questions, just let us know. We have diverse majors here; physics, biochemistry, engineering, business, even medieval studies, plus Mark in history."

"Yes, just ask," JeFu said.

A nagging weight was on Nan. "I'm very concerned about Scott. It's a pity that he's under such pressure," she told Ethan.

"I know. I feel very bad for him. I wish there is something we could do."

Nan decided she should have a conversation with Scott. She asked Mark to invite Allison and Scott over for dinner the following Sunday and to arrive early to give them time to talk.

They did not show up for the Sunday dinner. Nan wrote a letter instead.

Dear Scott,

I have been thinking about you. I know the pressure you are under. When you cannot change your father's mind, you may have to change your perception and your approach.

First, we know your father wanted you to do well. His demand may not be reasonable, but his intention is for you to succeed. You may think he wanted you to have good grades so he can be proud. That may or may not be true. He may just be thinking for you and your future. Even if he wanted you to succeed so he can feel proud among his friends and his colleagues, you still need to accept that. He is your father, and he has invested heavily in you, financially and emotionally, I am sure.

Second, while we all know grades do not necessarily predict success or failure in the future, this does seem to be your father's viewpoint. If this is the case, unless you know of a way to change him, it is best you accept it and be at peace with it. Strive to get better grades using any means you can. Do extra credit assignments, get help from professors and fellow students, spend more time writing papers, reports, etc. We here at No. 12 are all willing to help in any way we can.

Third, if the reality proves you cannot attain what your father expects, you need to look and think beyond the immediate present, face it, and know everything is a process. We have to go through the process to reach the end regardless of how painful it may seem now. It is true that there is light at the end of the tunnel, no matter how long the tunnel may seem now. There will be an end, always. Stand up, no matter how difficult. You can handle it. One day, you will look back and you will be glad you did not give up. You will wonder why you let it seem so insurmountable to you now.

I also think your mother needs your support. I am sure you are very close to her, but I do not know if you share with her your thoughts, experiences, hopes, desires, and dreams for your future. Being so far apart makes it difficult, but please try to write often, if you have not yet. I know she wants to know everything that is going on in your life.

I hope you and Allison will come visit us.

Best,
Nan

III

Allison and Scott did visit No. 12 the last Sunday in January. Scott appeared relaxed. He thanked Nan for the letter when they were alone. "I read it many times," he said. Nan knew it would be a long road for him, and he would need continued support.

Winter was brutal and gloomy in Ithaca, especially for those accustomed to a winter temperature in the sixties as was the norm in Phoenix. Even the normally cheerful Allison felt a hint of boredom and misery. The sight of snow, though, was magical.

Scott had been studying hard. He wanted to get good grades. He knew he had to.

He sat at his desk for a long time, his eyes fixed at the quiz paper he just got back. Finally, he went to call Allison.

"How did you do on your history quiz?" she asked.

"Okay. But it's still below my father's standard. I'm disappointed."

"Don't worry about it. I'm sure you'll get better and better," Allison said. "Do you want to watch a movie tomorrow night? The Cinema Society is showing *The Producers* and *The Graduate*."

"We'll see."

"What are you doing now?"

"Just sitting here doing nothing."

"Do you want to come over? Or I can go over to your place too." Their dorms were not that far apart, and it had stopped snowing.

"I'll be over," Scott said.

It was nine o'clock in the evening. He sat for a while longer. Then he got up, put on his coat and boots, and walked out of his dorm. It was in the dead of winter. There was not a single soul around. He did not realize, but he was walking in the opposite direction of Allison's dorm. It was so desolate. The earth seemed to be at a standstill. All he saw was loneliness and his father's disappointed and angry face. Without warning, a miserable image appeared vividly. He saw himself lying on the floor in a hotel room sobbing hopelessly. He had been forbidden to sleep in bed; his father just discovered he had not practiced violin before their trip to Yosemite. He shuddered and almost stumbled. He approached the Thurston Avenue Bridge over the Fall Creek Gorge below. It was quiet. The familiar sound of rushing waters heard during the fall season was fading in the distance. The water had largely turned into icicles, and the icy waterfall had become gentler and tenderer. It looked so peaceful. It was dark and he could not see the bottom below, but he knew the gorge was covered with snow. He had seen it in the daytime. The scenery was so haunting, so lonely, yet so overpowering. Oh, the white fluffy stuff that was so soft, so comforting, and so inviting. It was waiting to embrace him. "There is light at the end of the tunnel, no matter how long the tunnel may seem now. There will be an end, always." He startled. *Nan was right. I hope she's right. But where's the end? I can't see it. Ten years from now? A hundred years from now? Forever?* He asked. "Stand up, no matter how difficult. You can handle it." *Can I? Maybe I can. But how? I hope Nan's right. It's too hard. I wish Nan were right.* His father's angry face was in front of him, along with the countless images of himself crying and shaking. *Where's the light? I see the long, long tunnel, but I can't see the light. Where's the light? It's impossible. I worked so hard, and I got a B+. How's it ever possible that I'll be able to get all As? How do I look beyond? How do I face it? I can't live every day like this. I only see the dark, dark tunnel. It's impossible. I can't escape.* His father was getting angrier and angrier. *No, it's impossible. I can never escape. Never. Never. Never.*

He never made it to Allison's dorm. He jumped.

Tragedies never claim only a single victim. Many lives would invariably be altered, some permanently.

Allison blamed herself, "Why did I suggest that he come over? Why didn't I go over to his dorm instead?" She was devastated.

"That might have put it off, but it would most likely still happen sometime later." Her friends tried to reason with her.

"No. He could get an *A* on his next quiz or paper. Then he would not have to take his own life. Then he would still be here. I want him back." She was frantic.

The house of No. 12 was in great distress. Besides trying to console Mark, they had to deal with their own emotions, especially Nan. She thought she had made some progress the last time she saw Scott. She was ready to guide him further. She blamed herself too. "I should have seen the extent of the urgency," she told Ethan.

"No, don't blame yourself. He apparently made an on-the-spot decision when the opportunity was there," Ethan said. "He was still too young. At that age, they're not mature enough to think through rationally. There's a saying, 'Suicide is a permanent solution to a temporary problem.' Unfortunately, he wasn't able to comprehend and separate temporary from permanent. It might be a coward's way out, but he's finally without pain."

"But what a cruelly irreversible permanent solution! What a waste of life!" Nan sobbed.

Jennifer cried interminably. JeFu tried to calm her while wiping his own eyes.

Scott's parents, the Fosters, flew in. His brother Andy, the MIT graduate who majored in physics and worked in aerospace, also came. So did the Coopers, they were worried about Allison and wanted to be by her side.

Andy was five years older than Scott. He had also been under his father's strict discipline, but it seemed Scott had generally been more severely punished. Andy could never forget the time his father went into a rage and struck Scott after reading his report card. Scott was six, in first grade. The teacher had suggested that "his handwriting could have been better if he had taken more time trying." Scott was finally allowed to go to bed. His father then turned his anger toward his mother as he always did whenever one of them was in trouble, yelling at her for not paying attention to her children. Andy went in Scott's room and saw he was trembling and sobbing. He lay down next to his brother, held him, and said, "I'll stay here until you fall asleep." He himself was only eleven at the time. Andy had also experienced corporal punishment. It had continued until they were in high school. He wondered if those sad images had come to Scott's mind at his last moments of life. He wept.

Scott's father was stone-faced. Although he appeared impenitent, he was obviously shaken. Poor Mr. Foster, he did not realize the pressure he put on his son; some of Scott's classmates murmured. Others blamed him. Scott's mother was heartbroken and sobbed uncontrollably.

The university security returned items found on Scott's body to his parents; his wallet containing his student ID, Allison's picture, some loose bills, his shattered watch, a history quiz paper in his coat pocket, and a letter addressed to him and signed by Nan that was retrieved from a buttoned-up pocket.

His mother read the letter. Some passages were underlined with red ink, apparently by Scott.

"Change your perception and your approach . . . It is best you accept it and be at peace with it . . . Look and think beyond the immediate present, face it . . . There is light at the end of the tunnel. . . There will be an end, always . . . Your mother needs your support . . . She wants to know everything that is going on in your life . . ."

Scott could not wait for the light that was waiting at the end of the long, long tunnel.

Her tears flowed again. She was awoken, and she wanted herself back. She asked her husband for a divorce when they returned home.

Mark introduced the house of No. 12 to his parents. They saw the camaraderie among his housemates and were reassured. Please help Allison too, they asked the group. The sparkling Allison had become quiet and subdued. It would take time to heal, and her friends at No. 12 were patient. Mark brought her to their Sunday dinners whenever she was willing. By the end of the school year, Allison had partly recovered from the trauma. Nightmares lingered, nonetheless.

There had been student suicides in the alluring gorges at Cornell. Scott was not the first and certainly would not be the last. Although the suicide rate at Cornell was comparable to the national average and to the student suicide rate on other college campuses, those gorge suicides at Cornell were somehow more publicized and exaggerated. Did its occurrence in such hauntingly beautiful gorges tempt a mystical connotation?

When Ezra Cornell proclaimed "I would found an institution where any person can find instruction in any study," he built Cornell in Ithaca, high above the Cayuga waters, with the Cascadilla Gorge on the south and the Fall Creek Gorge on the north. The peculiar site was chosen "to protect us from uncongenial neighbors," according to his words. It might have walled off adverse external power, but, alas, it cannot guard against internal struggles that propelled some students to succumb to self-destruction.

IV

It was spring again. Nan went for an early morning walk, feeling the crisp air and listening to the singing birds. She saw Ethan walking toward her and remembered that spring morning two years before.

"Got on campus too early again?" Nan teased him.

"You remembered!"

"How can one forget?"

They walked side by side. Nan was still amazed by the charming environs of Ithaca. She stopped and looked at a spring beauty closely.

"So many colors and shades—white, pink, purple, yellow, and green—all in a single flower," she said. "How amazing nature is!"

"I didn't notice. I just saw the flowers but never thought I'd examine them."

"Sometimes we become complacent with ourselves and lose the desire to explore and appreciate."

"That's right. But you're more sensitive to beautiful things, and ugly things too I suppose, than anyone I know."

"What a beautiful spring morning!" Nan exclaimed, taking in the sight of newly bloomed flowers, the sound of twittering birds, and the fresh and fragrant smell of the air.

Ethan smiled. *So sensitive to the beauty, exactly what I was just saying.*

"What time do you need to be at your lab?" he asked.

"Before noon. My experiment comes out at twelve."

"Let's go to Ithaca Falls. I'll make sure you get back in time."

The sight and the sound of this massive body of water cascading down more than one hundred feet of drop and of comparable width were altogether imposing. They sat on the rock at the bottom of the fall, watching, listening, feeling, and enjoying all it had to offer.

Nan thought of Scott.

"I'm still sad over Scott. Sometimes I wanted to scream," she said.

"I've been thinking about it too. It did seem odd. He had a *B+* on the quiz, for heaven's sake! Why would that kind of grade push him to take his own life?"

"Perhaps the pressure his father put on him was much more than we can imagine. He did seem extremely worried about his grades."

"What I don't understand is why his father was so driven, as if the success of his children was the only thing he lived for."

"I must admit my competitive nature," Nan unintentionally disclosed, "I used to always want to be the best; I couldn't fail, I couldn't lose to others, I couldn't relax."

"I don't really see that." Ethan said.

"I've come a long way."

They were quiet, sorrowful for the loss of a young life much too soon.

"We all have to leave this beautiful place when we graduate," Nan reflected after some time.

"Not if one wants to stay at Cornell, join the faculty, raise family, and make it a permanent home."

"That's true. But most people leave and find their callings somewhere else."

"I asked you this before. You said you wanted to find a job in your field, either here or Taiwan. Is that still what you are thinking?"

"Yes, it is."

"You know, your calling might be in Boston," Ethan suggested.

"I don't know. I still have a year and half. No one can predict what might happen then."

"Will you consider applying for a postdoc position in Boston?"

"Yes, if it is available."

Ethan was relieved.

"Have you heard the legend about the Suspension Bridge?" It came to Ethan's mind.

"No, I only know the one about Beebe Lake."

"If a girl refuses a kiss in the middle of the Suspension Bridge, the bridge will collapse into the gorge."

"Ha, that's an excuse for guys to steal kisses!" Nan laughed.

Ethan asked, "What do you expect in a relationship?"

After a few moments, Nan replied, "I'm not looking for a perfect partner, but I do want a perfect relationship—a relationship in which I love as deeply as I'm loved." Then she added, "Relationships cannot be analyzed, they can only be felt."

Ethan impulsively took Nan's hand and held in his own. She did not pull back.

Nan knew of a story of her sister Lily's best friend. She married right after she graduated from college to one of her classmates. She had broken up with her boyfriend, and the man she married had been after her for a long time. The tragedy was that she did not have real feelings for her husband. He loved her much more than she loved him. She married him out of spitefulness toward her old boyfriend for leaving her for someone else. Lily had advised vehemently against her friend's rash decision, but she insisted on taking the temporary solution to what she perceived as a permanent problem. Her husband soon realized his love was unrequited. Out of desperation, he began drinking and became violent with her. It was a painful marriage that destroyed both of them. *A temporary solution that greeted her cruelly with eternal regret*, Nan thought.

When Nan got back to her dorm that evening, she found a letter in her mailbox from Andy Foster.

Dear Nan,

Please excuse me if this letter seems too abrupt. My mother shared with me the letter you wrote to Scott, and we felt obligated to let you know how much we appreciate your concern for Scott and how much wisdom was in your letter. It had obviously made an impact on him. He had underlined multiple passages in the letter. I am sure it was on his mind at the last moments of his life. Unfortunately, the hopelessness he felt must be too overwhelming to overcome. We wish he had known you much sooner, and perhaps you could have opened his eyes in time to avoid the tragedy.

My father had been extremely strict with us, more so with Scott than with me. There had been abuses, both emotional and physical. Scott was so afraid of my father he would do anything to avoid having to face him. We lived in constant fear of saying or doing something that was wrong in my father's eyes. He treated my mother almost the same as he treated us. She was also a victim whenever we were in trouble. After so many years of abuse, my mother had accepted and erroneously believed it was her fault for whatever we did or said to trigger my father's anger.

My mother is now in the process of getting a divorce from my father. She wants to stand up and speak up against unwarranted spousal and child abuse. There must be many families living in the same unspeakable and never-ending darkness like ours.

Scott was carrying a load too great for him. It is heartbreaking that it took the loss of him to wake us up.

We owe it to him to make it public. We hope the tragedy of my family might save some others from similar fate.

With gratitude,
Andy Foster

It was not that Mr. Foster was a callous person by nature. He himself grew up in an environment under the absolute dictatorial control of his much older brother. Their father had died shortly after he was born, and his big brother took over the disciplinary role. Scott's father was programmed to the strictest regimen of what his big brother believed to be the way of proper upbringing. That belief had been carried through from the generation before. Once when he was in third grade, he came home with a report card that had a score of 84 on one subject. He knew he was not supposed to have anything below 90, but his friends were playing outside, so he left the report card on the table and went to join them. Not too long after, his big brother came out with a stern expression telling him to go home. As soon as he stepped in the house, his brother slapped him on the face. The bruise was so severe it took over a week to fade away. He never had a score below 90 again. He was proud of his own achievement and trusted that was how his children should be disciplined. He never realized its flaws, unfortunately. It had destroyed his family.

PART FIVE

First Taste of Love

I

Nan's letter home began to mention Ethan more frequently and in more depth.

"I had always thought Ethan is confident of himself and has a clear vision of his future. I have now also found the other side of him. He is kind, generous, and thoughtful. I have witnessed many of his such deeds. Just yesterday, when he was walking me home, we saw a student fall from his bike after hitting a construction barrier on the road. The student was more worried about his bike than the scratches on his legs and arms. Ethan went over to help him, making sure he was all right. He took money from his pocket, put it in the boy's hand, and told him to get his bike fixed. We walked on as if nothing had happened. I know this was a common act of kindness; many would do the same. But it did validate my perception that he is the person worthy of my love. He does what he says, he is true to himself. Of course, it is also the love he has for me that touched my heart."

As Nan understood Ethan better, she learned to appreciate him and to love him. She was now truly happy and content.

The Delaneys came to Cornell to attend Ethan's graduation. Ethan introduced Nan and other members of No. 12 to his parents and his younger sister. They too had heard a lot about No. 12, Nan in particular.

"So nice to finally meet you all," they said.

Mrs. Delaney turned to Nan and asked, "Ethan told us you came here alone by yourself. Was it hard for you?"

"Yes, it was. But I was fortunate to have met Ethan and his friends in this house right after I arrived. They made it easier for me."

"Do you still miss your folks back home?"

"Yes, very much. I dream about them too. I'm afraid it will never go away completely. But it's manageable."

"She still writes letters to her family at least once or twice a week," Ethan volunteered cheerfully.

"Your parents are lucky," Mrs. Delaney said, winking at Ethan.

"After three years, they still look forward to my letters. I know how it feels. I still look forward to their letters too. We are physically so far apart. Letters are the only way to quench some of the worries and the yearnings," Nan replied.

"You're right," Mr. Delaney said.

"Ethan said we'll see you in Boston in a few days?" his sister Mary asked.

"Yes, indeed."

The Delaneys liked Nan immediately.

A few days after the graduation ceremony, Ethan cleaned and packed up his belongings and four years of memories, bid a difficult good-bye to his housemates, and got on the road. Nan went with him to Boston.

It was a long ride, more than three hundred miles. That gave them time alone before the anticipated long separation.

"Oh, Nan, I'm so glad you came to Cornell," Ethan said, full of gratitude.

"I'm glad too. I asked myself many times, is this my destiny? Is this God's will for me?"

"So what's the answer?"

"I don't know. I think yes, but I'm waiting."

"Waiting for what?"

"For God to tell me."

"How would you know?"

"I think I'll know when God answers. He gives us free will to choose. He does not answer our prayers if he disapproves. Sometimes he halts and delays because it is not time yet."

"Well, I can never understand," Ethan continued. "Remember that first time when we had our home-cooked Sunday meal together, the first time you went to church with Eric? I wanted to know why you thought the pastor was genuine, and why you believed in God. I remember your answers. I remember sitting there watching you presenting your argument confidently, and I remember thinking how passionate you were. I was very impressed with you."

"But I didn't convince you, did I?"

"It put a seed in me. Seeking is a long process. You said it yourself, it took you ten years. Maybe it'll not take that long for me, now I've you behind me."

"I hope. I'll pray for that," Nan said. Then a feeling of sadness befell. "I dreamed of Scott a few nights before. He was standing at the edge of a cliff waving at me, smiling. I said, 'What are you doing there so close to the cliff? You'll fall off'. He said, 'I was looking for my paper.' 'Did you find it?' I asked. 'No, but I don't need it anymore,' he said indignantly, 'I'm done with it. I'm free.' 'You are? I'm happy for you,' I said. He walked toward me with a cynical look on his face. I was scared, and I started to run. He followed me and cried out, 'You failed. You failed!' I finally woke up and realized my pillow was wet. It's odd I remember that dream so vividly."

Ethan pulled off the road and stopped the engine. He held Nan and said, "Let it go. Something good will come out of it. Andy said in his letter that it woke his mother up, and she's taking actions. I think Scott would be happy if he were here to see it."

"Yes, only it's too late for him." Nan sighed.

"Unfortunately, there are tragedies in this world that we can't control. Scott was a victim, but his death might have a purpose. We need to look at the bright side rather than the dark side and hope the world will get better and kinder with the lessons we learn from each of these tragedies."

His words comforted her. They got back on the road.

"Time is so unforgiving. It moves forward without any mercy," Nan lamented. "Now it's you, JeFu, and Jennifer. All the five No. 12 originals have graduated. Oh, I wish it never had to end."

Ethan cradled Nan's shoulder with his right arm and said, "Everything has an end, but there are other bright futures ahead. We just need to accept them."

"The perpetual optimist." Nan smiled. She knew she could trust him to always hold her up.

"I'm so happy for JeFu and Jennifer," she said.

"I too. They're a lucky couple, love and respect each other."

"JeFu is taking Jennifer to Taiwan to ask for his parents' approval for marriage."

"Is that how it works in Taiwan? The man has to ask his parents first?"

"I think that's the unwritten rule. Then they'll ask the girl's parents. If either side says no, the marriage is off. Unless they elope, of course."

"What do you think? Will JeFu's parents approve?"

"I think so. I certainly hope so. Jennifer is a good person, she has a soft heart." Nan continued, "I wish I had gone to see JeFu's parents when I went home last time. It would have been nice to know them."

"You didn't go home last year, and you aren't going home this year. It'll be two years in a row."

"I miss them badly. But I need time working on my thesis. Now I'm losing another four days with you." Nan smiled.

"That's well worth your time." Ethan was happy.

"Actually, seriously, I dread the departure following the visit. It was so hard last time."

"I'll go with you next year after your graduation. Then it won't be so bad since you'll have me."

She felt assured.

"Do you want to take a rest and stretch your legs?" Ethan asked.

They turned off the highway and went on a country road. "Fresh Fruits," a sign said. They stopped and walked around the fields. Air was warm, but the gentle breeze felt good on the skin. Ethan held Nan's hand, overflowing with happiness. *I will protect her till I die*, he told himself.

"I'm grateful for all the things this country has to offer. I lived in Taipei, the crowded city with little greens. My original hometown in mainland China was as rich in natural resources and beautiful landscapes as here. But we lost it to the communists. Then they destroyed it because of the self-serving agenda of their leader."

"Yes, you mentioned it when we were debating whether we should stay in the Vietnam War."

"It seems there are more wars than peace in the world as a whole. Will lasting peace ever be a reality?" Nan reflected.

"Probably not," Ethan said. "But one can always find bright spots here and there. We should never lose hope."

Nan appreciated his confidence. They walked on for a while.

"Let's go get some fruits," Ethan said. But there was no one at the fruit stand.

They got back in the car. Nan began the detailed story of how her mother, leaving behind all her possessions—house, land, and all—was able to take them and fled to Taiwan. She told Ethan what she had once told ShiMin.

"My mother is a woman of wisdom, courage, and vision. Everyone was against her idea of fleeing with her aging mother-in-law and three young children. They said it was too dangerous, she would not make it, and life might be okay even if the Communist won. But she knew escaping was the only choice she had if we were to survive." She added, "So many families were separated in the chaos of the mass exodus from the mainland at the last moment."

Ethan was overcome. He did not realize there was so much tragedy in this world. This one was close to home. It was the history of the person he loved.

"I'll protect you from all harm, always, till I die," he said impulsively.

"I know," Nan said. "I'm blessed, and what if I die first?"

Ethan squeezed her hand. He could not envision life without her. He could not answer.

"I have your mother to thank. I wouldn't have met you if it weren't for her," he said instead.

"Now tell me something about your childhood," Nan said.

"There was nothing as exciting as yours."

"Well, then tell me something boring about your childhood." She smiled.

"Okay, just don't fall asleep on me," Ethan joked. "I was a disappointment when my parents were told 'it's a boy!'"

"So was I when it was announced 'it's a girl!'"

They both laughed.

"My father wanted to have a girl as pretty as my mother so he could be proud of. But he soon changed his mind and was quite happy to have a son," Ethan said.

"My parents felt disappointed not because they had a particular preference for a boy but because my grandmother wanted to have a grandson to 'continue the Yang name and bloodline' as was the prevailing concept among the Chinese people."

"I'm glad you're a girl," Ethan said, then realized the absurdity of his statement. They laughed again.

"There was one thing that I've not thought about all these years," Ethan said. "The neighborhood around our family home was quite spread out, and we didn't have playmates like you had. My mother would drive me and my baby sister once a week to her friend's house to play with their two children, a girl my age and a boy two years older than I was. Emma liked to play with dolls, and she begged me to play with her. But I was more interested in following her brother Robby around, and most of the time, she just followed us around. They had a very large yard with many trees. One day, we went further in the woods and wandered into their neighbors' yards. We kept walking and came across a gazebo surrounded by trees that was not easy to see. I found it first, and Robby and Emma came running after me. I was startled by a mourning sound and then saw a boy in a wheelchair. The boy's face looked old, but he was very small. He was alone, so we tried to talk to him. He looked a little scared in the beginning, then he became excited and waved his arms around and laughed. A woman came and angrily shooed us off. When my mother took me there the following week, we went straight to that gazebo. We hid behind the trees and watched. The woman was feeding and talking to the boy. The boy moved his arms, hit the spoon, and spilled the food. Emma laughed. The woman jumped up, and we ran as fast as we could. We went back again the next week. He was alone, so we approached him. Emma touched his hands and started to ask him questions. He looked at her and mumbled. I just stood there watching. I'd never seen someone like that before. Then I realized the woman was standing behind us. We ran. From then on, we went back there often and played with that boy. He always laughed when he saw us. The woman was his caregiver, not his mother, but she loved him. Years later, when we were old enough to understand, we were told that prominent family was ashamed of having a handicapped child. They kept him away from the society to protect him, and themselves."

"What a sad story. Did you know what he had?"

"Cerebral palsy, according to Robby."

"Weren't your mother worried where you went?" she asked.

"No, not for a long time. They just thought we were in the yard or neighbor's yard. Robby's family had been there for generations, and they were very familiar with the neighborhood. They knew we were safe."

"What happened to that boy?"

"Robby told me he died from pneumonia a few years after I started school and stopped going to his house."

"We have a saying, 'Every family has its own demon.' We may never know what demons other families have to fight against," Nan said. She thought about her mother's struggle during their early days in Taiwan. MayAnn did whatever she could to help support the family, including learning to embroider. Nan was too young then. But Lily had told her, "I woke up late at night, lay there listening to the rhythmic sound as the needle passed through the tightly stretched silk, 'tze, tze, tze . . .' It was like my heart being stabbed by the needle, one after another, repeatedly." Nan's eyes watered every time that image came in mind. MayAnn was able to sell her embroidery. In fact, she became so good at it that she entered in competition and two of her pieces won prizes.

"How were your school days like?" Nan asked.

"It was easy as pie. I was bored most of the time. My parents considered having me skip a grade when I was in fourth grade, but they took my teacher's suggestion and gave me extra assignments instead. I was class president a number of times, both in high school and college."

"I wouldn't doubt."

"I ran against a girl in my senior year of high school," Ethan said, recalling. "She was very pretty and quite popular. My campaign slogan, 'Choose Knowledge and Creativity over Beauty, Elect Ethan,' among a number of others apparently worked, and I was leading the poll. She became anxious and came to me asking me to tone down and go easy with that slogan in exchange of a date after the election."

"Did you agree?"

"Of course not."

"I didn't think so." Nan smiled.

"Anyway, she cranked up her campaign, and we ended up a deadlock, the first time in the school's history. Neither one of us wanted to be a co-president. Finally, the school decided to have each of us give a one-hundred-word speech to the entire school. Only teachers would vote, and it was to be based on the speech alone. I worked hard on my speech, counted the number of words, making sure it was exactly one hundred. My opponent's speech came to one hundred and nine. She either didn't count carefully, didn't think it needed to be so exact, or she was not able to edit it down. I won."

"What was your speech?"

Ethane recited, "I have run my campaign vigorously and relentlessly because I believe I can contribute to the well-being and prosperity of our entire school community. School is a place to learn and to be prepared to serve, not just ourselves but the larger society we live in. I have always demanded of myself a positive attitude of acceptance, tolerance, compassion, selflessness, and cooperativeness as you all have witnessed. Help me in spreading this principle so we can become a cohesive body worthy of the investments our parents, our school, our greater community, and our country have so generously bestowed on us."

"I'm impressed. I think you would still have won even if your opponent's speech were also exactly one hundred words," Nan said.

"That's what one of my teachers told me afterward."

"I'm proud of you. You say and do what you believe."

Out of the window, Nan saw a sign, "Eric's Market." She recalled what her mother said during a conversation when she went home two years ago. "He will find the right person someday," her mother had said about Eric.

She said, "I hope Eric will find his girl."

"ShiMin too," Ethan said.

The Delaney's home was in Southborough, approximately thirty miles west of Boston. The house was old but large, well maintained, and beautifully landscaped with an impeccable green lawn, lush mature trees, sculptures, and rows of roses of various colors along its perimeter. It was one of those grand houses that enticed admiration. The family was happy to see Nan again, Mary especially. Like her brother, she was outgoing. Unlike her brother, she was not interested in pursuing higher education.

Ethan introduced Boston to Nan. They went to the Esplanade on the banks of the Charles River. He showed her the Hatch Shell where the Fourth of July concerts by Boston Pops were played and fireworks were displayed every year, the large parklands, the running and biking trials, the bridges linking Boston and Cambridge where Harvard and MIT stood, and the sailboats. Yes, the sailboats! Nan thought of her undergraduate thesis advisor and his homesickness in the foreign land, counting days to return home.

They walked across the bridge to Cambridge, visited Harvard Square, went to the campuses of Harvard and MIT, and admired the buildings that housed many brilliant minds. Nan was excited and touched, imagining herself being nurtured in this academically extravagant environment.

Then there were also the Museum of Fine Arts, the Boston Symphony Orchestra, the New England Conservatory, the Freedom Trail, the imposing buildings, and the many churches. And the history! Oh, the history, the pride and grandeur of the country. Nan fell in love with the city.

Ethan had been offered a postdoc position at Yale. He was waiting to hear from Harvard and MIT.

Four days later, Nan flew back through connecting flights to Cornell.

Ethan called the next day. "It's MIT!" he almost screamed. Nan was elated for the promise of his bright future.

II

In the last year of her graduate studies, Nan spent most of her time in the lab finishing up her research. She was getting some unexpected and exciting results. Dr. Thompson was quite satisfied with her progress.

She walked around the campus in her spare time, taking in the beauty of nature and reflecting her experiences with her friends. Her old roommate Lauren stayed at Cornell after graduation as an instructor in the classics department. She and Tom had married. They visited Nan sometimes and invited her to their apartment for meals. She talked on the phone with Ethan, read his letters, and wrote letters to him. And, of course, continued to write and read letters from home. Time was not too difficult to pass. Only an unexplained melancholy would envelop her every now and then.

Christmas finally approached. Nan flew to Boston for the few days Ethan could squeeze out of his demanding work. This time, he was able to take her inside the lab at MIT and tried to explain to her all the magnificently impressive instruments and graphs and all. She was excited.

The Delaneys were happy to have Nan with them. They all went to the Christmas Eve service. Ethan's parents were Christians, and they hoped Nan would be able to move Ethan to accept Christianity.

Ethan's sister Mary had just graduated from college after four and half years. She was an average student and decided to pursue a modeling career, to her parents' chagrin. The extended family had been loaded with high achievers, and they were not going to have a daughter with a career in modeling.

"You didn't have to go to college to be a model," Mr. Delaney said disappointedly.

"But I like modeling. I can't think of anything else to do."

"Even a regular desk job is better than modeling," her mother said.

"What kind of regular desk job? It's not like I can pick and choose."

"Anything is better than modeling," her mother insisted.

"I like modeling. That is it."

"Neil, what are you going to do with your daughter?" Mrs. Delaney was desperate. She turned to Nan for reinforcement. "Nan, what do you think?"

"I think the chance of success in any career is much higher if we are allowed to do what we are passionate about. Disastrous consequences sometimes occur if people are forced to do something they don't like or can't do," Nan responded thoughtfully. "I don't think a career can be considered desirable or undesirable. If it's something Mary likes and has the aptitude for, then it's desirable regardless of what other people may think. I think as long as she keeps her focus, follows ethical standards, and not be influenced by any promises of shortcuts, she should be fine."

"Brilliant," Ethan whispered.

"That's what I thought. Thank you, Nan," Mary said happily.

Her parents were not too thrilled with what they heard. But they had to agree there were some truth in it. They relented eventually. Mary became a rather successful fashion model.

When Nan was a sophomore in college, her psychology professor, who was a prominent psychologist in Taiwan at the time, had assigned her and two other students to go and interview students at a junior high school that had a special program for emotionally disturbed young teenagers. The boy she interviewed was thirteen. He was from a well-established family, unlike most others whose families were generally poor and less educated. He was a loner, and he was defiant. With his lips tightly closed, he stared at Nan indignantly.

"I'm Nan. I'm a student too, second year at the National Taiwan University. I'm here to share with you some of my experiences."

No sign of acknowledgment. He continued staring at her.

"I was not born in Taiwan. My mother took us and fled from our hometown in the mainland. I was not even four years old yet. We had to rebuild our lives from nothing. What about you? Did your parents come from the mainland too?"

Silence. Nan had to continue her monologue.

"Life was very difficult for us in the beginning; I was told when I was old enough to understand. Then I began to realize the world was not all roses. There were always disappointments. Once I wanted a beautiful doll that I saw in a small neighborhood store. My mother told me it was too expensive for us. I was unhappy for a long time. When I looked back, I laughed at myself and wondered why I let such unnecessary stuff bother me for so long. You probably didn't have that kind of experience. I know your parents are quite rich, and they probably let you have whatever you want."

Still silence. But the stare appeared to thaw slightly.

"I also learned money is not everything. Instead of money, my parents gave me love. They supported whatever I wanted to do or to be as long as it was a good decision. They said a good decision is one that will make me happy and that does not harm anyone. That's why I'm in college now. I want to be a scientist. What about you? Have you thought of what you want to do for your life yet? Or maybe it's too early to think about that?"

"I want to be a dancer," the boy said.

Nan was surprised, not because of the answer per se but merely because he answered.

"Ah, dance. You must be good at it."

"I always liked to dance since I was little. My parents were proud of me in the beginning, and they always wanted me to show off to their friends what I could do. Then when I was still dancing when I was ten years old and told them I wanted to be a dancer, they flipped out. No, no way there should be a male dancer in our family, over our dead bodies, they said."

"How did you react to that?"

"I was very angry. I said that was what I wanted. It was my dream. There was nothing else I wanted to do for my life."

"I guess they didn't agree." Nan knew very well that the Chinese society as a whole at that time valued doctors, teachers, politicians, and men in leadership positions. Male dancer was almost unheard of and definitely considered an oddity, if not looked down upon.

"No, but I don't want to do anything else."

"Do you want to give it some time? Do you want to enjoy your life now with your friends like everyone else? You are still young. No one can predict the future."

"But they wouldn't allow me to take dance lessons."

She was not able to respond to the boy's agonizing disappointment. "At least make some friends now. You can pick up dancing later," was all she could think of to say.

Nan wrote a detailed report after the interview. "When parents impose on their children a career choice according to what the society at large prized, they might compel them to desolation. And it could extinguish the flame in the young hearts that might otherwise have led to great success," she concluded. Her report was so insightful that the professor dedicated an entire class to the reading of her report followed by a very lively discussion among all students over that topic.

Sadly, for that boy, it had more than extinguished the flame in his heart. In one of the letters from home years later, Nan's mother mentioned the death of that young man at age twenty. He had leukemia, and he refused treatment. It was in the newspaper.

The day after Christmas, Nan flew back to Cornell and immediately immersed herself back in her research and began the tedious yet exhilarating task of thesis writing. She was meticulous by nature and had to go through many copies of drafts.

Then she began the process of applying for a position in Boston.

Four years after Nan left Taiwan and embarked on further education in this then unknown foreign land, she received her PhD degree. So much had happened in those four years. She met this group of complete strangers who had become her closest friends; one of them would soon be her husband. She came a girl with a heart never before stirred, she was now a woman destined to be wed. *What a journey!* she exclaimed.

Ethan came for her graduation. She was happy. He was beaming.

"I'm going to ask your parents for your hand!" he declared.

III

They arrived in Taipei after an exhausting flight. The whole family was at the airport eagerly waiting: her parents, Lily and her new husband, Shane and his wife Sue, and their one-year-old son. They had heard so much about Ethan in Nan's letters; they felt they already knew him.

The Yang's home in the Military Dependents' Village stood the same. Her father had it repainted, inside and out, preparing for their arrival. Only MayAnn and WayLee stayed there now. Lily and Shane had moved out to build their own families.

"No. 12!" Ethan looked at the number on the front door and exclaimed.

"Yes!" Nan smiled happily.

They had a traditional family reunion dinner. MayAnn, Lily, and Sue prepared the dishes, all ten of them.

"I hope you like it—the genuine Chinese food, un-Americanized!" Nan smiled at Ethan.

"What's that word? Did you just make it up?" Ethan said teasingly.

"I sure did," she said, laughing.

MayAnn kept piling food on Ethan's plate. WayLee tried to discourage her. "Don't stuff him," he said. Nan winked at Ethan, translating, "My father is trying to rescue you."

"There's enough food to feed twenty," he said.

"You'll make them happy if you eat more." So Ethan tried his best.

Nan woke up first the next morning. She stood outside of Ethan's room and knocked lightly, no response. *He's exhausted.* She smiled.

Her parents were already up. They sat on the sofa by the window.

"How was your sleep?" MayAnn asked.

"Not bad at all. I didn't have much jet lag."

"You look happy. I think you have found the one."

"Yes, Mama. Ethan is very good to me. He's a good person; smart, straightforward, and dependable. I know I can trust him."

"Are you certain you are committed to him and want to spend the rest of your life with him?" MayAnn persisted.

"Yes, I'm sure."

MayAnn needed to know the truth of her daughter's heart. "What about ShiMin? What's your feeling?" she asked.

Nan had already examined herself. She answered calmly.

"He's like a mirage to me. I cannot touch him. I've given him many opportunities, but he wouldn't allow me to get in the wall he built around himself. Whatever was bothering him is too great to break through. I've accepted it."

"Life certainly has its perplexities that are beyond our understanding," MayAnn lamented. "Ethan appears very open. There is no hiding of his admiration for you. But I need to remind you, don't let your pride get in the way. Some frictions between husband and wife are bound to happen. Don't insist on your opinion, even if you think you are right. Accept and acknowledge what he is better at than you are."

"Your mother is right," WayLee chimed in, "That's how we have such a good marriage, an everlasting one. And, as you know, this is not only between husband and wife; it's a general principle for a healthy relationship between all people. We all have our own weaknesses and strengths, just because you are not as good as someone in certain things, you cannot dislike that person and try to dismiss their achievement."

"I know, I am really working on it."

"That's good," WayLee said. "We're getting old. The world is now yours."

"No, Papa. You're only sixty. Isn't there a proverbial saying that life begins at seventy?"

"I guess you are right. But we are on our way down, and you are on your way up. You have the entire future ahead of you. Just remember not all will be what you desired. There will for sure be some bumps and hurdles along the way, some may even be seemingly indomitable hardships. Don't lose your focus when that happens. Remember there's always light at the end of the tunnel."

Nan thought of Scott, his desperation and despair that prevented him from seeing the light at the end of the tunnel. It still hurt her, and she still wished she could have done something more.

Ethan came into the room. He could not wait any longer.

"Mr. and Mrs. Yang, I ask your permission to marry your daughter Nan."

"What is it about Nan that makes you want to marry her?" MayAnn asked.

"Her intelligence, her kindness, her electrifying personality, her poetic sensitivity, everything about her." Then he added, "I adore her. I have found my jewel. I will never let her go."

"We are going to ask you the same question we asked Nan," WayLee said. "Are you certain you are committed to her and want to spend the rest of your life with her?"

"Oh, I most certainly do! Wholeheartedly."

"That is the confirmation we need from you," MayAnn said.

"We know Nan is certain that she wants to be with you for life. She is yours. Just remember, a good marriage is not by luck. It needs continued nurturing by both of you," WayLee reaffirmed.

Ethan was in seventh heaven.

Watching them, MayAnn was reassured, even though she was convinced that in the depth of her daughter's heart, a special place was held for ShiMin. She could not figure out why he was holding back. Nan never told her of his father's abandonment of him.

The family hosted a celebration dinner, announcing Nan's impending marriage to Ethan. They reserved a private room in a restaurant and invited their neighbors, their colleagues, and some of Nan's college and high school friends. This would be in lieu of the wedding banquet that was going to take place in the States. Lily and Shane were especially happy for their sister.

"Nan, I'm so happy for you. I think it's a good match. Ethan will be good for you," Lily said as the three siblings gathered in Nan's room after they came home from dinner.

"I believe so too. He's smart and seems to have a good heart," Shane agreed.

"Yes, I'm fortunate. Hard to accept we are all grown-up. Where did our childhood go?" Nan sighed.

"We had fun, didn't we?" Shane smiled.

"You little rascal. Papa had to tell us the moon story to warn you not to put bugs on me."

"Yes, but that was fun watching you screaming and jumping!"

Ethan knocked at the half-open door.

"Come in, Ethan. Join us. We're just remembering our childhood." Shane gestured him in.

"I was reminded that Shane used to play pranks on me," Nan told Ethan.

"Really? Like what?"

"He caught those dragonflies and put them on the back of my neck when I was doing my homework."

Ethan laughed, imagining Nan screaming at Shane.

"Remember you used to ride your bike to school when you were in junior high?" Lily said, recalling. "I was scared of riding on the streets, and my school was further than yours, so I just took the bus every day. One day, it was raining, and you didn't come home the usual time. We got very worried, and Papa walked out in the rain to look for you. It was almost halfway to your school when he saw you hunkered down, still trying to put the chain back on its track. Papa told us later that your face looked strong and determined. You did not cry. But when you saw him, you held his fingers so tight it hurt."

Nan remembered that incident. She could still feel the worry and panic she felt inside and the utter relief the moment she saw her father.

"Somehow you seemed to have it all. You were good academically. You were also good in sports. We used to go watch you compete in swimming and eighty-meter hurdles."

"That's right. Those were my two sports."

"Wow, I wouldn't have known." Ethan was impressed.

"Writing was the other thing Nan was especially good at," Lily said. "She always got high marks on her compositions and creative writings. She used to come home and told us 'teacher read my writing to the class today.' We heard it so often that we took it for granted."

"That, I can vouch for. I've seen her writings." Ethan was very pleased, remembering especially the letter Nan wrote to the house of No. 12 with that beautiful essay just a few days after she arrived Cornell.

"Remember your literature teacher wanted so badly for you to choose it as your major?" Lily said. "She even wrote to Papa and Mama, trying to convince them you could become a great writer. I guess she forgot you could be great in whatever you decide to study."

"We were so sad the day you left for the States." Shane remembered that day. "We came home from the airport feeling so lost."

"Mama cried often, and she would wake up finding her pillow wet," Lily said. "She worried so much about you. Papa tried to reassure her, but I didn't think he was very sure himself either. We just waited for your letters."

"Now no one needs to worry about me anymore. Ethan will take care of me." Nan felt blessed. Ethan was glowing.

"We were so excited when we got the first package you sent," Shane said. "I loved the shirt you gave me. I wore it proudly, showing off. My sister sent this to me from the United States, I told my friends. And those cookies, I can still taste it."

"I loved my dress. I still have it. Mama loved the dish detergent. It did work wonders," Lily added.

"You sent them dish detergent from the States?" Ethan thought he heard wrong.

Nan laughed. "Yes; dish detergent, dish pads, laundry detergent, paper towel, lotion, shampoo . . . Those things you took for granted. At that time not many stores carried them and they were expensive. I knew my mother would never buy them herself."

"Incredible," Ethan said.

"I just remembered," Lily said, "that time a group of us were outside our home talking. Your playmate next door ran out of her home all of a sudden, and without any warning, she stabbed your face with a pencil in her hand. You were so angry. You got in a fight with her. The stabbing didn't cause much damage, but the fight resulted in scrapes and bruises on both of you," Lily said.

"Ah, I had long forgotten that. I asked AnLing later why she stabbed me, but she wouldn't tell me. I asked if it was because we were too loud, and we were bothering her doing her homework. She said no. I said if it was because I didn't call her to join us. She wouldn't answer."

"I see the fierce side of you." Ethan winked at Nan.

"Yes, be careful. She certainly can be ferocious, if you're on the wrong side of her," Shane said. "Our mother told us a tale about her when she was not even five. A group of children were playing ball. A boy forcefully took the ball off Lily's hands. Lily stood there crying with her arms stretched out for the ball. Nan ran after the boy, kicked him, and got the ball back to Lily."

"Stay on the right side of her, you'll be safe," Lily said rather embarrassedly.

"I'll not only be safe, I'll be blessed." Ethan smiled.

They carried on their reminiscence late into the night. Ethan was grateful for hearing the past stories of the woman who would soon be his wife.

Nan took Ethan and visited a number of famous tourist destinations around the island, including some of the places she had gone with her schoolmates during their "Day of Outing." It brought back memories that made her nostalgic. Then she reminded herself, "The past is no more, the future not yet, only now." Looking at Ethan by her side, her heart overflowed with thankfulness.

"Let's go visit JeFu's parents," Ethan suggested.

"Ah, you remembered!"

JeFu and Jennifer had married. They were now in Indiana, both doing postdoc at Purdue.

Nan made arrangements, and they traveled to TaiChung to see JeFu's parents.

The Fongs were excited to meet their son's friends. They had heard so much about them.

"We are so glad to finally meet JeFu's good friends in the United States," Mr. Fong said.

"So when are you two getting married?" Mrs. Fong asked cheerfully.

"We don't have a date yet. We'll figure out after we get back to the States," Ethan answered, sparkles in his eyes.

"Jennifer is a good daughter-in-law. We like her very much," Mr. Fong said.

"When did you see them last?" Nan asked.

"In February. They said they wanted to escape from the cold in Indiana. But it was cold, rainy, and dreary here. We think they wanted to come to tell us in person that they are expecting a child." Mrs. Fong was delighted.

"How wonderful!" Ethan said, looking at Nan lovingly.

Mrs. Fong said to Nan, "JeFu told us you brought them together. He would not have met Jennifer if it were not for you in the first place. Then you pointed the direction for him. Otherwise, he would probably not have the courage to pursue her."

"I'm just happy they are together. They were born for each other," Nan said what she thought.

They were invited for lunch, the typical Chinese enthusiasm at the table with piles of food. They both were stuffed. Nan was happy she finally met JeFu's parents.

Ethan asked after they left the Fongs, "What did Mrs. Fong mean by your pointing the direction for JeFu?"

"I knew you'd ask. I hinted to him that Jennifer had an interest in him." Nan laughed.

"I never knew that. How come no one gave me a hint that you were interested in me?" Ethan joked.

"You wish!"

"Seriously, Nan, anyone would be lucky to have you as a friend."

Nan squeezed his hand, thankful for his appreciation.

They had limited time in Taiwan. The night before their departure, the whole family sat around the dinner table and chatted. One of Nan's college classmates who lived in the same Military Dependents' Village had just got back from her graduate school in TaiChung. She came to visit. Nan was very happy to see her, and they began to reminisce their college days. They recalled their psychology professor. The image of the boy Nan once interviewed appeared immediately in her mind. It was an image of a thin and depressed boy dancing gracefully, an image Nan had formed in her own mind.

"What a waste of life and talent!" she blurted out sadly.

"What do you mean?" Ethan was in a fog.

"Remember our discussion when your sister Mary wanted to be a model? Our psychology professor in college assigned me to interview this boy who wanted to be a dancer, but his parents wouldn't approve a career that they deemed unworthy. He later died of cancer. He refused any treatment."

"Ah, that's sad," Ethan said.

"I remember that class well," Nan's college classmate said. "We had an in-depth discussion of how society in general evaluated the merits of various careers, whether it is right to have a standard to determine what is or isn't a good career, what parental roles were in guiding the development of their children, whether one should go with one's heart or go with the expectation of their parents, what were the possible consequences if one is forced to do something one doesn't like to do."

"That was a good class. I can still remember some of the arguments." Nan recollected. "Education in Taiwan was more of teaching only, no discussion. We rarely had opportunity to discuss and explore our own ideas and views. Students generally accept whatever they were taught without questioning. It's changing though, I think."

"Yes, it's certainly better now," her friend said.

They changed to happier topics.

"Remember, Nan, we were so poor and could only afford occasional special lunches at one of the dorms for out-of-area students? We pooled our money, five dollars each; purchased two dishes; and shared."

"Yes, I remember that very well. Those were the good lunches we longed for."

"Five dollars for lunch, I wouldn't call it poor," Ethan said.

"But five-dollar Taiwan currency was less than fifteen cents U.S. currency!" Nan explained.

They all laughed.

"Oh, Nan, I almost forgot. Remember SenLan?"

"Sure, she was one of my lab partners in our organic chemistry class. She was very quiet but very smart. She only had her father here in Taiwan, I believe."

"Right. Her mother and her younger brother were not able to flee mainland China. They got separated from SenLan and her father. Guess what? They managed to escape to Hong Kong. From there, they came and were finally reunited two years ago."

"Wow, that's about twenty years of separation." Nan was amazed and excited for her college friend.

SenLan had told her friends the story of her mother's and her brother's miserable lives under the Communist. In the 1950s after they failed to flee, her mother was sent to labor camp. Her brother was only five and was cared for by his grandmother. The Great Leap

Forward movement led by their party leader Mao began in 1958. Mao wanted to convert the country rapidly from an agricultural society to an industrial civilization. Instead, the movement resulted in the Great Famine. Millions of people starved to death. Then the ten-year Cultural Revolution ensued in 1966 that brought schooling to a halt. More than a million people were killed and many more were imprisoned, tortured, and harassed. SenLan's brother, like many others, was unfoundedly accused of having bourgeoisie thoughts and was sent to a remote countryside in the province of Gansu to be 'reformed' in very harsh conditions; later he was moved to a factory to operate heavy machinery. He had difficulty adjusting to life in Taiwan when he first arrived. He later commented, "Before I left mainland China, I never knew what Freedom was."

"Many families got separated when the country tried to retreat to Taiwan," Nan's father said sadly. "Now this Vietnam War, we can expect many more will fall upon the same fate."

WayLee was right. Saigon fell to the North Vietnam Communist three years later.

It was late. They said good night and good-bye reluctantly.

The next day, Nan and Ethan bid good-bye to Taiwan. The entire family was again at the airport, seeing them off. But Ethan was right. He was with Nan, and that made the good-bye easier for her.

IV

Nan was offered a research fellow position in the department of pediatrics by Harvard University and the Massachusetts General Hospital. Her home base was at Mass General, the first teaching hospital of Harvard Medical School. She and Ethan were ecstatic. Not only because of the prestige of Mass General but also the assurance they could now stay in Boston, the city they both loved. Further, MIT and Mass General were so close physically, just across the Charles River.

Neither Ethan nor Nan wanted an extravagant wedding. They only invited their extended families and close friends. The house of No. 12 was at the top of the list. Nan wrote individual letters and sent them with the invitations.

Dear ShiMin,

It has been more than two years since you left Cornell. Now I have also completed my journey. Looking back, I realize so much had happened in such a short period in the large scheme of our lifetime, issues and changes I would never have foreseen. But there is nothing we can do but to embrace what might have been destined for us. I am finally at peace with myself.

Ethan and I will be married next month. We will call Boston home, the city we both love. Ethan has been at MIT for a year, and I will be starting at Mass General soon. He supports me emotionally and keeps me happy. I am grateful and know I am blessed.

I hope you will explore and accept the beautiful things as you have once commented. I hope you too find peace.

Nan

ShiMin had been expecting this letter and the wedding invitation. Still, it was heartbreaking when he did receive it. He went to the beach, took long walks up and down for hours while listening to the heartbeat of the ocean and watching the starry sky, at times letting his tears flow. He was happy for Nan. She had finally arrived at her destination. But why this stabbing aches in his heart?

For days, he struggled. Finally, he put on Mozart's *Requiem*, sat, and wrote.

"That day we took you to tour the campus when you first came to Cornell. At the top of the Libe Slope, all of a sudden, you spread your arms and turned around and around. You were radiant, you were glorious! That image has etched on my mind."

He removed the last sentence.

And I fell in love with you right then and there. An emotion so strong he had to stop. He got up and went to the beach. The waves were rough that evening, and the beach was deserted. He sat on a small rock, watching the ocean and begging for solace. Then he noticed someone was walking into the water, fully clothed. He instinctively ran over and dragged the man to shore. The man struggled to get away, but ShiMin was able to restrain him and coaxed him to get in his car. He started the engine, turned off the radio, and put on heat to dry themselves.

"I wish you didn't stop me," the young man said. He appeared to be in his late teens or early twenties.

"Life is precious. Nothing in this world should allow us to take our own lives."

"Easy for you to say."

"No, it's not. I've thought about it myself when the feelings of hopelessness seemed too overpowering to bear," ShiMin said. "You need to find an avenue and direction to give your life another meaning."

"How? I just lost my father, the only relative I had in this world. Now I lost my job. I don't know how I can survive."

"I'm very sorry for your losses. But what do you think your father would have wanted you to do? Would he have wanted you to die with him? You need to stand up and carry on. Find something else to do. Take on whatever job is available. There are also lots of charity assistances you may want to look into. Haven't you heard 'when God closes one door, he opens another'? There are options. Taking your own life is not one."

The conversation was therapeutic for ShiMin. He went home and completed his letter to Nan.

"I am happy for you. I will forever be grateful you came to Cornell. Fate was kind to me and brought us together. I treasure the friendship we shared and know it will never fade in my heart. May your life with Ethan be filled with the joy you felt at that moment on top of the Libe Slope."

Then he added, "I am sorry I will not be able to make it to your wedding. Please give Ethan my apology."

Nan had to cover the wound in the depth of her heart. Then she told Ethan, "ShiMin said sorry that he will not be able to make it."

"Does he have a girlfriend yet?" Ethan asked.

"He didn't say."

They found a small apartment close to both of their workplaces, paid the deposit, and waited to move in after the wedding.

V

MayAnn and WayLee flew in from Taiwan for the wedding. Nan was overjoyed to have them by her side. She introduced them to her parents-in-law to be.

"Welcome, Mr. and Mrs. Yang. I'm so glad we finally get to meet." Ethan's mother greeted her soon-to-be in-laws happily.

"We feel the same," MayAnn said.

"We love Nan. She's a wonderful person," Mr. Delaney said.

Ethan's little sister walked in cheerfully. She would be the maid of honor in the wedding.

"Mr. and Mr. Yang, I'm Ethan's sister, Mary. I'm so glad Nan will be my sister-in-law! I love her so much."

Nan had told her parents the conversation she had with Mary's parents. MayAnn said to Mary, "I think you'll be a good fashion model." Mary was delighted.

Except for ShiMin, the members of the house of No. 12 were all there, including Mark and the two newest members, Bob and Rodney. Mark's sister, Allison, also came. Allison had regained some of her spirited personality, but she was quieter than before. She had not been dating; Scott was still on her mind. Larry and Amy pursued their careers in Baltimore. Amy stayed at the Johns Hopkins Hospital as a pediatric resident. They already had a son. Jennifer and JeFu were expecting their first child soon. Unexpectedly, Eric brought his new girlfriend. He had finally found the right person, just as MayAnn had said. Lauren and Tom also came. They wanted to delay expanding their family until they were better established. Everyone was at a place they had hoped for.

"Too bad ShiMin couldn't be here," Larry said regretfully.

"I miss him," JeFu said. "He used to be more vibrant, somehow he became quieter the last year or two."

"I think so too. I just thought maybe he was too preoccupied with his study and career," Ethan said.

"What about you, Nan? You two were very close. Have you heard from him?" asked Jennifer.

"No, only in the beginning."

"I called him a year or so ago," JeFu said. "He seemed satisfied with his work and was expecting to get a junior faculty position at UCLA. He spent almost all his time in the lab."

"I wonder why he felt he needed to work so hard. He used to be more relaxed and he still did extremely well," Larry commented.

"Did he have a girlfriend?" asked Eric.

"No, at least not at that time," JeFu answered.

There were so much old memories of their lives together at Cornell to share. They retold their impressions of Nan when she first arrived at Cornell, and they recalled that memorable Labor Day barbecue in the park, their Sunday meals together, their discussions on religion, the Vietnam War that was still ongoing, and many other issues large and small.

"It sounded like you really had a great experience," Tom said. "No wonder people called you 5+2. I'm envious."

"We certainly had a swell time," Eric said. "Nan was the glue that put us together. That's Larry's conclusion at his wedding."

The topic then turned to their trip to Baltimore to attend Larry's wedding.

Amy recounted her impression of Nan the first time she met her. "I've not told this to anyone before," she added, "but I was thinking to myself, I hope one of you will be fortunate enough to win her heart."

"It's a reality now," Ethan said blissfully.

"I just came across an article in our local paper," Mark said. "Mrs. Foster was giving an interview about the tragic death of her son Scott. She described how she was brainwashed into believing it was always her fault for whatever her husband perceived as failures of their children. She spoke against domestic violence and child abuse, and wanted to bring the dark secrets out in the open. She also gave credit to Nan for providing her the impetus to take action now."

"At least something good came out of the tragedy," JeFu said.

"We probably shouldn't talk about that sad event on this happy occasion." Jennifer had become teary.

"That's quite all right, Jennifer," Nan said with empathy. "Good or bad, there is always an end. Everything will come to pass in the end. We need to remind ourselves to not be caught up in a situation that is only temporary."

"Well said," Ethan agreed.

"I imagine most people think college is the best years of their lives. But my grad school experience surpassed my college experience. I think ours was unique. Thanks to Nan," Eric reflected.

"That is so true," JeFu agreed, holding Jennifer's hand tightly.

The future was bright for each of them. There was no reason to think otherwise.

It was a simple and elegant wedding. Nan had chosen the same music that had been played at Larry's wedding. She thought those were perfect, and she had always loved them. The music of Bach's *Cantata, Jesu, Joy of Man's Desiring* began, and Ethan entered in absolute ecstasy. He walked confidently, his eyes bright and his face glowing. Mrs. Delaney watched her son. Suddenly, her tears began to flow, to her own surprise. Then the music that Nan thought could only be heard in heaven, *Canon in D Major* by Johann Pachelbel, was played. Everyone stood as Nan entered on her father's arm. She walked down the aisle gracefully, looking flawless, radiant, and glorious. Tears were in MayAnn's eyes as she watched her daughter take the first step into her new life.

Ethan gave his wedding vow to Nan.

"Nan, I had always been looking for the jewel in my life. I found it in you, and I will never let you go. I promise I will love you, take care of you, respect you, and honor you. I know there will be trials and tribulations in our life. I promise I will always be at your side, protecting you from all harm, until I die."

Nan was touched. She knew Ethan meant every word he said. She had her vow prepared. But after hearing Ethan, she decided to improvise.

"Ethan, I came to this country four years ago without ever having tasted love. Then I met you. My love for you developed gradually and became stronger and stronger, until I was overwhelmed. I love you unconditionally. I promise I will accept you as you are. I will always be with you and support you no matter what life may bring us. You will be my life partner, and I will be yours. Forever."

They looked deeply into each other's eyes and framed their vows in their hearts.

The recessional music, Wedding March from *A Midsummer Night's Dream* by Mendelssohn, signaled the end of the ceremony as the new Mr. and Mrs. Ethan Delaney exited.

When guests sent off the exuberant newlyweds after the reception dinner, MayAnn prayed for them a lifetime of happiness and contentment.

Mrs. Delaney told her husband, "I don't know why, but tears just poured out of my eyes as soon as I saw Ethan walking onto the aisle. It was such a happy occasion. I never imagined I'd cry."

Nan had arranged guided tours of the city and other parts of New England for her parents after the wedding. This was MayAnn and WayLee's first time in the States. Everything was new to them. On the other hand, some of the natural landscape looked familiar—the lush rolling hills, the deep blue waters, the gorges and canyons, the vast expanse of unspoiled nature—as they had seen in various parts of mainland China when they were moving around with the air force before the children arrived. That made them nostalgic and wishful for the day they could return to their true homeland. Nevertheless, they enjoyed their two weeks in the States. WayLee was particularly impressed with the Glass Flowers Exhibit at the Harvard Museum of Natural History. This was a collection of more than three thousand life-size and life-like models of flowers and plants made of glass. It was created over a span of fifty years beginning in the year of 1887 for the purpose of teaching botany at the university.

"They looked so real. Many are very small, and some even have bees attached to show pollination. It was amazing! How they were able to make them is definitely beyond my imagination." WayLee could not stop talking about it. He told MayAnn many times, even though she was there with him and had seen those life-like objects herself. That was one major topic of his conversations with friends after they returned home.

They went back to Taiwan reassured, knowing Nan was under the unmistakably wholehearted care of Ethan.

PART SIX

New Life as Husband and Wife

I

Ethan and Nan started their new life as husband and wife, deeply in love. It did not take long for Nan to get in the groove of her new position. She soon identified her research topic under the guidance of her mentor, Professor Brown. When Brown realized Nan had the ability to intelligently and perspicaciously critique manuscripts submitted for publication, he asked her to review and prepare draft comments before he finalized them to send back to journal editors who sought his opinion. Nan took them home to work on at night, as the days in the lab were continually fast paced, and she never had time to work on any manuscripts. She enjoyed the process, and it proved to be a good learning experience for her.

They did not waste the little time they had outside of work. They attended Boston Symphony Orchestra's performances and frequented the Museum of Fine Arts. They spent their time with nature; the fall foliage, the magnificent mountains and ocean. They visited places of rich history of the country; the Plymouth Rock, Mayflower II, Plimoth Plantation, Walden Pond, JFK Library, Bunker Hill, and Cape Cod. They walked the Freedom Trail and many more. Life was good.

Nan was never tired of John Singer Sargent's *Oyster Gatherers of Cancale* and *The Daughters of Edward Darley Boit* in the Boston Museum of Fine Arts. "Oh, I feel so rich and so blessed whenever I step in this museum. Look at all these paintings! Absolutely astonishing! So many, one after another! How could one put a price on them? It was the heart and soul of the artists. No amount of money should be able to buy them."

Ethan would tease her. "Your expression is what's priceless." He had learned to love what she loved and to believe what she believed in.

He had submitted an abstract of his research. The abstract was accepted for presentation at a conference in Rome. Nan was excited. She had always wanted to witness the grandeur of ancient history and civilization. She managed to take a week off and went with Ethan.

Rome did not disappoint her. They toured around the city together whenever Ethan could steal some time from the meeting. They also scheduled to stay two extra days after the conference ended.

"Rome is human spirit in all its splendor," Nan exclaimed.

"What do you like the most?" Ethan asked.

"I can't say. I like all. It's almost incomprehensible that without modern tools, such splendid structures could be built and so many of them." Nan was full of appreciation. "Ah, the ingenuity of the human mind!"

They were then in St. Peter's Square, waiting in line to get into the magnificent St. Peter's Basilica, described by Ralph Waldo Emerson as "an ornament of the earth . . . the sublime of the beauty."

Nan turned around and took in the panorama of the entire square.

"I think this is more than an ornament and inspiration. It is a stupendous magic to the utmost," she said.

"And the art, of course," Ethan said as they stepped into the church.

"Art, of course!" Nan echoed as the great expansion of art unveiled before them. Endless paintings and statues surrounded them. They were in awe.

They stood for a long time in front of Michelangelo's *Pietà*. This famous marble sculpture depicted Mary holding the body of her son Jesus on her lap after his Crucifixion. Nan was engrossed with the amazing love of Christ and the miraculous skill of the sculptor.

Coming into the Sistine Chapel, they witnessed the history of Christianity from the Creation to the Last Judgment painted on the ceiling and the altar wall by Michelangelo. For Nan, this was beyond comprehension.

She said to Ethan, "How is it possible this was done by man?"

"It was done by God through man," Ethan responded impulsively.

Nan was so touched by his statement, she instinctively kissed his cheek. Ethan held her hand firmly, elated.

The art in Rome seemed limitless. The collections in the Galleria Borghese, including the marble sculptures of David, and of Apollo and Daphne, were yet again breathtaking for them. They felt they were immersed in a rich and plentiful medium with endless supply of extravagance.

The evening before they headed back to the States, they visited the famed Trevi Fountain. The fame was not exaggerated. The sight and sound were altogether abundantly luxurious. They kissed, in front of the fountain, happy and content.

The couple standing next to them smiled. They asked, "Are you from the States?"

"Yes, Boston," Ethan answered.

"Wonderful city. We lived there for ten years. Always loved it. Our son and daughter-in-law are in Burlington, Vermont. They are expecting their first child. We will stop to see them for a couple of days on our way home," the man said. He appeared to be in his fifties.

"We now live in Indianapolis," his wife said.

"Two of our good friends are in Lafayette, not too far from you, I guess," Ethan said.

"No, not at all, just about an hour's drive. Are they at Purdue?"

"Yes, they both are on staff there. They should be on faculty soon."

"Are you newlyweds?" the wife asked.

"Not really. We have been married for about ten months," Nan answered.

"You looked like you are just married, the way you looked at each other."

Nan blushed. Ethan was happy.

"It's almost dinner time. Do you have anything planned?" the man asked.

"Not really. We thought we'd just settle on whatever we come upon on," Ethan replied.

"Why don't we have dinner together to continue our conversation?" the man said.

"They might want to have a romantic dinner by themselves," his wife interrupted.

"It sounds like a good idea to share a meal together. What do you think, Ethan?"

"Of course, I'm all for it."

The man liked to talk and had many stories to tell about his days in the Army. Nan and Ethan enjoyed.

"Good food, real Italian. And good company." The man was satisfied.

"We enjoyed very much. This is an unexpected bonus to our trip," Nan said.

They exchanged names and phone numbers.

"Come visit us if you are in Lafayette visiting your friends. We will take you around Indianapolis. You may want to see the Motor Speedway too," they said.

A few days after Ethan and Nan returned home, a Delta Airlines plane crashed into the seawall at Boston's Logan Airport while trying to land, killing all eighty-nine people onboard. The new friends they met in front of the Trevi Fountain were among the victims. They were on that flight from Burlington to Logan and were then supposed to fly home to Indianapolis from Logan.

Ethan and Nan were shocked and saddened.

"What a disaster, unimaginable!" Ethan said.

"It was only a few days ago. The imagery of our encounter and the stories he told are still so fresh and vivid." Nan sighed. "These are the verses in the Bible: 'I have seen all the works that are done under the sun; and behold, all is vanity and a chasing after wind.' Life can change in a moment without warning. We need to do our best and make every day worthy of living."

II

Although MayAnn had wished for more grandchildren soon, she understood Nan and Ethan's intention of putting career first. *They are young, they have time.* She accepted.

And life was perfect for them. They were deeply in love, and their researches were going well. Within three years, they both had been promoted to faculty positions. There was nothing more they would have desired. Now they began discussing the prospect of rearing children.

"How many would you like?" Nan asked happily.

"Two."

"Sounds good. Boy or girl?"

"At least one girl."

"Okay, I'll take note." Nan laughed without a care.

So it was settled. Two children, a family of four. What a wonderful prospect.

Nan was thirty-one then. They were certain they will have their first child within a year, or two years at most.

That did not happen, to their dismay.

Nan became somewhat anxious. She recalled a story her mother told.

"A good friend of your grandmother's, Bao, was married into a family of power and wealth," MayAnn had told Nan and her sister Lily. "The family had only one son and one daughter. Girls in China in those days were generally considered as 'other people's property' since they would be married off, and 'married daughter is like a bucket of splashed water.' They were lost forever. So the lone son was their only hope to carry on the family name. It was therefore all the more important that Bao be reproductively successful. When there was still no sign of any baby two years after the marriage, her mother-in-law began threatening her. 'I will send you back to your mother if you cannot get pregnant,' she told Bao. Bao couldn't get pregnant, but she and her husband loved each other, and they did not want to be separated. They ultimately concocted a scheme. They padded Bao's abdomen with cloth, adding layers as time went on, pretending she were pregnant. In the meantime, they had Bao's closest and most trusted servant girl go and find potential pregnant women who were too poor to raise more children and were willing to sell their baby as soon as they were born. The servant girl identified three such women to guarantee at least one would be a boy. They waited till the women went into labor. When one of them delivered a boy, Bao told her mother-in-law that her own mother was gravely ill, and she needed to go visit her. Her mother-in-law was reluctant noting she appeared near delivery, but her husband reassured her and accompanied Bao to 'visit her sick mother.' They went and returned three days later with a baby boy."

That was outrageous; the distance people were willing to go to have a baby! Nan had been astonished by the story. Now it had a new meaning.

Nan visited the obstetrics and gynecology department in her own hospital. The physician ordered a number of laboratory tests after an initial consultation and examination. They were normal. The tests were expanded to include rarer possible causes. Then Ethan was tested as well. Nothing abnormal was found in either of them.

"Is it because I'm too old?" Nan asked and then realized how foolish the question was. *I am not quite thirty-three. I am not old.*

"No, many women have their first child after they are thirty."

"Why then?"

"We don't know. All lab tests have been normal. This would be considered idiopathic infertility, infertility without a known cause."

"What's next?"

"I would recommend keep trying, while we consider options for infertility treatment."

Ethan tried to comfort her. "It may take a while but don't be discouraged," he said. "Besides, I love you all the same whether we have children or not. It wouldn't be the end of the world. We'll always have each other."

Nan knew how much Ethan wished for a daughter. Nonetheless, she was comforted by his reassurance.

They decided to defer treatment and hoped for nature to take its right course.

In the meantime, they tried to live their life as normal as possible. They dedicated themselves to their work, published papers, and continued to climb the academic ladder. Museum and concerts were still their favorites. And they spent as much time as possible enjoying the beauty nature had to offer. Boston was still their city.

By this time, the Hancock Place, or commonly known as John Hancock Tower, had been completed. Despite all its initial engineering flaws, it boasted to be the tallest construction in Boston. The tall skinny skyscraper with lightly blue-tinted glass windows all around stood gracefully and splendidly. It became Nan's favorite building. She was especially fascinated by the reflection of the magnificent Trinity Church on the glass windows of the Tower. On her way to and from work, she would, as much as possible, take the streets that allowed her to observe the building with the image of the church in it. It always gave her a sense of amazement and gratitude.

Two years later, they opted for infertility treatment.

It was not an easy and innocent process. Nan experienced side effects from the medications she was given. Treatment had to be suspended several times. After two years, in late 1982, she became pregnant. The joy she and Ethan experienced was overwhelming.

Nan was thirty-eight when Becky was born, very late by usual standards at the time. The year was 1983.

III

"Oh, Nan, she's so beautiful!" holding Becky, Ethan was on cloud nine for days.

"As beautiful as you are, if you were a girl," Nan said happily.

Both their families were overjoyed. Becky would be the third grandchild for the Delaneys and the sixth for the Yangs. Ethan's sister, Mary, had two children. She had moved to Los Angeles years before to pursue her modeling career. She was quite successful there and had married a fashion designer. Mary remained close to Nan and was glad she now had a niece.

"I think about you often, and I have been praying for you," Mary wrote. "I am so happy that you now have Becky. She is absolutely adorable. I am sure she will grow up to be a person of wisdom, just like her mother."

MayAnn and WayLee had been having frequent conversations about Nan having difficulty conceiving.

"Nan wants to be a mother, I know that. But it seems Ethan is even more eager to have children," MayAnn said. "I am worried for Nan. They have good doctors and hospitals there but that have not helped her yet."

Now with the birth of Becky, they were finally free of their worries. We can now relax and enjoy, they assured each other. Lily and Shane also felt relieved. Like their parents, they too had been worried for Nan.

Ethan's parents visited them often and helped as much as they could. They fell in love with their new granddaughter as soon as they saw her. "She does have the image of Ethan, and Nan too," Mrs. Delaney commented with satisfaction.

MayAnn and WayLee made a trip to the States. They had not seen their daughter and son-in-law for ten years, although the letters continued all along. By then Nan and Ethan had moved to a townhouse in a very nice community called Bishops Forest in a suburb west of Boston.

"You're so beautiful, my little darling," MayAnn held Becky in her arms and watched closely at her long-awaited granddaughter. "I think she looks like both of you," she felt blessed. They stayed on for three months after Nan returned to work.

Becky was an easy baby. She did not fuss very much, and she usually slept well. When the weather was nice, MayAnn and WayLee would put Becky in a baby stroller and push her around the neighborhood. Small clusters of townhouses were scattered among this large grounds of mature trees, plants, birds, squirrels, and gentle hills. There were also a few small playgrounds within the community. "My little Becky, you can play here when I come next time. You'll be big enough then," MayAnn had said. To her, the setting was what she would find in storybooks. It really was like a small forest in the middle of a city. Sometimes they would encounter neighbors, who invariably stopped and exchanged greetings, and commented on how beautiful the baby was. MayAnn was very happy. Her memory of that feeling of absolute contentment during this time lasted forever in her heart.

They left the States reluctantly after three months.

At Becky's six-month checkup, the pediatrician ordered a complete blood count. "Becky looked quite pale," she said.

Nan had noticed that, but she convinced herself and brushed it off as probably just her fair skin, like Ethan.

Three days later, the pediatrician called. "The blood test confirmed anemia," she said. "The hemoglobin content was low, and the red blood cells were smaller than normal. We will need to do additional test to find out the cause of the anemia."

"What kind of test?" Nan asked.

"It's called hemoglobin electrophoresis to determine the types and proportions of hemoglobin in the red blood cells. That will give us an indication of the cause of her anemia. We will also consider mutation analysis if necessary."

Nan took Becky in for a second blood draw.

The bombshell dropped when the test was completed. Beta-thalassemia major, a genetic disorder affecting the red blood cells.

"How is it possible? It's a recessive disorder, isn't it?" Devastated and refusing to believe, Nan argued. "I understand the carrier frequency for beta-thalassemia is higher in the Chinese population, and I could be one of the two or three people in a hundred who carry the mutation. But it's so much lower in where Ethan is from; the odds that he also carries the mutation are so small. Becky couldn't have two copies of the defective gene." Nan was almost pleading.

"It's unusual that Becky should be affected with beta-thalassemia major, given it is a recessive disease as you already know. But I don't think the diagnosis is wrong. I will check both of your blood for carrier testing. I will also refer you to a hematologist," the pediatrician said.

The world changed for them in an instant. They were thrown into a bottomless abyss of anguish and despair. They waited for their blood test results, still hoping Becky's diagnosis was wrong.

The night before their appointment with the hematologist, the pediatrician called Nan.

"We have received your carrier testing results. Do you want to see the hematologist alone first and maybe come with your husband at a later date?"

"No, why?"

"The results are sort of complicated. Perhaps it is better that you are by yourself first."

"No, Ethan is a scientist. He will understand even though he is not a biologist."

They went in the next day. The hematologist, Dr. Smith, discussed the disease in detail with them.

"Beta-thalassemia is a recessive genetic disorder caused by abnormalities, known as 'mutations,' of the gene called beta globin gene that controls the production of one component of hemoglobin. Hemoglobin is the molecule in our red blood cells that is responsible for carrying oxygen to tissues and organs in our body.

"Children with beta-thalassemia major usually have poor weight gain, progressive paleness, feeding problems, and later enlargement of the liver and spleen.

"Treatment is by red blood cell transfusion. The problem is that transfusion has to be done frequently to keep the hemoglobin at a reasonable level. Unfortunately, frequent transfusion can cause iron overload that can then result in organ damage, including heart failure. Therefore, iron overload will in turn require treatment by iron chelation therapy. With adequate treatment, normal growth and development and improvement in the overall prognosis are possible. This is a lifelong disease, but it is not without treatment."

"Do they get to live a normal life?" Ethan asked with an aching heart.

"More or less. It's just they will be in and out of hospital and with frequent needle sticks."

"What's the life expectancy?" Nan's heart sank.

"It's shortened compared with the general population because of various factors and complications. But survival beyond age forty is possible."

"Ah!" both Nan and Ethan exclaimed in despair.

Although Dr. Smith was not a geneticist, he had seen many patients with beta-thalassemia and had gained enough knowledge to be able to explain the genetic basis of the disease.

"As far as how mutations of the beta globin gene can cause beta-thalassemia major, it's best to start with chromosomes," he began. "Chromosomes are structures in our cells that contain genes. Each cell has twenty-three pairs of chromosomes. One set of the twenty-three chromosomes is inherited from the father, and the other set is inherited from the mother. Therefore, there are two copies of each gene, one from each parent. In thalassemia major, both copies of the beta globin gene are defective. The body will not be able to make hemoglobin effectively, and severe anemia will occur. That will result in beta-thalassemia major as is found in your daughter."

Dr. Smith waited a few moments. Then as delicate as he could, he started the topic.

"As I mentioned, this is a recessive disease. That means the gene on both chromosomes, one inherited from the father, the other from the mother, needs to be defective for a child to have the disease. We tested both of you. Nan, one of the two of your beta globin genes has a mutation as expected. Ethan, though, does not have a mutation . . ."

"What does that mean?" Nan asked. *That doesn't make sense*, she realized immediately.

"We don't quite know. There can be many possibilities, theoretically. For example, Ethan may have a very rare mutation that cannot be detected at this time, or in the very early stage when the embryo was forming, a mutation occurred on the chromosome that was inherited from Ethan, so both copies of the gene in Becky became defective, or some other theoretical possibilities. But all these would be extremely rare."

"Or perhaps the diagnosis is wrong. Perhaps Becky has only one mutated gene. Perhaps she is only a carrier just like me." Nan was holding on to the slim hope that Becky was not affected with the disease.

"Yes, we would certainly wish the diagnosis were wrong. Unfortunately, all tests and indicators of her red blood cells are typical of thalassemia. You are in one of the best institutions in the country. Some of the leading researchers working on thalassemia are in Boston."

Nan was a scientist, she understood. But as a mother, she could not accept.

Dr. Smith had to bring up the most likely possibility in this kind of cases, mistaken paternity.

Nan was stunned. "No, there must be an explanation, but nonpaternity is not the one," she declared. She realized this was why the pediatrician had suggested that she came to the appointment by herself.

Somehow Dr. Smith believed Nan. *Perhaps there really is a yet undiscovered mechanism,* he thought.

Nan and Ethan returned home heartbroken. They both were silent in the car, mulling over the conversation they had with the hematologist and trying to make some sense of it.

As soon as Becky's caretaker left, Ethan spoke in a saddened rage. "It's ShiMin, isn't it?"

He tried to justify it for himself. "When you first arrived Cornell, they took you to the Libe Slope. Afterward, Eric and even JeFu couldn't stop talking about you. They said you looked like an angel on that hill. But ShiMin was silent all the time. It wasn't like him. But I thought Eric and JeFu had taken all the words out of his mouth."

He ranted on. "I had always wondered. But I didn't want to accept it. I lied to myself that the reason you were so attached to him was because he was the first one you met, and he helped you settle in. Now I know why he didn't want to consider Princeton. It's too close to Cornell. What I don't understand is why he gave you up." He was desperate.

"You are out of your mind!" Nan was stunned and deeply hurt by the accusation. She burst out crying.

"You heard the hematologist. What else could it be other than nonpaternity?" He felt helpless.

In desperation, she said, "Look at your daughter, look at her Caucasian features. She is more like you than me, she even has your wavy hair!" She stormed out of the house.

Ethan was bewildered. He went into Becky's room. She was awake, and she smiled at him and giggled. His heart melted. "My daughter," he admitted. He picked her up. She reached her hand and touched his face. His tears streamed down.

All the happiness and contentment he and Nan had embraced together rushed back into his heart. "What happened to me? What happened to my promise to protect her from all harm, always, until I die?" he asked himself. "Now I've committed the cruelest crime, accusing her of being unfaithful." He could not forgive himself.

Nan ran furiously, her head pounding, her heart full of rage, sadness, and disappointment. She kept running aimlessly, wanting to get away from all the cruelty of the life she was trapped in. Eventually she slowed down, still sobbing. But rational thinking set in. *Becky needs me, she needs both of us. We have to give her a stable home; I can't leave now.*

Ethan was worried, scared, and panicked when he did not see Nan. He rushed out but realized he could not leave Becky alone by herself. He went back inside and walked about agitatedly, repeatedly watching the door and looking out through the window. His soul was so tortured that he cried out loud, "Come back! Nan, please! I need you, I love you. Oh, please come back!" Each minute seemed like an eternity. He had never experienced this much anxiety in his life. As soon as he saw Nan, he grabbed her, held her tightly, and cried.

"I'm so sorry. I was so confused and didn't know what I was thinking. I can't forgive myself for having ever doubted you, even just for a second. I broke my wedding vow to you. Please forgive me. I can't live without you." He begged.

Nan understood. Although it still hurt her heart, she knew he was desperately confused.

Nan's burden was heavy. But like her mother, she was a strong woman. *Becky and Ethan need me. I have to be able to carry them forward.*

Ethan's parents could not accept the fact their new granddaughter had a genetic disease that had no cure. They went to see their own family physician.

"Ethan's new baby was just diagnosed with a genetic disease called beta-thalassemia major. Is it possible?"

"It is quite rare in people of your background. What did the doctor tell Ethan how the diagnosis was made?"

"They said Becky has severe anemia, and they did a special test, hemoglobin electrophoresis, I think, and that confirmed the diagnosis," Mr. Delaney answered.

"The diagnosis seems quite reasonable then," the family physician said, then added, "Although the possibility of having the mutation is very small in your ethnic group, it is not unheard of."

The Delaneys also talked with two of their friends who were pediatricians. They also tried to read whatever they could find about the disease. But every effort pointed them back to the diagnosis they were told.

There was no escape.

IV

Nan's heart bled every time Becky had her blood drawn or had red blood cell transfusion. Most of the time, Becky cried and fought; sometimes she was quiet as if she accepted her fate. Nan felt guilty, even though she knew it was beyond her control. At times, the day felt so dark that she would cry out, "Lord, why?" The family had fallen under an unremitting cloud of misery.

She usually took Becky to the hospital by herself to spare Ethan the torture of having to endure the agony of witnessing Becky's suffering. Watching her, all she could say was "my darling Becky, don't cry. It will be over soon." The physical and emotional burden was so heavy that she had to take an extended leave from work to care for Becky.

It took much longer for Ethan to accept the tragedy. He would forget his pain temporarily when he was absorbed in his work. But the perpetual agony returned as soon as he turned away from work.

Becky responded to medical treatment and was able to grow, although she was smaller than others her age. She also developed appropriately, in fact, more advanced. Before age one, she was already starting to say words. Dada was her favorite. She called "dada, dada" and waved and jumped excitedly whenever Ethan came home. He would hold her close to his heart, trying to forget the merciless reality of her disease.

Nan's letter home had become shorter and less frequent. She had not yet told her parents. *It would only make them worry and sad. There was nothing they could do*, she decided. She knew it would be a long and lonely road she will have to confront by herself.

After nearly a year, she was finally able to face what she needed to do.

"Dear Papa and Mama, Lily, and Shane." She wrote. "We have been dealing with an adversity. Becky is not well. She was born with a disease called beta-thalassemia major that causes severe anemia and requires frequent blood transfusion. But she is otherwise normal and very smart. She already has quite a few words: dada, mama, no, bye, go, want, etc., and she tries to repeat what we say. She calls Ethan dada, and she loves him. Ethan had a difficult time coping in the beginning, but he is adjusting, and for that I am grateful.

"Since beta-thalassemia is a genetic disease, I want to let you know you need to be tested to determine if you are a carrier. At this time, the most reasonable approach is to test Lily and Shane. Hopefully, you don't have a defective gene for this disease. There is nothing more you need to do if your tests are normal. In case you are a carrier, your children will also have to be tested before they get to reproductive ages.

"We are moving on all right. I take it one day at a time and appreciate what I do have."

MayAnn had suspected something was happening in Nan's life, judging from the way Nan's letter had been in the previous year. But she knew her daughter, Nan would have told her. So she consoled and convinced herself it was the burden of her work while also having to care for Becky.

Yes, indeed, something was happening in Nan's life but never had MayAnn imagined it could be of this magnitude. The ultimate test in Nan's life that MayAnn had feared for finally arrived. "Can she handle it? Will she be able to survive this trial that she would most likely perceive as her failure?" MayAnn asked.

The family was in disbelief and despair. "Blood transfusion? How can such a little baby take it? How could this happen? Why does tragedy of this enormity happen to them? How? Why?" they asked.

There was no answer.

V

Dr. Smith, the hematologist, was rather satisfied with Becky's progress, considering she appeared to have a more severe form of the disease. Her onset of symptoms was relatively early, and her initial anemia was quite severe. He had been thinking of what Nan had said, that there must be a reason, but it definitely was not nonpaternity. He decided to have Ethan, Nan, and Becky's DNA tested and compared to see if it might provide some information.

It took quite some time before the test was completed. The results were astonishing.

"We have some very unusual results," Dr. Smith began when Ethan and Nan came for the meeting. He had been very excited with what the lab results showed, but he also understood the toll and suffering the family was experiencing. He suppressed his excitement and approached them compassionately.

"As we discussed before, we inherit one set of chromosome from our father and one set from our mother. In Becky's case, she inherited both of her number 11 chromosomes from Nan, none from Ethan. Chromosome 11 is where the beta globin gene is located. Furthermore, her two copies of chromosome 11 are exactly the same. They both have the defective beta globin gene. The research lab also tested other chromosomes, and they all show she inherited one copy from Ethan and one copy from Nan as they should be."

That explained everything. But it did not make Nan feel any better. Becky still had to fight her battle.

"How did it happen?" Nan asked.

"I'm not sure. I'll refer you to a geneticist. He should be able to explain and answer your questions."

Then he said, "Nan, you were right from the beginning. I'm very sorry."

"That's all right. You based your conclusion on the knowledge that you believed to be right. I based mine on the fact that I knew to be true," Nan replied. *And knowledge could be wrong, but fact is always true. Truth triumphs over knowledge, that is the irrefutable fact.* She knew all along.

Becky was anxiously waiting for them when they got home. She was now more than two years old. Like a sponge, she was absorbing whatever was taught to her.

"Dada, read book to me." She brought a picture book and opened it.

Ethan picked her up, kissed her cheek, and said, "We have to eat first. After dinner, we will read."

Becky put down the book and walked toward the kitchen. "We have to eat first," she said.

A wave of warmth came upon Ethan. He was now ready to face the reality.

Nan smiled. She knew they were at last able to move forward.

Nan wrote to her parents. "I think we are finally able to begin a new phase of our life. It had been a long and painful journey, but Ethan now appeared to have accepted what we were dealt with. I thought of a quote in the book *A Soldier of the Great War*. 'God compensates perfectly. You cannot fall and expect not to rise.' We are now able to rise."

She began responding to her close friends of No. 12, their multiple letters filled with love and compassion. She had put them aside, never was able to complete drafting a reply until then.

Dear Jennifer,

I am sorry for not writing to you. But I knew you would understand. Thank you for offering repeatedly to come and help us. We had been in a perpetual darkness the last two years. I felt so inadequate. I was unable to do anything besides just taking care of Becky and Ethan and struggling to survive. At times I wondered if hell could not be any worse. Watching Becky's sad face enduring the painful needles was worse than being stabbed in my heart. Still, I had to remain the strong one to hold both of them up. Ethan was so afraid of losing her that he did not allow himself to be too attached to her. I think he finally realized Becky is a normal two-year-old little girl. She is not defined by her illness. You know how confident and dependable he was. I pray he will get himself back soon. I thank you for your friendship; I hold it preciously in my heart.

Nan

They went to see the geneticist.

"I discussed your test results with Dr. Smith," the geneticist told them. "We looked over the actual laboratory data and the plots of DNA analyses. Becky inherited both copies of chromosome 11 from Nan, none from Ethan. This fits well the descriptive term of uniparental disomy, that is, literally, 'one parent, two chromosomes.' In Becky's case, the two copies of chromosome 11 are exactly the same, and both copies of the beta globin gene are defective and have the same mutation. That is the reason she unfortunately has the disease beta-thalassemia major."

"How could this uniparental disomy happen?" Nan asked.

"We can only speculate, but here's a reasonable hypothesis. Normally, egg and sperm each contains twenty-three chromosomes. Embryos generally do not survive if a fertilized egg is missing a chromosome, unless somehow a rescue mechanism by nature occurred. For example, the sperm contains only twenty-two chromosomes and is missing one chromosome 11, the fertilized egg now has forty-five chromosome with only one copy of chromosome 11. But it corrected itself by duplicating the one chromosome 11 that was in the egg. Now the fetus can survive with the normal total chromosome number of forty-six, but both chromosomes 11 are maternal in origin and are exactly the same."

"Now I understand." Nan finally had her answer.

"How common is this uniparental disomy?" Ethan asked.

"Not common at all. In fact, the concept is very new. The term was only introduced in 1980. And it seems only to be a theoretical possibility, so far in 1985, there has been no reported cases I can find in the literature."

"What is the risk of this happening again?"

"It would be extremely small. It occurred as a sporadic event, it is not inherited."

The discussion aided, especially for Ethan, the understanding of how Becky had the disease. It did not change the course or management. But for Ethan, knowledge did foster acceptance, and that was important for him.

Ethan was able to love Becky without reservation. He was going to love her and protect her, "always, until I die," as he promised Nan. He was even able to take Becky for her red blood cell transfusion. He held her little hand, whispering in her ear with a broken heart, "Don't cry. It will be over soon. Dada loves you. Everything will be all right."

The family established and accepted its new normalcy and was at last able to move on as much as could be expected under the shadow of Becky's lifelong incurable disease.

The hypothesis that uniparental disomy can be a cause of recessive genetic disorders when only one parent is a carrier for the disease was later confirmed. In 1988 and 1989, two independent reports were published in the *American Journal Human Genetics*. Both patients in these reports had cystic fibrosis as a result of uniparental *iso*disomy of chromosome 7, on which the gene responsible for cystic fibrosis resides. The term *isodisomy* signified that the two copies inherited from one single parent were exactly the same, as was the case in Becky.

PART SEVEN

Last Reunion

I

In the summer of 1986, Lily visited Nan in Boston. The two sisters embraced and sobbed. There was so much unspoken sadness in their hearts.

It did not take long for Becky to get used to Lily. Lily would take Becky, holding her little hand to walk around the beautiful grounds of the Bishops Forest community. MayAnn had described their days with Becky so often and in such detail that the picture of her parents pushing Becky in the stroller with absolute contentment had been ingrained in Lily's mind. Now she was experiencing it herself, thinking of her mother all the while.

They stopped at one of the small playgrounds. Becky liked the swing, and Lily pushed her gently. "Auntie, please carry me. I'm tired," after a while Becky would ask. Lily picked her up immediately and planted a kiss on her cheek. "Good girl. Let's walk around a little more and let dada and mama have some rest."

Lily's heart was troubled. She could not yet summon the courage to tell Nan the news about their mother.

This was Lily's first time to the States, and Nan wanted to show her the city. The whole family went together, a rare event since Becky became ill. It had been a long time since Nan was able to appreciate this city she loved so much. Sitting next to Ethan in the car, she watched the long-forgotten yet familiar surroundings and buildings. She longingly reached her hand to Ethan. He held it tightly.

Around lunchtime, they arrived in Chinatown and went in a restaurant. It was still early, and the restaurant was not crowded. They sat. Nan ordered Ethan's favorite dish, and Lily ordered the rest. As they were waiting, Lily suddenly realized someone at the next table behind her was saying something familiar. ". . . forgiving, and compassionate; love your country and love your . . ." She quickly turned around. There were four people at the table: a couple, a baby, and an older man. She fixed her gaze on the older man. Everyone was now looking at her. Her heart racing, she asked, "Are you Chong or Liu?"

"I'm Chong. Why?"

"Oh my lord," Lily cried out. "I'm Lily. This is Nan. More than thirty-five years ago, you carried us on your backs to visit my grandfather's grave with my mother."

"You are Teacher Yang's daughters! Miracle! My wish is granted. Now I can leave this world without any regrets." He wept.

Among her siblings, Lily was the main audience of their mother. Like her mother-in-law, MayAnn had fallen in the habit of retelling old stories and old memories. She talked often about their last visit to her father-in-law's grave, her reading classes, and the students, especially Chong and Liu.

"The night before I took you to join your grandmother at my father's house, I gave them the last reading class. I wanted to leave them with something they could try to learn themselves, something of substance. So I wrote down this phrase for each of them—Be kind, forgiving, and compassionate. Love your country, and love your countrymen. I wonder if it had made any impact on them," MayAnn had told Lily many times. Nan had heard it too.

"My father recited that phrase to us often," the younger man at the table was saying.

Lily was crying almost inconsolably.

Becky said, "It's okay, Auntie. Don't cry. It will be over soon," those same words her parents uttered agonizingly whenever she was having blood transfusion or iron chelation therapy.

With a start, Nan held her daughter and let her tears flow. Becky looked at her mother's face closely and said, "Don't cry, Mama. It will be over soon."

With tears in his eyes, Ethan embraced them both.

Chong introduced his son, daughter-in-law, and his new grandson.

"Thank you for carrying me that day," Nan said rather embarrassedly.

"Oh, I remember that day very well. It was the day that changed my life. I never forget what Teacher Yang taught us. She was such a good teacher. We learned so much in four weeks. More importantly, we learned that there were good and kind landlords like your family. When we went for class the next evening, there was no one in your servants' quarter. We waited. Finally, we realized you must have fled. We didn't say anything to anyone. The next morning, our leader, Chang Din, found out your family had disappeared. He was very angry and ordered us to search the neighborhood. I and the others in Teacher Yang's class rushed to as many homes as possible, just in case someone in the neighborhood knew where you went and might tell. But no one was able to get any information from anyone about where you might have gone."

"How did you end up here?" Nan asked.

"I came a month ago to visit my son's family and my new grandson; I will go back to China next month. Because I was a peasant and a communist soldier, I was considered a good class and was able to get promotions. Teacher Yang had given me the chance to know I can learn. After you left, I studied by myself and asked people who could read to help me. Now I have a good position in my hometown in Jiangsu. I owe everything to Teacher Yang."

"I wish Mother were here. Perhaps we can arrange for her to come next time you come to visit your son," Nan suggested.

Lily almost burst out crying again. She tried to suppress her tears.

"I will write to her today. I have to get the letter out from here," Chong said.

Communication between citizens across the Taiwan Strait had not yet been permitted at the time.

"We will call our mother. She will be very happy to know we found you," Nan told Chong as they parted.

"Lily, you were so impressionable. I would not have expected to see that much emotion from you for having found Chong," Nan wondered.

There is no better time than now to tell Nan, Lily decided.

"Nan, Mama is ill." Her tears flowed again.

Nan was struck. *How much suffering can one endure?* she cried in her heart.

"She has a problem with her lung that started almost three years ago, soon after she and Papa came home from visiting you when Becky was born. They did all kinds of test but could not find a cause. She coughs and sometimes has difficulty breathing. It is slowly getting worse. The doctors said there is no cure, and she has to let it take its course."

"Did they say what it is?"

"They said idiopathic pulmonary fibrosis, I think."

"What's wrong with her lung?" Ethan asked.

"Basically it's getting scarred slowly with no identifiable cause," Nan said. "Lily, it's not the end of the world. I think it's a very slowly progressive disease. Maybe someone will find a cure before it gets too advanced," she continued, trying to convince Lily and herself. "Let's hope for the best."

Becky had fallen asleep in the car. Ethan carried her in. Her peaceful face was comforting to him after learning the grave news of his mother-in-law, the person his wife so loved.

As soon as it was day time in Taiwan, Lily and Nan called.

MayAnn was surprised to get the call. She was worried if anything was wrong. Lily delivered the good news right away.

"Mama, we found Chong!"

When MayAnn finally realized the miraculous reality, she exclaimed, "God has rewarded me."

II

Even though she told Lily that a cure might arrive in time for her mother, Nan knew it would take a miracle. Besides the constant agony over Becky's condition, she now also had to endure the burden of the unending anxiety about her mother's chronic and incurable illness. She wanted to be at her mother's side, but she couldn't travel because of Becky, and her mother couldn't travel to visit them because of her condition. Nan was torn. "Why?" she asked. "Why?" The images of those happy and content days at Cornell floated in her mind. *That was another lifetime.* She sighed with an aching heart. She wasn't sure if her faith was wavering.

Ethan finally became the stronger of the two. He would have to be the one to support her. "It's time that I carry her forward," he told himself.

"Why don't you take a couple of weeks and go home to your mother?" Ethan proposed.

It was unexpected. The impulse to see her mother had come to her initially, but it had been immediately forced out of her mind.

"I've been thinking," Ethan continued, "Jennifer and JeFu had repeatedly volunteered to come and help us. Their son is now almost fifteen. If they can make arrangements for him to stay with a friend or someone, they might be able to come and help me when you are gone."

"We can't ask them that. That's too much to ask." Nan suppressed the idea.

"Why not? You would have done that for them, wouldn't you? Nan, you have always thought for others. Sometimes it's harder to receive than to give. To be able to accept kindness can also be a blessing to the giver."

Nan realized she had at long last regained the Ethan she knew. It had been a long journey. Her heart was filled with love and gratitude.

"Yes, we give, and we take. This is how humanity works. We all need one another. We cannot exist in solitude," she concluded.

She wrote to Jennifer.

Jennifer replied immediately. "I am so glad you wrote," she said in her letter. "I have been waiting for this for a long time. I will make arrangements right away and let you know our plans."

Within a week, Jennifer called. "Would it work for you if we come in two weeks?" she asked. "That will be from Saturday, March 21, to Saturday, April 4."

Nan made reservation for flights to Taiwan, called her brother Shane's home, and spoke with her mother. MayAnn was excited. She will be able to see her beloved daughter soon.

It had been fifteen years since the two couples of No. 12 saw each other at Nan's wedding. The reunion under the circumstance was heartbreaking. Jennifer and Nan embraced and wept. Even JeFu and Ethan were hugging with tears. They had all grown older. Cornell seemed so long ago. Nan heard herself once telling Ethan, long ago, "Everything will be fine. Things happen for a reason." *Do they?* she questioned.

"I'm so sorry, Nan," Jennifer was finally able to speak. "I had asked over and over why these tragedies have to happen to you, of all people. Then I realized only you are able to endure and survive. You have so much love. It's enough to keep you standing."

"You are right. Our bond is as strong as it's always been," Ethan admitted. "Actually, she made me stronger. I'm the luckiest guy."

"That's the best I've heard. I'm so happy you think so." Jennifer was moved. It was a testament that Ethan had accepted the bitter reality.

"All of us were worried," JeFu said. "Everyone called Jennifer, including Lauren, hoping to get some information about you. We all love you."

"We haven't been able to get in touch with ShiMin. He apparently moved," Jennifer added.

Nan had been preparing Becky. She talked to her about Auntie Jen and Uncle Je and showed her their photographs. Becky took to Jennifer and JeFu quickly. Nan was relieved.

When Nan put Becky to bed that night, she reminded her again, "Tomorrow morning, Mama will go to Taiwan to see Grandma. Dada will take me to the airport, but he will be back after he finishes his work. Auntie Jen and Uncle Je will take you to school and pick you up after school. They will take care of you until I come back."

"Why do you have to go see Grandma?" Becky asked again.

"Because Grandma is sick. Grandma is my mother. I love her, just as you love me. And I love you so, so much."

Becky was satisfied. Nan kissed her good night.

Early the next morning, Ethan took Nan to the airport. He parked the car and went in with her. They held hands as she waited to board.

III

Lily and Shane met Nan at the airport. There were some excitement, but there were more sadness in their hearts.

"How's Mama?"

"She's a little worse. But there are still good days here and there," Shane said.

MayAnn opened the door as soon as she heard voices. She embraced Nan, looked at her from head to toe and all over her face. She was satisfied.

"How's my Becky?"

"She's growing all right. She's smaller than all her classmates, but she's smart."

Ethan and Nan wanted Becky to have as normal a life as possible. They started her in preschool earlier in the year. Becky had to be out of school often for blood transfusion and sometimes iron chelation therapy. She did well regardless, and she would become a first grader in the fall of the following year.

"She's in school already?" Shane asked.

"It's a preschool, kind of like kindergarten in Taiwan," Nan said.

WayLee was preparing some Chinese cough medicine for MayAnn. When it was ready, he quickly turned off the stove and walked in.

"Papa!" Nan was not able to repress her emotion any more. She burst out crying. Her father had noticeably aged.

WayLee was finally able to speak, "This is a happy occasion. Let's have a celebration at your mother's favorite restaurant."

Shane's wife and their three children, a boy and two girls, came home after Sunday services. Later, Lily's husband brought their two boys over. Only Ethan and Becky were absent.

MayAnn was having a good day. She coughed only sparingly, and her breathing was smooth without much difficulty.

That night, Nan was awoken by her mother's cough. She got up, walked toward her parents' room. Standing outside, she could hear her father patting lightly on her mother's back. "Shall I get you the medicine?" he asked. "No, wait a bit. Let me sit up. Maybe it will go away." Nan stood there, feeling a stabbing ache in her heart. She went back to bed, lying awake.

MayAnn took out the letter she received from Chong and showed it to Nan.

"How you found him was a miracle beyond belief," she said. "We have a saying, 'If it is destined, you will find each other even if you were thousands of miles apart.' I think I was destined to get the closure."

The letter read, "Dear Teacher Yang, I am happy I saw Lily and Nan. I am glad now I found you. I did not forget what you taught us and the phrase you gave us the last day. I can write it: Be kind, forgiving, and compassionate. Love your country, and love your countrymen. I still learn from my son and other people. Liu can read too. He is in Shandong. I will tell him when I go back. Hope I can see you. Thank you. Chong."

MayAnn was very proud of Chong's accomplishment. Nan gave the credit to her mother.

"Mama, only you would do such worthy deeds. You changed people's lives."

"I'm getting old. There would not be very much more I can do."

"You have already done so much. In fact, we are here because of you. You had the courage and wisdom to bring all of us out of the tyranny. We would have all died in communists' hands."

"It was thirty-seven years ago now, hard to believe." MayAnn sighed. "But I am still not able to move your grandma back to be with your grandfather." She said determinedly, "I have to fulfill my promise before I go."

There was nothing Nan could say.

"How is Ethan handling Becky's condition?" MayAnn had wanted to know.

"It was very hard for him in the beginning. It made no sense that Becky could have this disease. He was also very scared that we would lose her. That put a lot of burden on him, and he did not know how to handle it. I was so afraid he might not be able to get up after that heartbroken fall. But he did. He has accepted it and is dealing with it healthily."

"That's good. I'm glad you kept the promises you made to each other when you married."

"Yes, I do love him. We both are committed to spending the rest of our lives together."

MayAnn had an episode of cough and shortness of breath. WayLee brought her oxygen and medicine. It quieted down after a while. "I have to get your grandma back to be with your grandfather," she said again.

Mother and daughter cherished their time together. They took slow walks in the neighborhood and visited some neighbors. They were no longer in the Military Dependents' Village. The atmosphere was different; the ambience of camaraderie was lacking. Nevertheless, people were friendly and kind.

A middle-aged woman pushing a child with a twisted body in a wheelchair came toward them.

"Good morning, Mrs. Yang. You look good this morning," she greeted.

"Good morning to you, Mrs. Yu," MayAnn responded. "This is my second daughter, Nan. She is visiting me from the States."

"You must be very happy to see her."

"Yes, I am. It was one wish I had."

MayAnn told Nan after Mrs. Yu walked away, "That's her son in the wheelchair. He's twenty-two, but he looked like eight. He has cerebral palsy and some other disease."

"We all have our own nemesis to battle against, don't we?" Nan said, more to herself.

A week later, they had surprise visitors.

"Mr. and Mrs. Fong!" Nan exclaimed as she opened the door.

"Jennifer and JeFu told us you are here. We decided to take a trip and try our luck," Mrs. Fong said. She looked at Nan closely, making sure she was fine.

Nan was not fine. She recalled the last time they met. Ethan was by her side. They were on top of the world, happily engaged to be married, and ready to embark their professional career that promised brilliant future. With a carefully planned parenthood, it seemed a guaranteed lifelong success awaited them. She became emotional and could not speak.

Mrs. Fong put her arms around Nan. "Jennifer said you were given the ultimate test because only you are able to withstand it."

Things happen for a reason, the voice arose in Nan's mind again.

"We talked about you and Ethan often since you visited us last time. It was, oh, fifteen years ago now," Mr. Fong said. "You two looked so happy, so good together, and we were so happy for you. We thought your children would be so brilliant and . . ." Mrs. Fong tugged at his arm and stopped him. Nan fought back her tears.

MayAnn and WayLee had heard much about JeFu and Jennifer. The two couples took to one another immediately. The men talked about their days working for different branches of the military, and the women conversed about their children and grandchildren. Nan listened with a grateful heart for having Jennifer and JeFu in her life. She recollected the first time she and Jennifer met in Dr. Thompson's office. They did not realize then that they would become lifelong close friends. Despite the nagging anguish she was feeling, *humanity and humility are truly wonderful gifts from God,* she had to admit.

"We hope the best for you, Ethan, and Becky. We just have to come to see you and to tell you in person," Mrs. Fong said as they were leaving to go back to TaiChung, approximately one hundred miles away.

IV

Nan accompanied her parents to MayAnn's regular medical check-up two days before her scheduled departure. The lung function had deteriorated slightly since the previous visit, the specialist told them. "But that is expected. It is a slowly progressive disease. We will make sure to keep her as stable and comfortable as possible," he added.

Nan went to the pharmacy to pick up her mother's refilled medication. As she was walking away, she realized someone was staring at her. She looked back and saw a remotely familiar face. She searched her memory, then they both recognized.

"Nan Yang?" the man in his early sixties asked.

"Dr. Lee!" Nan exclaimed.

Dr. Lee was Nan's undergraduate thesis advisor who spent a year as a visiting scholar at Harvard, the one who watched sailboats on Charles River, counting days to come home. It had been more than eighteen years since they last saw each other at Nan's graduation before she embarked on her journey to Cornell to pursue her advanced studies.

"How wonderful to run into you. Are you back in Taiwan?" Dr. Lee asked.

"No, I just came to visit my mother for two weeks. She has been ill, and we are here for her regular follow-up appointment. I'm picking up her medicine."

"I'm sorry to hear that. I just got medication for my blood pressure."

"Dr. Lee, do you have a moment to meet my parents?"

"Sure, I'm done here."

Nan took him to where her parents were waiting and introduced them.

"Dr. Lee, we have heard a lot about you from Nan. It is an honor to finally meet you." WayLee was happy to have the chance to get acquainted with one of Nan's favorite professors in college.

"Nan was one of my best students. I still remember her thesis. I never had a student who wrote thesis so well that required little correction."

"Urinary hydroxyproline excretion in rats." Nan was thinking of Ethan's reaction when he heard she had to handle rats. *It seemed like a lifetime ago.*

"Dr. Lee, would you have time to come to our home, and we can have more time to talk?" MayAnn asked.

Dr. Lee came to Shane's home with them. He had recently retired. His wife died of nasopharyngeal cancer a year before. His son was eight years younger than Nan and had been doing quite well in the financial sector, until he was dragged into a scandal involving many of his colleagues that landed them in prison.

Nan described to Dr. Lee her PhD thesis at Cornell and her marriage to Ethan.

"Ethan is from Boston, and we have made Boston our home. Every time I saw Charles River and sailboats, I thought about you. I told Ethan so many times, even he thought of you too. It always gave me a feeling of melancholy."

"I have not thought about it for a long time. Now the image is in front of me, even though it seemed a century ago," Dr. Lee lamented sadly. His entire life raced through quickly before him, from his youth as a brilliant child, his days at Harvard then back to teach at the best university in Taiwan, his own marriage, the demise of his wife, the fall of his son, to now his aged body. He was overwhelmed. His eyes watered.

Thinking of her own life growing up carefree, her luminous Cornell days, and now this bottomless anguish over Becky's illness, Nan was reminded of "Behold, all is vanity and a chasing after wind."

Dr. Lee stayed for dinner. Nan wept when she said good-bye to him, suddenly realizing that she too had become hopelessly sentimental.

MayAnn took a nap after lunch the next day. She felt good when she awoke.

"You had an aunt on your father's side," she told Nan. "But she died when she was seven." Nan had heard the story before, still, she listened as usual.

"'She was such a beautiful child, everyone said so.' Your grandma told me," MayAnn continued. "She was also very smart. There were already matchmakers trying to arrange marriage for her when she turned five. But as the proverb goes, 'A beauty's life is usually doomed.' She died just after she turned seven. She was sick for a few days. Your grandfather consulted the best doctors, and your grandma burned incense continually for Buddha. But nothing could save her. Your grandparents were crushed. They couldn't understand why such severe calamity should happen to them. It took your grandma a long time, but she was eventually able to recover. By the time she had your father, she was already in her thirties," MayAnn's voice quivered. "After so many years, your grandma still talked to me about it. She never got over the pain of losing her daughter."

It was time for Nan to leave. The separation this time was excruciating, knowing this would likely be the last time they were together. Nan held onto her mother for what seemed like an eternity. Lily was sobbing. WayLee and Shane too were weeping. Shane finally pried Nan from their mother. "Nan, we have to go."

MayAnn stood, watching them drive away.

PART EIGHT

Disasters Struck

I

In 1988, the promise MayAnn made to her mother-in-law was finally fulfilled, twenty-one years late. The government in Taiwan opened the door the year before, allowing its citizen to visit their homeland in mainland China. Overcoming all procedural and practical hurdles, MayAnn and WayLee were finally able to have the coffin exhumed and the remains gathered. WayLee, now seventy-six, accompanied by Lily, would bring his mother's remains back to his hometown.

"I have been waiting for this day all these years," choking, MayAnn said to her husband. "No material wealth can ever replace the love mother gave me."

"I know, and Ma knew. And you know how much Pa loved you too. I wish you could go with us. We will be back as soon as the mission is completed."

MayAnn had been fighting the chronic lung disease for five years by now. She was getting weaker with increasing difficulty breathing. The cause of the illness had never been diagnosed. Her doctor forbade her to travel, knowing she would never be able to tolerate the journey. When the possibility of fulfilling her mother-in-law's wish finally came in sight, she had for a brief moment felt the impulse of taking the trip. *Ah, that is a fool's dream*, she told herself and was immediately seized by an overwhelming sense of sorrow.

They had already reestablished contact with WayGuo's wife, YeLin. She was still in ZhouShan, now living with one of her daughters married to a farmer who had come back to ZhouShan to work in a fishery. They had tried to maintain the grave as much as they could. But after so many years under the Communist, it had been largely unattended.

The grave was still standing on top of the small hill, obscured by some overgrown vegetation. The writings on the monument had mostly faded, but the kind and loving eyes on MayAnn's father-in-law's picture remained vibrant.

WayLee realized the same kind and loving eyes had looked at MayAnn nearly forty years ago just before she fled mainland China. A mix of memory and emotion struck him—the difficult life during the war against Japan then the Communist, the anxiety he bore waiting for his family to safely arrive in Taiwan, the passing of his mother and his brother, the ill health of MayAnn, and now at last, the fulfillment of his mother's dying wish. He finally broke down.

"Brother, it is all right," WayLee's sister-in-law, YeLin, who herself endured much suffering for many years under the brutality of the Communist, touched his shoulder and spoke. "Let the bygones be bygones. Life will go on one way or another."

"This is the tragedy of our generation." Wiping his eyes, WayLee sighed.

Lily embraced her father, trying to comfort him. She was six and Nan was not quite four when their mother brought them there the last time. The two soldiers, Chong and Liu, accompanied them. *Ah, where did time go? Now I'm already forty-five! So many changes in our lives*, she thought helplessly. *One can't hold time back.*

YeLin had already hired a construction crew. When they arrived, WayLee instructed them what he wanted done. The foreman indicated that the work would be ready for final closure in two days.

YeLin and her daughter took them around WayLee's hometown XiangShan. Their family home had been torn down. Two large apartment buildings now stood in its place. There was not a trace of the carved redwood front gate. Lily vaguely remembered the day her grandmother and siblings left on rickshaws at the gate. Two days later, she and her mother journeyed away to join them. They never returned. That was the last time any of them had seen their home. She fell in mourning.

"Sister, do you know what happened to MayAnn's cousin, Jon?" WayLee asked. "He helped them flee the mainland."

"Ah, that was a sad story. He was sent to the far north to do hard labor and to be reformed. He was not able to adjust to the severe treatment; he soon got sick and died within six months. One of the people who was also sent there was fortunate to be able to come back after two years. He told us."

"That's not what MayAnn would want to hear." WayLee was sorrowful.

They took a ferry to YeLin's home in ZhouShan Island. The next day, YeLin's daughter accompanied them to the famous Mount Putuo, one of the attractions MayAnn visited before she left the mainland. With mountains and waters, the scenery was at nature's best. "This is my homeland, big and rich," WayLee lamented in despair. "Where is the day when China will be reunited in a democratic society devoid of the misshapen Communist ideology?"

When the reconstruction was ready, WayLee placed the urn holding his mother's remains in the grave next to his father's coffin. The site had been cleaned, and the carved letters on the monument had been repainted in gold color.

WayLee took out from his wallet a carefully preserved, perfectly heart-shaped leaf encased in clear plastics. He said, "Pa, this is the leaf that flowed onto MayAnn's chest when she came to see you before she fled China. Although it has withered, it maintained its shape. MayAnn wanted to bring this back to you herself, to return the fallen leaf to its roots." He stopped, unable to continue. Lily and YeLin were crying. "MayAnn . . . she has been ill and cannot make the trip. She asks for your forgiveness . . ." Tears streamed down from WayLee's eyes.

After regaining control, he continued, "Ma, I'm here to fulfill your wish. MayAnn and I are sorry for this prolonged delay. Please forgive us.

MayAnn loved you like her own mother. But she is ill now. The doctor does not allow her to travel." He struggled. "I'm afraid she will not be with me too much longer."

He put the leaf on his father's coffin. "Pa, Ma, you are now together forever."

The work crew sealed the grave. WayLee and Lily flew back to Taiwan the same evening.

MayAnn sighed in relief. But her heart was troubled for not having been able to witness it herself. WayLee held her lovingly, knowing nothing could ease her sorrow and agony.

That night, in her dream, MayAnn heard her mother-in-law calling her, "MayAnn, my dear daughter."

A month later, she left this world, leaving behind her heartbroken husband and without seeing the day of reclaiming mainland China she so longed for.

Her last letter to Nan was received on the day she died. It said, in the last paragraph, "I miss your grandma very much. I am grateful for having her, your father, Lily, you, Shane, and all my grandchildren. I had a full life, and I cannot have any complaint or regret for what God has given me. My heart is with Becky. I am grateful for having those three months with her. I can still feel that absolute contentment, pushing her in the baby stroller, your father by my side, walking around the charming grounds of Bishops Forest. My only grief is that I will not be able to see her grow up, and I am not able to wait for the day when we retake our beloved country."

II

Becky's disease was more severe than most other patients with beta-thalassemia. Her anemia and iron overload were harder to control. An episode of acute illness scared her parents. She developed fever, headache, and vomiting. They rushed her to the hospital, and there she had a seizure. Eventually she recovered. Thrombosis, or blood clot, in a vein in the brain was the cause, they were told.

Becky started first grade in the fall of 1988, not too long after her grandmother died. She was not quite six and she was very small, but she was ready intellectually. She liked the school and made many friends. Blood transfusions and iron chelation therapies continued. It was difficult for her young friends to understand, but they accepted her. And Becky was happy.

Nan was still mourning her mother's death, and she dreamed of her mother often. At times, Ethan had to wake her up. Once she saw her mother holding Becky, saying, "My little angel, you are here. I found you." Nan held out her arms to embrace them, but they disappeared. Fighting, she cried, "Come back, come back, please!" she implored desperately and found herself awoken, in Ethan's arms. She got up and went in Becky's room. Becky was soundly asleep.

So this challenging life went on while they tried to cope as well as they could until April of the following year when they noticed Becky became tired easily. Nan took her to see the hematologist. He ordered a battery of tests, including an EKG.

"It showed some signs of heart failure," Dr. Smith told them when all test results were available.

"How can that be?" Both Ethan and Nan would not believe.

"In general, with adequate transfusion and iron chelation, the risk of heart damage due to iron overload is small. In Becky's case, we have had more difficulty trying to control her illness, even though you, and she, have been fully compliant. Perhaps there are some other modifying factors that contributed to the severity of her disease."

"What do we do?" distraughtly, Nan asked.

"I have discussed with other hematologists. Perhaps we can try different chelation protocol. We need to monitor closely and provide her with all supportive measures."

They were thrown into the dark abyss again. But they were now stronger and were able to face the utter cruelty together. They did everything they were supposed to do, and they followed every instruction given by the doctors. They loved Becky ceaselessly.

Even though she was weaker, Becky nonetheless loved school and maintained her attendance as much as she could. Her classmates, yet at the tender age of six, were able to recognize Becky was different. She was sick. They treated her gently, and Becky was still a happy child.

The heart failure progressed, albeit slowly. She became paler, and her breathing gradually became labored. Five months after the initial discovery, Becky had to be hospitalized. Her classmates' parents brought them to visit her at the Boston Children's Hospital. Becky was not able to talk. She was in an oxygen tent, and she was weak. But they smiled at one another, and Becky was happy to see her friends.

Nan and Ethan stayed by their daughter's side, day and night.

A week later, she left this world, leaving behind all her love and all the love she had received. Before she died, she managed to tell her parents, "Dada, I love you. Mama I love you." It was September 22, 1989.

The universe went dark on Nan and Ethan.

III

Ethan thought he had been prepared for this outcome. He was wrong. The grief was so monumental that he was not able to function for weeks. With her own broken heart, Nan needed yet to carry Ethan; the man she so loved, the man so confident and so dependable, the man supposed to protect her always.

But losing Becky wounded him to the core. He was broken. He could not withstand.

The burden once again fell on Nan.

How do you mend a broken heart? she asked.

The old members of the house of No. 12 were devastated for their friends. They came to mourn with them. But what could one say to comfort the tortured soul of those who had lost their child? Jennifer and JeFu, in particular, were deeply distressed. The two weeks they spent with Becky more than two years before had made an everlasting memory for them. *This beautiful, smart, and happy child, why?* they too asked.

Ethan's parents had also been preparing for this tragedy but they too were crushed nonetheless. Since it was harder for Becky to travel and visit them, they had been making frequent trips to visit Becky. They longed for Becky's happy voice calling grandma and grandpa.

Mary came from Los Angeles to stay with Nan and Ethan. She loved Nan, and she knew she owed her career to Nan for convincing her parents to let her choose the profession in which her heart was.

Back in Taiwan, the family was buried in a constant gloomy cloud. Lily asked her school for two weeks' leave and came. But there was nothing she could do to ease any of Nan and Ethan's misery. She could only make sure they ate and slept.

Ethan struggled to get back on his feet. But a part of him had gone with Becky. The image of this happy child was constantly on his mind. He should be happy because she had been happy. But he could not face the unrelenting fact that he would never be able to hold her in his arms and hear the sweetest sound of dada from his beloved Becky. For him, the wound, so deep, so fierce, even time might not heal.

Yet Nan had to bear the heartlessly heavy load of both Ethan's and her own grief and devastation.

After a month, Ethan went back to work. It was reassuring when he was able to absorb himself in the science of his calling. But the anguish and sorrow returned as soon as he was forced back to the reality. He was not able to overcome or to escape.

It was bone-chilling cold on December 22, 1989, snow and ice were on the ground. On his way to work, Ethan was hit head on by a truck. It was three months to the date after Becky died.

He had left for work that morning as usual. He kissed Nan and said good-bye. He was still in deep grief as was Nan. Recovery, if ever, would be a long and painful process.

As he was driving, Ethan's mind was again filled with images of Becky. The first night when she was admitted to the hospital, he sat by her bedside, watching his pale but courageous daughter, he had instinctively reached out and embraced her. Becky felt his wet face, she said, "Dada, don't cry. Everything will be fine. It will be over soon." Nan had immediately held his head, letting him bury his face in her chest to muffle his cry of pain.

His eyes blurred.

The ambulance pulled into the emergency entrance of Mass General. He did not survive.

Nan was told later that the truck coming from the opposite direction swirled around suddenly. A witness who was behind Ethan's car reportedly said, "I saw the truck skidding, in a panic, I honked the horn desperately and yelled at the car ahead of me 'slow down!' I don't think he did."

Ethan's parents were utterly broken; two heartbreaks within three months. *Lord, why such heavy tribulations?* they asked. They both noticeably aged overnight. There were not many tragedies more grievous than the old having to bury their young.

Ethan's sister, Mary, and her husband flew in from Los Angeles as soon as they were informed of the accident. Mary loved her brother and her sister-in-law dearly. Losing her niece and now her brother was too great to bear. She was not able to comfort Nan. She was in perpetual mourning herself.

The house of No. 12 made the second heartbroken journey in three months. Bewildered by the inconceivable calamities, JeFu said to his friends, "We have an old adage back home, 'The beautiful and talented are unfortunately doomed with a tragic life.' I never imagined it could happen to Nan. Ah, but it did!" Jennifer broke into tears again.

Lily took two weeks off from work again and came to take care of Nan. Shane had to stay home with WayLee who had recently been hospitalized for a minor heart attack. The family was stricken. They begged to understand the incomprehensible.

"Why, Lord, why?" Nan cried out. "I have trusted that things happen for a reason. But I can't find a reason now."

She was the strong one. It was she who provided the support to those in need. Who could provide the support she now desperately needed? *Am I really put here to be tested of my strength and faith to the ultimate?*

Her heart was broken when Becky died. Her heart was now shattered a thousand pieces when Ethan joined Becky. There was nothing left in this world for her.

How do you mend a shattered heart?

She buried Ethan next to Becky.

Three weeks later, Nan went to church for Sunday service. When they were standing singing *Great is Thy Faithfulness*, the woman in front of her reached her hand to her husband, he held hers, and they continued to sing. Nan was already in tears, now she was not able to stop weeping for those beautiful moments she would never have again.

"Those wonderful moments once captured, forever they are ours," her own words came to her. In desperation, she asked, *Really? Could they?*

She went to the cemetery after church. As she was walking toward Ethan and Becky's graves, she saw a white-haired couple. The man had a bouquet of flowers in one hand and his wife's arm in his other hand, carefully guiding her through the pavement. *Whom are they visiting? Their daughter? Their granddaughter?* Her tears pouring down her face.

She became exceedingly fragile emotionally. She was shrouded in an unremitting anguish.

A colleague and friend of Ethan's came by to see Nan.

"I'm so sorry for your loss," he said. "It was a huge loss for our department too." He had an envelope in his hand.

"I found this in Ethan's drawer. This note was attached to it. But I thought I'd bring it to you myself instead of mailing it."

The note read: Please mail this letter for me. It was addressed to Nan Delaney, sealed and stamped ready to be mailed.

Nan, my dearest wife,

I had always been grateful that you came to Cornell and into my life. Then the arrival of our beautiful Becky perfected our union. I wish the wonderful life we had together could have lasted forever, but perhaps it was too perfect and nothing so perfect could be allowed to last. Still, I know I have been blessed to have you. I would not have traded my life for anything else. We have been together twenty years, and except for those last six years, we had been on top of the world in absolute bliss. We were dealt with the tragedy of Becky's illness, but we also experience the gift of invincible love and happiness of our treasured and beloved daughter. I have no complaint, and I have no regret.

Becky is gravely ill. I recognize that. I cannot imagine life without her. I love her, and you, with all my heart and soul. I wondered why she has to suffer so much, what is the purpose of her being here if she were to be blatantly taken away so early. But then I realized she has always been happy, and she has given us happiness. She has enjoyed and experienced the essence of life. Is it not what we are supposed to get out of being put in this world? The length of time cannot be a measure of the worthiness of a life. Becky has lived her life the best she could. Her life has not been in vain.

Thank you for giving me the precious and extravagant gift of time. For two years, you patiently waited for me to get up from the most cruel and pitiless fall. I knew how heartbroken you were yourself, yet you continued standing by my side. You kept your wedding vow and never wavered. You loved me unconditionally, accepted me as I am, and supported me when life brought us the most unforgiving reality. You have been my life partner just as you promised.

I do not know what I have done to deserve such a beautiful being like you. Knowing you and having you made my life complete. Even if I die today, I believe I have already achieved what I was put here for.

I pray you will not have to read this letter. Let me bear the grief and anguish of losing you so that you will not have to experience the pain of losing me.

But in case I leave before you, I want you to continue living, and remember what you once said, "Existence is a blessing. We should live our life intensely, feelingly, and passionately." So continue to live it intensely, feelingly, and passionately, to honor my life and Becky's life. I pray and I know someone worthy of you will come and love you as much as I love you and walk with you through the rest of your earthly days. Becky and I will cheer you on.

And I know you would have wanted me to do the same if you were to die before me.

I want you to be happy. Remember those wonderful moments once captured, forever they are yours.

Love forever,
Ethan

It was dated Saturday, September 16, 1989, the day after Becky was hospitalized.

Nan held the letter close to her heart and cried.

PART NINE

Healing and Triumph

I

ShiMin had moved to Palos Verdes, the gem on the ocean he loved, and buried himself in work to cover up his anguish and sorrow for not being able to pursue the only woman he truly loved. He was still at Harbor-UCLA and had been spending more time at the UCLA main campus approximately twenty-five miles from his home. He taught undergraduate and graduate courses at UCLA and collaborated research with other faculty members based there. During the seventeen years since he last communicated with Nan, he had spent one year for sabbatical at Stanford and one year at UC Berkeley. Being frequently out of his Harbor office and not particularly eager to be connected with anyone since Nan's marriage, he made no effort in keeping his contact information current. Jennifer and JeFu had not been able to reach him.

Jennifer was frantically trying to find ShiMin. She sent another letter to his office address, hoping it will get to him somehow.

"The catastrophe is so great beyond imagination . . . We are at a complete loss . . . We don't know what to do . . . When she lost her daughter, we thought she had hit the bottom and couldn't go any lower. Then Ethan . . . You were her closest friend. Only you can help her now. Please! I pray this letter reaches you."

ShiMin fell in a state of disbelief and confusion. *How could this possibly be? Could there really be tragedy so profound in this world?* he questioned. He had wanted Nan to have a good life without having to worry about any uncertainty. Who would ever foresee that she could not be spared of the tragedy after all? His heart ached for her. *Moreover, I made Ethan an additional victim.* He blamed himself in bewilderment. He argued that if he had listened to his mother, all these might have been avoided. He and Nan might be happily together now. And Ethan, he was so handsome and so talented. He would not have had any problem getting whomever he desired, and he would still be alive. *What an irony! The malicious game fate played on us!* he cried out in despair. *Why? Oh Lord, Why?*

He called Jennifer.

When Jennifer heard his voice, she burst out crying and was not able to talk. JeFu took the phone from her.

"ShiMin, we need you," JeFu said, choking.

He took the first flight available out of Los Angeles and flew to Boston.

II

Nan read Ethan's last letter so many times, she had memorized it. She ruminated over and over. "I would not have traded my life for anything else . . . I cannot imagine life without Becky . . . I want you to continue living . . ."

These words were heart-wrenching for her. Her heart trembled every time she read it. Gradually, she came to the realization it was Ethan's gift to her. Anticipating the ending of his own life sometime, Ethan had released her to continue living on happily. But her anguish and sorrow remained intractable. She was very fragile emotionally, easily bruised with the slightest trigger that reminded her of her happy times with Ethan and Becky.

She was thrown into a depression. Her days were long. At times, she found herself sitting impassively for hours. She tried to go back to work but realized immediately she was not able to concentrate to be productive. In this respect, she was not as disciplined as Ethan who was able to push himself to face what he had to accomplish even when he was under the tremendous anguish and grief surrounding Becky's illness.

She went to the cemetery often, even in the winter. When the weather was brutal, she was usually the only one there. In that solitude, she felt so close to Ethan and Becky that she could hear them and touch them. Beautiful and happy images appeared in her mind, but reality invariably set in, and she was left with a feeling of emptiness.

One day in February, the temperature rose up to sixty degrees. Nan went to the cemetery, so did many other families. An older woman walked over.

"They must be your husband and your daughter," she said cordially.

"Yes," Nan replied, not really wishing to carry on a conversation.

"I've seen you once before, and I can see your despair," the woman said. "I know, I've been through it myself."

Nan had paid no attention to other graves.

"I'm visiting my late husband. He died eight years ago."

"Oh, eight years!" Nan had not thought of the long road ahead.

"Yes. We were in a five-car accident on a snowy day. I had minor injuries, but my husband was in a coma for ten days until they disconnected his life support. It was very hard in the beginning. Like you, I was in tears constantly, and I thought I would never get over it. I remember clearly how sometimes I would forget he was gone, that he was not with me anymore." She was thinking. "Once my sister took me out to a new restaurant, and they had a dish I knew my husband would have liked. Right away, I said I will tell Joel about it when I get home. My sister looked at me with sympathy. She thought I was crazy. That happened a few more times during the first five or six months."

"Ah, that happened to me too. I knew I was not crazy, but I had never realized it could be possible to, in a moment, forget they were gone. I had wondered if I was the only one."

"No, you are not the only one. In fact, it was quite common. Apparently, many people who lost their loved ones have the same experience."

"I dream of them often, but none of the dreams made any sense," Nan said.

"I believe that is common too. How long have you been married?"

"Seventeen years."

"I wouldn't have known; you look so young," the woman said. "And your daughter? I noticed she died three months before your husband."

"She had a genetic disease that caused severe anemia and heart failure that took her life."

The woman was touched. She said thoughtfully, "I just want to tell you to have faith. Right now, the memories you have of them make you feel sad because they are only memories that you cannot physically hold on to anymore. The world looks very dark to you now, but gradually, you'll find those same memories will bring you comfort and assurance. It did to me, and it did to my friends who lost their loved ones. It may take longer for some people, but it invariably does."

But the most precious possessions had been stolen away from Nan. There was absolutely nothing she could have done to avoid it. She was left with a perpetual sorrow, treading slowly on the long road to recovery.

When Nan returned home, she put on the recording of *Canon in D Major* by Johann Pachelbel, the heavenly music she had chosen for her wedding, and then heartbrokenly for Ethan's funeral; the music that was so beautiful, so peaceful, and yet so sad. She listened to it over and over. Her tears flowed profusely. She could only wait for the day to arrive when it would bring her comfort and assurance instead.

III

Three months after Ethan's tragedy, Nan opened her door to find ShiMin standing before her. A rush of emotion seized her. She could not move or speak.

"Nan!" ShiMin was finally able to utter the name.

It was nearly twenty years since they last saw each other. The Cornell days had been long gone. Their focuses at that time were study, learn, work on their research, get the degree, and to enjoy the anticipated bright future ahead of them. Like all their friends then, they did not think youth was not forever, they paid no attention to the merciless time clock that ticked and trod constantly forward. Now they too had to ask themselves, *where did our youth go?*

"I'm sorry I'm so late," ShiMin managed to speak. Nan broke down and was not able to control herself.

ShiMin stood there, unable to move.

This person whom he loved with all his heart, one so strong, so brilliant, so courageous, was now standing in front of him helplessly and hopelessly, waiting to be rescued.

He finally attempted to speak, "I had wished you a lifetime of happiness without any worry. You were so perfect in so many ways. You deserved a perfect life." He paused, overwhelmed by the tragedy. "We don't know why things happen the way they happen. I beg there is a reason." Looking back at his own life and realizing he had let it be defined by his not-so-serious birth defect, he was besieged by his lack of confidence. *What have I done?*

"I just wanted you to be happy!" he cried out in desperation.

He had been very successful academically. He channeled all his energy into work. Other than out-of-town meetings and conferences, the only places away from work he ever visited were the Palos Verdes beaches and trails. In that solitude, he felt connected with her in the depth of his heart, accepting the reality that he would never have her.

He stayed in Boston for two weeks. He called on her and spent time with her every day, trying to bring her out of her hopelessness and desolation.

"It's natural that we want to keep our loved ones with us forever. We don't want them to leave even if it might be a better place for them. In a way, that might be our own selfishness," he said gently, "Ethan is now with Becky in God's Kingdom. I think he was confident you'll be able to live on for them. Otherwise, he would have waited for you."

"Nan, I know how raw and how deep the wound is," he continued, "But gradually, it will get better. The pain will always be there, but it will become bearable, and you'll eventually be able to deal with it." ShiMin understood. "I know, I lost my mother two years ago."

"Oh, ShiMin."

"She was the only one I had in this world. What made my regret so deep was that I didn't go back to visit her all those years. I couldn't handle her inquisitive eyes and her constant questioning about my personal relationships. She brought that up in almost every letter." His voice became hoarse. "I knew she held onto her life waiting for me. She died the day after I made it back to Taiwan."

For the first time after her own tragedies, Nan became truly aware of the universality of the inescapable fate of humanity.

"We all have to face our final destiny of death," she said.

"But I do believe there is more beauty and kindness in this world than ugliness and cruelty. That made up for the unfortunate finality that we all have to confront," he continued. "Birth, death, one generation after another. That is the principle of nature. Just like the waves in the ocean, they continuously push the ones before them. You cannot stop. You have to make way for the ones after you."

"Yes, that's the way of life. It's a continuum, in a sense." Nan said.

She got up and walked to the fireplace to look at the pictures on the mantels. ShiMin followed her.

"Becky looked so beautiful and so happy, very much like you," he said.

Nan ran her fingers over the pictures of Ethan and Becky. She became emotional again.

"You and you alone will have them forever. Nobody can take that away from you," he said confidently.

He picked up the record by the fireplace. "May I?" he asked.

"Sure."

He put it on. It was *Canon in D Major* by Johann Pachelbel.

"This amazing piece of beautiful music, it used to give me peace. Now it brings me tears every time I listen to it," Nan said tearfully.

ShiMin was fully aware it would be a long and challenging journey to recovery for her. He was prepared.

The day before he had to return to California, they strolled around the Bishops Forest grounds. Nan had not noticed, but spring was already creeping in. For the first time in years, she stopped, looked carefully, and smelled the fragrance of the newly bloomed flowers. ShiMin watched her.

"Do you want to go back to work?" he grabbed the opportunity.

"I tried on and off for months, but I couldn't concentrate and was getting nowhere."

"It takes time. You might want to try again. It will do you good."

IV

Nan went back to work. There were some bad moments and days when her longing for Becky and Ethan became nearly insufferable. When it grew to be too painful to bear, she would drive about, park her car, and walk around her favorite building, the John Hancock Tower, staring at the image of the Trinity Church inside the Tower. She would then come to her favorite spot on the banks of Charles River, and watch the Hancock on one side and sailboats on the other. Painful as it was, she would force herself to look forward. She would eventually be able to overcome and was beginning to make progress. Yes, time would heal, albeit very slowly.

ShiMin was able to arrange a sabbatical at Dana-Farber Cancer Institute, another Harvard Medical School hospital. He moved to Boston to be close to Nan. On Ethan's anniversary, they went to the cemetery. It was bone-chilling cold a year ago, the coldest day of that year. It was now near sixty degrees, the record high for that day thus far. It was the winter solstice.

Nan was engulfed with heartache. A year and three months had passed. The graves were no longer new. But the wound was still fresh, and ShiMin knew she was still emotionally imprisoned.

"We thought we had finally achieved our goal in life when Becky was born. We had been successful in our career and then we had our child, the circle was complete. But the happiest days in our lives were short lived," Nan said in agony, "Becky had an unusual disease, no, the disease was not that unusual. It was the mechanism of her having the disease that was extremely unusual."

He did not interrupt. Nan had never talked about the circumstances surrounding the death of either Ethan or Becky, and he did not ask. He had been waiting for her to be ready.

"She had beta-thalassemia major as a result of uniparental disomy. She didn't stand a chance. There were other complicating factors that made her disease much more severe. Ethan justified Becky's short life by the fact she had enjoyed and experienced the essence of life. She was a happy and courageous child even though she suffered so much from her illness. There was so much love amongst the three of us. I would not have exchanged it for anything, not if I had to give that love up."

"I understand. You had been rewarded with love that was irreplaceable. Remember, it belonged to you, and you alone will have that forever." ShiMin said.

"Ethan, he was so broken when Becky died. He had accepted Becky's disease and was willing to face the challenge. But he couldn't recover from losing her." She paused, looking at Ethan's gravestone. "He wrote me a letter the day after Becky was admitted to hospital, anticipating her imminent demise. At times, I wanted to join them too." She broke down.

"Ethan wanted me to live on, reminding me of what I said of existence being a blessing. He knew I would have wanted him to do the same if I were to die before him."

A pair of sparrows flew over and landed on the grass near her. "Ah!" she exclaimed, reaching out her hands, sobbing. The pair remained still, fixing their gaze on Nan, then flew away. She knew that was a miraculous sight; all migrating sparrows should have gone south a month ago.

They would never forget that magical image.

ShiMin realized her revelation was cathartic for her. He continued to wait patiently.

Nan was finally functioning at work as normally as could be expected. Being able to get her research and teaching back on track was quite comforting to her. Her colleagues had been very patient and supportive. Nan was grateful, knowing the sacrifices they had made for her, covering for her duties while she was not able to.

The seasons continued to revolve steadily, and it was spring again. Everything woke up; the water, the waterfall, the trees, the birds, the squirrels, and the hearts that might have been hibernating.

"How have you been all these years?" Nan was now able to think beyond her own misery.

"Work was good. I'm happy with what I've achieved."

"You should be. You have done very well. I read all your publications, and I was impressed. You had quite a few prominent collaborators too."

"I read yours too, and I can say the same about you," ShiMin said.

"In fact, I reviewed two of your manuscripts." Nan decided to divulge.

"I know which two. One reviewer's comments were so well-written with a somewhat poetic quality that was unmistakably yours."

"So you realized."

"Yes. I also think we might have reviewed the same manuscript once. My anonymous co-reviewer's report had your writing style."

"Now I have lost most of my last six or seven years in academics."

"Publication and success are not the most important things in life. It will take some time, but you'll get your place back, I'm sure," he reassured her.

"What about your personal life?" Nan asked.

"I really didn't have much personal life. The only thing I did was walk on the beaches and trails and watch the night sky. Oh, I saw the play *Long Day's Journey into Night* four years ago on Broadway. I was in New York for a meeting at the time. I also saw the musical *Les Misérables*. I thought about you and," he paused, then with determination, "I wished you were there with me."

Nan was startled. She repressed her emotion and asked instead. "Haven't you found anyone you liked?"

"No, I never looked for one."

"I'm sure there are ladies who would like to have your attention."

"Yes, there have been."

"You built an impenetrable wall around yourself. I could never get through."

"I have a birth defect," he couldn't imagine he said it.

"I know, hemifacial microsomia. What does that have to do with *your* ability to love?"

So she knew all along! A birth defect that bothered no one but himself.

"Ethan was too impeccable and too ideal. You two were a perfect match," he said regretfully.

They went to church for Sunday service. As they were standing up to sing, the band began to play *Great is Thy Faithfulness*. Without thinking, Nan reached her hand to ShiMin. He held hers tightly. They sang together.

V

Autumn began to edge in. Trees around the cemetery were starting the process of transformation. Hints of yellow, gold, and red were peeping through here and there. It was Becky's second anniversary.

"Mama, look how pretty this leaf is." Nan heard her daughter, holding a half-yellow half-gold leaf. Becky was four then. Nan had impulsively picked her up and kissed her with a heart filled with thankfulness. *Bless her heart,* she had thought. *She is able to enjoy and appreciate despite her illness. I hope this will last forever.*

It did not last, of course. Her life was cut short too prematurely. Nan's heart ached. "She has enjoyed and experienced the essence of life . . . Becky has lived her life the best she could. Her life has not been in vain." Nan heard Ethan's voice clearly. And she knew neither was Ethan's life. No, his life had not been in vain. He had loved and was loved deeply. He contributed more to science than many in their lifetime.

"No, their lives had not been in vain," Nan said unconsciously.

Standing next to Nan in front of Becky and Ethan's graves, ShiMin understood what was going through her mind.

"No, of course not," he said. "We cannot measure the worthiness of a life based on its length. It is how we live that gives life its meaning." It sounded so much like what Ethan had recorded in his final letter. Nan became emotional.

But the gift of time was merciful, and she was finally making progress in her long journey to healing.

It was the third spring since the tragedies. After church, they went and sat on the large grassy slope by the harbor, watching boats and ships coming in and going out. It had rained earlier. Now the air was humid but clear. All of a sudden, Nan heard her parents—don't let your pride get in the way, acknowledge when others are better, don't dislike people because they have more talents than you. She startled. "God opposes the proud but gives grace to the humble," the Bible verse appeared in her. The inescapable fate of losing both Becky and Ethan had utterly humbled her. *Jesus is the King of kings, yet he came to serve, not to be served. Who am I to think I shall be better than others?* She felt the last trace of pride exiting from her soul, her subconscious resentment against those better than her melting away. She felt completely relieved, completely free. She triumphed over her pride, at last.

A little girl was running around, her mother following her, her father trying to capture the image with his camera for an everlasting memory. Nan watched and became teary.

ShiMin held her tightly in his arms, her teary cheek pressed to his face. He felt intimately connected with not only Nan but Ethan and Becky as well.

"Let them go, release them, and you will be released. Don't try to hold them back. Ethan wanted you to live on, he told you so," he whispered in her ears. "They are in God's Kingdom, and you know 'with the Lord, a day is like a thousand years, and a thousand years are like a day.' Ethan and Becky would want you to be happy all the days you are here on earth. Don't waste the precious gift God gives you."

The voice of the beautiful person she had so loved rose. "Nan, continue living your life intensely, feelingly, and passionately. Honor my life and Becky's life. Becky and I are cheering you on."

The happy and content images of her grandmother, her mother, Ethan, and Becky flashed across her mind, those she loved but no longer on this earth. True, she could not hold them in her arms, but she could indeed hold them in her heart, forever!

Those beautiful memories finally brought her comfort and assurance. *Death has been swallowed up in victory,* she reminded herself.

She looked up.

"Double rainbow!" she exclaimed.

Bible verses roll onto her heart.

"Blessed are those who mourn, for they will be comforted."

"Blessed are the merciful, for they will receive mercy."

Full of gratitude, she feels God's presence and love all around her.

The chain is finally broken and the tightly locked gate is let loose.

The heart, once broken, once shattered, is again whole.

A new day has dawned.

She is set free, at last.

What a Journey!

Edwards Brothers Malloy
Oxnard, CA USA
February 12, 2016